M000285114

# SPILLED
# INK

# SPILLED INK

## NADIA HASHIMI

Quill Tree Books
*An Imprint of HarperCollins Publishers*

Quill Tree Books is an imprint of HarperCollins Publishers.

Spilled Ink

Copyright © 2024 by Nadia Hashimi

All rights reserved. Printed in the United States of America. No part of this book may be used or reproduced in any manner whatsoever without written permission except in the case of brief quotations embodied in critical articles and reviews. For information, address HarperCollins Children's Books, a division of HarperCollins Publishers, 195 Broadway, New York, NY 10007.

Library of Congress Control Number: 2023943575

ISBN 978-0-06-306049-4

Typography by Joel Tippie

24 25 26 27 28 LBC 5 4 3 2 1

First Edition

*To Fawod, Yolaine, Nyla, and Kylie*
*Always a knock away*

*What we speak becomes the house we live in.*
—Hafiz, fourteenth-century Sufi poet

**I**

Even with my comforter pulled over my head, I hear the tap, the pause, the two quick taps, and one final tap. I peek at my alarm clock and groan to realize ten minutes have already gone by since it buzzed.

I roll over and rap my knuckles against the wall in reply.

*Tap. Tap-tap. Tap.*

*I'm awake*, I tell him. Barely.

It's been hard to fall asleep lately. I remember seeing midnight come and go. What time did I drift off? I feel around on my bed and my finger snags on the fraying threads of my comforter, nothing more. I roll over onto my stomach and hang my arm off the side of the bed, patting the carpet until I find the spiral binding. I pull the sketchbook onto my lap, the reading light still clipped onto the back cover. I click it a couple of times but it stays dark. I've drained yet another battery.

I sit up and blink the grogginess away. Pens hidden in the folds of my comforter roll onto the floor. At least I remembered to cap them. Archival ink pens aren't cheap, and I just bought this ultra-fine-tipped set of twelve. Is it possible that in my insomnia, in some half-conscious state, I channeled my inner muse and came up with an inspired drawing?

I look at the page, creased where my hand must have been when I fell asleep. I've been working on this drawing for a month now, and something just doesn't feel right about it. Yusuf calls my drawings edgy. I just like an image with a twist. I flip to the previous page. Two weeks ago, I drew a winged woman walking away from a tree with a stiletto heel impaled into its trunk. I stopped showing my drawings to my parents after they wanted me to explain what I meant by a cow wearing a crown in a frying pan. I thought "a picture is worth a thousand words" meant that you don't have to say the thousand words.

I throw off the covers and slide the sketchbook into the bottom of my nightstand drawer, where I keep an old inhaler and a snow globe from SeaWorld. I wonder if someday I'll outgrow drawing, the same way I've outgrown asthma or a tolerance for animals in captivity.

I hear footsteps next door, much to my surprise. The wall between us is thin and the floorboards in the house all creak so I know Yusuf was up at least as late as I was last night.

A door opens in the hallway.

"Not today," I say, and burst out of my room, my hair wild around my face. Yusuf and I collide as we reach for the bathroom doorknob. Yusuf's hand lands on it first.

"Third day in a row, Yalda," he says with a grin. He has a towel over his shoulder, and his T-shirt is rumpled from sleep.

"Oh, come on," I groan. Every morning is a race to the bathroom we share. It wasn't such a big deal when we were five years old and two of us could brush our teeth together without elbows jamming into each other. But we're seventeen now. I don't need him teasing me while I wash my face with apricot scrub, especially when I know he uses it sometimes. I know he doesn't want me in there while he's painstakingly shaving the twelve and a half hairs he's grown on his face since puberty. The hair on his head is another wormhole into which he disappears and loses all sense of time as he arranges his dark waves in a way that's supposed to look like he doesn't care about his hair at all.

My hair, on the other hand, could actually use an hour's worth of attention, and yet all I do is twirl it around my finger and tie it up into a messy bun—the hairstyle that has saved my sanity.

"Oh, come on!" I whine. I don't do well on little sleep. "Would it kill you to give me a turn to go first?"

"You know what, fine, you go ahead," Yusuf says. He shrugs and takes a step away from the door, which makes me pause. I'm wide awake now and on full alert.

"Nah, you go," I say, because after years of these games, I

know when I'm about to walk into a setup.

A smile erupts on Yusuf's face as he reaches for the door. It *was* a setup, just not the kind I was thinking. My reflexes kick in and I step toward the bathroom door, blocking my brother with my right leg. He starts to nudge me away with his shoulder but stops when my mom calls out from the kitchen.

"Please, if you love me, give me a break for just one day," she pleads.

I look up at Yusuf and watch his face go flat with resignation. Mom's guilt-tripping works wonders on him. I'm susceptible too, but for Yusuf it's pure kryptonite.

"Just be quick," he says, snapping upright. "Keith's going to be waiting."

I close the door behind me and glance at the clock on the wall, even though it's been stuck at five o'clock for the past few months. Mom has decided that this is our bathroom and we should change the battery ourselves. Yusuf and I have decided clocks are outdated. We're all stuck in this moment, trying to teach each other lessons, I suppose. While I brush my teeth, I look at the perfectly arranged toiletries on my brother's side of the sink. Because we're twins, people expect us to be similar in all ways, but we're not. Yusuf is organized but not pathologically so. His shirts aren't in rainbow order and he doesn't have perfectly aligned wicker baskets in his closet. He's just naturally neat. My mother says he and I have been different this way since we were babies. Yusuf would line up his toy cars like a parking garage's employee of the month. My chaos was

4

legendary and frustrating, especially to my mother, who likes to recall the time she found my stuffed panda in the oven and my rock collection tucked into her makeup drawer. I keep the clutter under control now partly because I realized I would stare at the piles of stuff instead of falling asleep and mostly because I was tired of being compared to my brother.

I check my phone. We need to be out of the house in twenty minutes. Keith will be waiting for Yusuf.

Or maybe Keith will be waiting for both of us?

I take another serious look at my face. People tell me I'm so lucky to have such thick hair, but I look at the girls in my school with barely a hint of fuzz on their arms or legs with hair so fair, it wouldn't do anything but sparkle if they didn't shave it off. That is not my reality.

I have only started tweezing my eyebrows into submission this year, which was late by society's standards. Some of my cousins have been plucking and waxing their faces and limbs since they were ten. One cousin has already had four laser hair removal sessions, and another told me her mom takes her to a salon where a woman with less hair than a reptile takes her into a small room in the back and spreads hot wax over her arms, then rips it and all her arm hair off with strips of fabric. Afterward, the reptilian lady rubs aloe vera and coconut oil onto my cousin's irritated skin as some sort of moisturizing apology. As much as I hate looking at the fuzz on my arms, what my cousin describes sounds like a satanic ritual and I am no friend of the devil.

"C'mon, Yal. You got that natural beauty going for ya," Yusuf calls from behind the door, as if he can hear my thoughts. "I'm the one who needs more time in there."

My brother is rarely in neutral. He's either plotting my downfall or pulling me out of a dark well. Maybe I misjudged his gear today. I smile and put my hand on the doorknob. I try to turn it but it slips right out of my hand. My fingers come away greasy. I didn't misjudge.

"What's taking you so long?" Yusuf teases, and I can hear the grin on his face. I wipe off the Vaseline with a wad of tissue. I look around and spot his clear-complexion face wash, then unscrew the cap and squeeze some hair conditioner into it.

"You think you're so funny," I say. But I must admit, this is reasonable revenge. Last week, I got into his phone and changed the names of half his contacts to "MARKETING" and the other half to "SPAM CALLER." He ignored a bunch of texts and let a few calls from my parents go to voice mail before he realized what I'd done.

"Pretty slick," I say when he opens the door for me from the outside.

"Thanks," he says, beaming.

"I was talking about the doorknob," I clarify, stepping aside so he can get into the bathroom. "Not you. That was amateur level."

Our pranks have been escalating for the past couple of years, and sometimes innocent bystanders are affected. One night, Mom stayed up late watching Turkish soap operas. On her way back to her bedroom, she stepped on a fake mouse Yusuf had left outside my bedroom door. Her scream woke us all up, and probably our neighbors too. Yusuf started begging for forgiveness from behind his closed door and took a prank break for about a month.

My mother does not appreciate pranks. She doesn't even like regular surprises, which makes me wonder how she took the news that she was pregnant with twins. Neither of my parents can think of any other sets of twins in their families or even among the other families they knew "back home" in Afghanistan. Dad has always told us that Yusuf and I were a special gift from God, but I also suspect that the way we surprised Mom is why we don't have younger siblings.

I change my clothes and sneak into my parents' bathroom to dab a little of my mom's foundation on the tender pink spot on my chin. Their bathroom shares a wall with ours, so I can hear Yusuf groan.

"My face soap? That's not okay, Yalda!"

Vindicated, I turn my attention back to my face. The circle of makeup hasn't concealed anything and actually draws even more attention to my chin. I wash it off and start over, using less this time.

"Yalda!" my mother calls. "You're late!"

Once I'm dressed, I throw my books into my backpack and dash into the kitchen. We live in a bi-level with three bedrooms on one end of the house, and down the hall are the kitchen and living room. Downstairs has another living room with furniture

Mom would love to replace. Yusuf and I both dreaded going downstairs alone as kids, and honestly, even now, I probably move extra quickly through there on my way to the garage. Our front door is on a landing between the lower floor and the upper floor. Mom hates the dated layout and went to a dozen open houses last year but stopped looking altogether when she saw how high prices had gotten in our area.

In the safety of our upstairs kitchen, Yusuf's tilting his cereal bowl into his mouth to drain the sugared milk. He can't spell *cinnamon* without autocorrect, but somehow he doesn't spill a drop, nor does any trickle down the corners of his mouth. I wouldn't attempt something like this unless I were home alone. I grab a banana off the counter and give my mother a quick kiss on the cheek.

"Yalda, did you post the coupon last night?"

She takes a deep breath and I know her sigh will carry a plea to God for patience.

I take my phone out of my pocket and open the neighborhood app. I find the flyer I made promising a free appetizer with the purchase of two entrées—Mom's idea since business has slowed down lately—and post it in the newsfeed.

"It's up," I say, showing her my screen to prove it's done. She squints and then plants a kiss on my temple.

"Thank you, janem!" she says. Mom may not approve of sugar in our food, but she goes heavy with the sweetness once we've done exactly what she wants us to do.

"Where's Dad?" Yusuf asks.

"At the restaurant," Mom says. "He has somebody there to fix the fridge."

"Didn't they just fix the fridge?" Yusuf asks.

"Just before Thanksgiving," I confirm. "That was barely two weeks ago. It's broken again?"

Mom closes the door she's just opened without pulling anything out of the cabinet. She sighs again. There's always something in need of repair. "He's coming home early this evening, so please be on time. I want us to all be together for the holiday. This is important. Family time."

Since we lost my cousin Rahim, family time has become a synthetic, scheduled event.

It's not that we weren't spending time together before last year. We had lazy Sunday mornings, trips to the mall on rainy days, or walks down a wooded trail. But nothing is casual anymore. Everything is calculated, like Mom's trying to make sure we reach some unknown quota to save us from what happened to Rahim.

My mother, dressed in her gym clothes, picks up the box of cereal from the counter and reads the label. She clucks her tongue in disapproval. Talking nutrition to us seems to exhaust her more than her most grueling workout.

"I wish you guys would let me make you my shakes for breakfast. This is all processed sugar," she says. She drums her fingers on the counter and jots another item on her grocery list. Because she doesn't have to be at the restaurant until eleven, she dedicates the mornings to getting us out the door, her workout routine, and researching foods that will render us immortal.

"Yalda Jamali, I'm leaving without you," Yusuf announces, using my full name and deepening his voice. It's an empty threat. We both know he wouldn't go farther than the front porch, but I still rush to get my jacket and backpack.

"Let's go," I say. Yusuf either has no idea that lately the walk to school has been giving me butterflies in my stomach or he pretends not to know. Either way, I'm glad my feelings are not a topic of discussion. We head down the sidewalk, Yusuf taking long, slow strides. Mine are shorter but quicker, which keeps us in step if not in sync.

Up ahead, a screen door creaks open and clatters shut. We don't pause or even slow down.

Yusuf nods at Keith, who plods at a diagonal across the frostbitten grass of his yard to join us on the sidewalk.

"Hey," he says, glancing at both of us. Keith's family moved into town a year ago so we didn't grow up together. I would probably stop speaking to my parents or at least threaten to stop speaking to them if they decided to move in the middle of my junior year. Keith has plenty of friends, but because most people here have known each other since middle school, he seems to float around the friend groups instead of being absorbed by one in particular.

"Hi," I reply casually. In the brisk air, our words form small, transient clouds before dissipating.

"How's it going?" Yusuf says.

The guys fall into a conversation about last night's basketball game. I watched the game with Yusuf and saw the same unbelievable three-point shot they're talking about. I debate jumping into the conversation but hold back because I have a bad habit of saying too much or the wrong thing and then I spend a lot of energy regretting it for the rest of the day . . . or month.

The end of the next block is a four-way stop, always busy at this hour of the morning. We wait for a driver to remember that pedestrians have the right of way at a crosswalk.

Two cars enter the intersection at the same time. A man leans into his horn and the other driver, a woman with sunglasses almost as big as her face, gesticulates at him to indicate the anger is mutual. We steal across to the other side while they mouth off at each other from behind their windshields.

"People need to relax," I say.

"Yeah, quick question—have you met people? That's not what people do," Keith replies with a laugh. He nods at the house on our left, with four yard signs out front, two in support of names I don't recognize for county council positions. The other two have been popping up since twenty-six Afghan refugee families were sent to a hotel on the outskirts of town. The signs bear benign-sounding messages we can all get behind like PROTECT OUR NEIGHBORHOODS, but it doesn't take an AP English class to read between those lines. If they were to say what they really meant, it would be harder to get people to put the signs up.

"Did you hear what the graffiti squad is claiming now?" Keith asks. A couple weeks ago, three students returned to the campus in the middle of the night with faces covered in masks and hoodies drawn tight. They had spray-painted a swastika and a crude schematic of male anatomy onto the brick exterior of the school. The school Wi-Fi connected to their phones while they were there, which made for digital fingerprints on their artwork.

"I heard Wyatt tried to argue his First Amendment rights were being violated," Yusuf says. Wyatt has always been trouble. He's the type who doesn't talk much in class and seems to be watching people from behind the mesh of his overgrown bangs.

"He would. I had two classes with him last year and I don't think he even got his name right on quizzes. Plus, I heard they were drunk. Wyatt's dad rewards them with a six-pack every time the football team wins," Keith says.

"Good thing our football team sucks," I say, and both Keith and Yusuf laugh. I feel a tiny tingle at Keith's reaction.

There isn't room for the three of us on the sidewalk, so Keith walks with one foot on grass and the other on concrete. Yusuf's in the middle and I'm closest to the street. In the fall, I felt like an intruder in these conversations, but then I noticed Keith would throw a question my way to include me. I don't do as much talking in the morning when it's the three of us, but because Yusuf leaves early for his independent study in the afternoons, the walk home is different. When Yusuf isn't there,

I feel like I'm a whole person and not just the extra from a buy-one-get-one-free deal.

Most of the time, I'm grateful for Yusuf. He takes up at least half my parents' attention and usually more. He laughs at my jokes and raps on my wall to wake me up. And up until his music took over his life, I've never *not* had someone to hang out with at home.

We save each other some days and strangle each other on others. I do wonder what I might look like if I weren't measured against my brother's neatness, his charisma, his easy smile. I have the same two friends I've had forever, whereas Yusuf seems to add new friends to his circle every week. The closer we get to graduation, the less we look like twins. There's so much we're not sharing at a time when my head doesn't feel big enough for the thoughts running through it. We share more with our friends than we do with each other. I can't guess his every thought the way I used to.

When I catch Keith grinning at me, his hair the color of cinnamon sticks, my palms get clammy.

I'm glad Yusuf doesn't know my every thought either.

# 2

"Where do you even find watermelons in December?" Keith asks.

I don't blame him for wondering. His family shops in the grocery store with a long deli counter, a whole aisle for sliced bread, and a floral section with orchids and bouquets of roses. We shop there too—sometimes. But mostly we get our vegetables and the ingredients for Mom's smoothies from the Asian grocery store where there are eleven different kinds of squash but only one kind of sliced cheese.

"Easy. We grow watermelons in our backyard," I say.

"False," Keith replies, giving me a skeptical look.

"False," I admit.

"And why watermelons?"

"They're supposed to represent happiness and love," I say, and feel my ears get hot. I could kick myself. When Keith asked if my family had any plans for winter break, I somehow stumbled into telling him about my namesake holiday, the winter solstice. I have managed to make it sound as sappy as a drugstore on Valentine's Day. Keith probably thinks it all sounds bizarre.

At the beginning of the school year, we walked home separately. Yusuf leaves school one period early as part of his independent study and Keith was his friend, not mine. Yusuf walks home alone, picks up the used car Dad bought for us to share, and either drives himself to the middle school to mentor a couple of kids who are learning guitar in an after-school program or goes to Crescendo, a music studio, to work on composing music. It's the perfect independent study for him. He's oddly patient with kids, and at Crescendo, where he also practices with his band, he teaches young, aspiring musicians about chords and how to hold a guitar. They like him because he's younger than the other teachers and he helps the kids learn to play their favorite songs to make them love the instrument. By the end of the semester, he has to turn in an original song and a paper on the impact music has on children.

I thought about doing an independent study in art, but I was afraid I'd have to display my work at school, and there's already enough judgment happening in the hallways. I stuck with regular classes instead.

Without Yusuf, I would trail behind Keith with my headphones on. One day, he stood at the corner until I caught up. He tapped his ear, and when I paused the music on my phone, he told me it wasn't safe to walk and listen to music.

I told him I was surprised he cared so deeply about pedestrian safety, though what really surprised me was that he'd noticed me behind him.

We walked the rest of the way home that day and every school day since, talking about music and climate change and debating whether our science teacher had performed his own hair transplant. Since Keith's house is first on our block, my parents don't see us walking together, which is a lifesaver. I don't need them flipping out about me talking to a boy.

I mean, it's not like we're dating.

We're just two people walking in the same direction and talking about matters of general interest. And that's why I'm struggling to understand why I told him something that's probably got him wondering what else goes on in my house. His family celebrates holidays that need no explanation and are guaranteed to be days off from school. But when I'd said tonight was our winter holiday, Keith seemed sincerely interested, so I rambled on.

"It's not just watermelon. We have pomegranates and dried fruits and nuts and my mom lights a bunch of candles. Then we stay up till midnight reading poems and stuff."

I look at him from the corner of my eye, unsure what he's thinking.

"That sounds a lot like telling stories around a campfire at night."

I feel relieved, like I was half-afraid Keith was going to accuse me of witchcraft. Yusuf's right. I really do need to chill out.

"Yeah. Except we do this in the comfort of our living room. I'm a big fan of indoor plumbing."

"That's wild. We have *so* much in common," Keith says in mock wonder, and I bite my cheek to avoid grinning. "So what poems are you going to read tonight?"

I shake my head.

"My parents read the poems. My brother and I just listen." It's kind of embarrassing that I can't read and write in the language we speak at home, so I leave that out. I also don't want him to ask me to say something in Dari for his entertainment. My first week riding the bus to middle school, a girl asked me to say something in my language. She and her friends leaned over the seats to get a listen. In my half-broken Dari, I told her that her teeth reminded me of burnt corn. The girls giggled and one tried to mimic the sounds. They asked me to repeat myself three times before they remembered to forget about me.

"I'm pretty sure the last poem my mother read to me was written by Dr. Seuss," Keith says. That gets my attention.

"Are you a Dr. Seuss fan?"

"A lyrical genius," Keith says.

"Just to clarify, was your mom reading this poem to you when you were five or last week?"

The look of faux outrage he gives me is golden. Keith is a walking GIF.

"You know what? That's cool. I'm a big boy. You can't hurt me," he says, then he stuffs his hands into his pockets. "I think he would have killed at a school visit."

"I dunno," I say. "A few of his books got pulled for racist images. And anyway, he was an introvert. Spent most of his time alone, writing, and pretty much stayed away from kids."

"Okay, I want to unhear that. But the introvert stuff—that seems like an artist vibe, so it makes sense. Yusuf said you're an artist."

"He did?" I ask, surprised to hear him say so. "I draw a little."

"That's cool. He said you're really good. Do you ever post your stuff?"

I shake my head. A knot forms in my belly at the thought of sharing my drawings. Why does my brother always need adult supervision? I'm not sure why Yusuf felt compelled to mention this to Keith.

"Not really," I say, trying to sound unbothered. "It's just a hobby. Not like Yusuf. He's the one who's really pursuing his art."

"Oh yeah! I hear Yusuf's band is going to be playing at WhereHouse. Do you get VIP tickets or something?"

WhereHouse is a funky, punky space on the outskirts of

town. I haven't been there but checked out some pictures online when Yusuf told me they were hoping to play in this year's Battle of the Bands there. The unimpressive but popular venue is four walls and a stage. Attached to it is what they call a restaurant, though it has fewer items on the menu than a food truck. There's also a bar next door in a place that's technically not part of WhereHouse but shares a wall, which is why Yusuf swore me to secrecy on this gig. Our parents would be less than thrilled to know he was playing so close to a bar.

"I don't know," I tell Keith. "I like watching them perform, but . . ."

Does Keith know Yusuf is hiding this from our parents? I don't want to out him. It always feels a little juvenile to have to sneak around instead of having parents who can be cool with what their kids are doing.

"But you don't want to go alone?"

What does Keith mean by that? I don't want to read this wrong but I'm too flustered to decipher any code.

"No, I didn't even ask my friends if they . . . also it's just not for everyone. You know?"

"Yeah. I want to go but I'm not sure what my mom will say if I ask her. She might offer to be a chaperone."

"Maybe I need to cut my parents some slack," I say. "I didn't think your mom would be like mine."

"Why not? Moms are moms." He shrugs. Are they? I've always thought American moms—the kind who don't have to explain their holidays to neighbors—wouldn't think twice about letting a high schooler go watch a band play. Things like sleepaway camp and coed hangouts make my mother break into hives. "My brother jokes that he enlisted so he could be somewhere that didn't have so many rules," he says.

"Ha! Well, maybe our mothers should hang out, then," I say, and immediately want to take the words back. Why would I want our mothers to hang out? Keith looks like he's picturing it, the meeting of the moms, and doesn't seem excited about it.

"Yeah, I don't think I'll be able to go with my parents' blessing either," I say to break the awkward pause.

"What if we don't ask?"

Keith smiles and then clears his throat in a weird way. He looks . . . uncomfortable, which I thought was my zone and mine alone until now.

"Now there's an interesting idea," I say while I try to wrap my brain around the idea of us going to WhereHouse without telling our parents. I'm a little bit intrigued but also unnerved even by the possibility of being dishonest with my parents about my plans for that night. Then again, Yusuf will be there, and my parents have spent all our lives telling us to stick together.

"We could go together. To the show. I mean, Yusuf's probably going early to set up. If you want. It's going to be cold, I think." Keith is speaking in bursts, a string of phrases. Is he asking me to go *with* him? I feel a flutter in my belly and somehow can't form a coherent response. Keith misreads my hesitation and starts filling in the awkward silence with more choppy musings.

"Or not. It was just a thought. My brother's been there and he says it's okay. Maybe a little shady. He saw a couple of rats hanging out at the dumpster outside."

"So it's a shady place with rats but otherwise okay. Have you considered a career in marketing?" I ask.

Keith shakes his head. "I'm sure they weren't rats. He probably said cats and I heard him wrong. Or maybe you heard me wrong? Anyway, I think a bunch of people and maybe some kittens are going to try to go. I probably will so let me know if you think you want to go together."

There's no mistaking it—he just asked me to go with him. And he's funny.

"Yeah, okay," I say, trying hard to sound casual and chill and not like the messiest hot mess to ever exist.

"Cool," he says. "You know, Brian Patton's band wanted to perform there too. His life goal is to set a guitar on fire onstage. He tried to do it at the school talent show last year but Ms. Callahan had him make cardboard flames instead."

"You can't be serious," I say. I picture Brian Patton, with his signature metal-studded black leather belt, cutting up red and orange construction paper with safety scissors, his pyrotechnic dreams reduced to an arts and crafts project.

"Dead serious. So we should also be there to make sure he doesn't burn the place down."

"We must have an extra fire extinguisher at our restaurant. Maybe I should bring it along," I offer. And then I stop talking because it seems we've just agreed to go together.

There is a long silence as we cross the street, looking both ways a couple of times like well-trained grade-schoolers. While I try to think of something interesting to talk about, the awkward pause balloons between us.

"So do you work at the restaurant every weekend?" Keith asks, and I breathe out in relief before I answer.

"Not every weekend. Just depends on the schedule."

*False*, I tell myself. I'm there every weekend, working right alongside my parents. Ever since Yusuf got the job at the music shop, I'm the only employee without kids, but I don't want Keith to think of me as some child labor victim.

"That's cool," he says.

"Working weekends is cool?" I ask.

"No. I mean, it is, but that's not what I meant. It's cool that you guys have a restaurant. And that you actually have a real job. I spent one summer at Swirl scooping ice cream for kids who needed forty minutes to choose vanilla."

"I love Swirl."

"I would have hooked you up with free sprinkles if you had come in on my shift."

"That would've been awful."

"Wait, what?"

"I hate sprinkles. Confetti shouldn't be edible. What is it even made of?"

"Fine. A topping of your choosing. But would you do the same if I came to the restaurant?"

"Well, we don't do sprinkles, but you would get the world's

22

greatest cuisine," I say without reservation. I can't help myself. My respect for our food allows no room for humility. "It's our bread that should be called Wonder. No joke. We don't just boil or steam anything. We marinate, sauté, fry, and broil. Besides salt and pepper, we use turmeric, mint, cumin, and a sprinkle of sumac. Over kebabs, it's perfection."

"Um, that sounds terrifying," Keith says.

I raise an eyebrow.

"I got some vicious blisters when I touched sumac. You guys can just eat it? What are you made of?"

"Oh, no. Different kind of sumac. No blisters," I promise, grinning. I picture Keith sitting at the corner table right below the poster of the *National Geographic* cover with the photograph of the green-eyed Afghan refugee girl, the one who haunts every Google search for "Afghan girl." Would he come alone or would he come with friends? What would my father say if he came in? Maybe I should have thought about this before I opened my mouth.

We turn the corner and reach his house with its sun-faded bricks and a tin star hanging over the front door. Keith's mother is standing behind the glass of their front door, watching us.

Keith waves at her and she raises a hand. I feel a warmth creep up my neck and raise my hand to wave, even though I'm not sure whether her gesture was directed at both of us or just her son. I know his parents aren't like mine and probably don't bat an eye at him walking with a girl, but I'm a little embarrassed all the same.

I readjust the strap of my backpack on my shoulder and take my phone out of my pocket to check it for no reason at all since my battery died an hour after lunch.

"See you tomorrow," I chirp. Truly, I sound birdlike.

"Yeah." He grins. "See you tomorrow."

I cringe at having this farewell play out in front of his mom but remind myself that she witnessed nothing more than a friendly conversation between classmates.

I pass a few more houses before I reach home. During the winter, our house looks like any other from the outside. During the spring and summer, when the bulbs Mom planted deep into the earth bloom into tulips and irises, our front yard becomes a splash of color on the block. I think that's why the winter solstice is so important to my mother. The seasons don't happen around her. They happen to her, like she too spins on an axis and rotates around the sun. My brother and I both take after her, though we seem to catch our light at different times of the year. The heat of summer suffocates me. I've never liked the buzz around the first day of school—maybe because I never come back with a new boyfriend, a beach tan, or pink highlights.

Winter is my spirit season. I live for bulky sweaters, peppermint mocha anything, and the bliss of an unexpected snow day. Sixty-watt bulbs guarantee that no one shows up to school with a beachy glow. It is the one season that—sort of—levels the playing field.

Yusuf's time is spring. He's like one of my mom's bulbs,

emerging with arms outstretched, ready to catch whatever life is throwing at him. This past March, he convinced his bandmates they had to start writing their own songs if they wanted to be more than a cover band. He went through two notebooks before he came up with something he liked enough to share. Over spring break, they played the song at the Plaza, a small downtown area with restaurants, and I watched people linger, impressed, before they went on their way. Every time someone didn't stay to hear the full song, I would look at Yusuf. He either didn't notice them leaving or didn't care. I never heard a hitch in his voice. I never saw his eyes follow their backs as they departed.

I unlock our front door. Evenings are when the restaurant is busiest, so Yusuf and I are used to coming home to an empty house. It was harder getting used to coming home to an empty house without Yusuf. I'm not sure what I'm worried about finding—aliens? Burglars? A backed-up toilet? A burglar causing a toilet to back up?

That's what I envy most about Yusuf. His time onstage is not plagued by thoughts of the infinite ways things can go wrong, with wondering if people are walking away because they don't like the sound of his voice.

I'm the overthinker, which is why I am more of a lurker than a poster on the Pic-Up app. I wring my hands, waiting to see if people will assign a precious star to a picture I've shared, whether it was the selfie I took the one time I went with my mom to the nursery to pick up geraniums for her summer garden or a picture of a rusted bicycle I spotted in the woods. If they do, I'm left wondering what they liked about it or if it's just a sympathy star so they can feel they've done a good deed for the day. I guess at how many people scrolled past, unimpressed or even annoyed. I can invent a million reactions that are unlikely, and yet the possibility haunts me.

I take out my sketchbook to make use of this quiet. I never post my art on Pic-Up because I already know it's not the best work out there, and if I receive a few polite stars, I will quickly forget them if I get even a couple of questionable comments. My sketchbook has been my safe place, my sanctuary. I'm free to draw what I want without worrying about whether my art will be liked. Maybe I'm just trying to return the favor by keeping the sketches to myself, guarding them from judgmental eyes.

I pick up a pen, a thicker one that I use for outlines.

I draw a glass bottle with a cork top, the kind that Alice drank from in Wonderland. I use a blue pen that is as close to black as possible and make the bottle half-full of a liquid. The liquid dips in the middle but then climbs the bottle's walls, creating a small whirlpool. Using my thinnest pen, I draw a tiny, inky figure standing on the surface of the water, at the center of that whirlpool, a raft under her feet. The figure is featureless, a shadow. Starting from the bottom of the bottle, I draw a vine that wraps around the glass, pointy leaves sprouting in all directions. Round and round goes the vine, wrapping itself twice around the bottle and then choking the cork top.

When I lift my pen from the page, I think what I've drawn

is not perfect or even amazing—but it *is* interesting. I almost want to show it to someone. Maybe Mom?

One more look at my drawing convinces me that's a bad idea. She'll read so far into it that she'll start taking me for long walks around the lake to increase my vitamin D levels. I flip through my last few pages of drawings. About a month ago, listening through the walls to Yusuf practice his music, I started to draw a seahorse, but not the tiny little wobbly creatures most people think of.

Yusuf's band is called The Hipper Campus, which is a twist on hippocampus, a mythological sea monster we first heard of in the Percy Jackson books. Poseidon sent the half-horse and half-fish sea monsters to take Percy and his friends. I don't know what made Yusuf think this was a good name for his band, but his friends must have liked it because that's the name they go by. For fun, I thought I'd try drawing a hippocampus.

I walk over to my brother's room with my sketchbook open to the page with the ink drawing of a stallion, front hooves in the air and nostrils flaring. The hair of his mane is wild, spread out as if he's underwater. His back half is scaled and ends with a curled-in flipper, like a dolphin. I sit in Yusuf's chair and debate ripping the page out and leaving it on his desk for him to find. That feels safer than being right there to see his reaction.

I'm about to tear the page when I notice a crumpled paper under his desk. He must have been aiming for the trash. Maybe it's the super-neat Yusuf energy in the room that makes me pick it up. Before I toss it into the trash, I notice it's a receipt from Room, the coffee shop by Crescendo. Room is actually called A Room with a Brew. According to a framed sign on the wall, the two owners were finance people who left their glass offices to fulfill their life's dream. The place is earthy and cozy and never rushes anyone out. My friends Mona and Asma love their organic lemon balls and I like that they sell books and magazines too. I feel less like a student and more like a creative when I have a mug and a notebook in front of me. It seems like a great place to draw too, but I'd have to go there alone to do that because I can't do anything more than casual doodles if anyone's watching.

The receipt in my hand is for a chai latte, an iced coffee with Yusuf's usual creamy, sugary additions, and one giant chocolate chip cookie.

Two drinks and one cookie.

I can't imagine Yusuf splitting a cookie with Liam or Chris. Who did he go with? I get the distinct feeling Yusuf hid this on purpose. I take my sketchbook back to my room and tuck it into my drawer without leaving my artwork on Yusuf's desk. Maybe I'm not the only one with secrets.

# 3

I'm at a red light, the smell of bolani filling my dad's car, when I look at the car next to me and feel my heart skip. The driver to my left is singing along to music, his hand tapping a rhythm on the steering wheel. He must feel my eyes on him because he looks over at me, and when our eyes meet, he laughs and waves.

It wasn't his singing that caught my attention. Plenty of people sing in their cars. But this guy resembles Rahim—or I think he resembles Rahim. The last time I saw my cousin, he didn't really look like himself.

We hadn't seen Rahim in years, not since Thanksgiving five years ago, which was the last time his family flew from Indiana to Virginia to spend the holiday with us. That had been tradition since Rahim's parents had a long weekend off from work, but our restaurant only closed early on Thanksgiving Day itself. I loved those visits. While our parents were gossiping about the far branches of the family tree and playing cards, the cousin crew got to hang out. Of my dozen cousins, no one was like Rahim. Because he was older than us, it felt like he had unlocked special knowledge. He could talk about the best player on the Manchester soccer team over lunch with our dads and then discuss orcas with the younger cousins over dinner. And he could mimic his mother's voice so perfectly that he'd even tripped up his father on more than one occasion. He had the kind of manners that made grandmothers swoon.

Mom loved that Rahim wasn't glued to his phone all the time. He said he didn't want to be a slave to the algorithms. Yusuf had suggested, in a half-joking, half-serious voice, that Rahim led some undercover life. There was a pause, then Rahim laughed and said that he wasn't a spy but even if he were, he would never tell. He'd laughed and I laughed too, surprised at how Rahim had made the comment light as a feather and blown it right out of the room.

Yusuf, Rahim, and I often stayed up late watching movies in the living room. One night, Yusuf went to bed early. We'd run out of decent options, so I put on one of those shows that Rahim and I agreed was so bad that it was almost good. It was about a strict boarding school for teen witches.

Uncle Zahir must have woken up thirsty. He stopped in the

living room with a glass of water in his hand and said we should get to bed. Then his eyes moved to the television screen, where three girls were trying on dresses for an upcoming dance. In two strides, he had crossed the room and grabbed the remote from the table. His thumb fumbled and the room went dark, but I could sense Uncle Zahir glaring at Rahim. Wanting to break the brick-heavy silence, I said something about being exhausted anyway. Even now, my stomach tightens to think of the look on Rahim's face when his father walked in.

But the next morning, Rahim acted like nothing had happened. He played video games with Yusuf for a bit but mostly sat outside on our deck reading a spy novel. They left for home two days later. After that, more time started to pass between calls from Uncle Zahir, until, at some point, our uncle wouldn't even call back when Dad left him a message. Rahim's mom, Ama Leeda, still took Mom's calls but they were short, empty exchanges. Rahim and his family never came back out to visit, and Ama Leeda always made some excuse when Dad suggested we could fly out to see them.

Yusuf and I had our suspicions, though *suspicions* isn't the right word because it carries judgment with it, and that's not what I meant to do. I can't remember which one of us said it first. With an extended family as large as ours, the odds were that someone didn't fit into the cishet categories. But then we didn't see Rahim for a couple of years, and we were certainly not sitting around debating his orientation. It was much easier to think it wasn't any of our business anyway—until the day I overheard Mom on the phone with my dad's cousin, who also lived in Indiana.

Mom was closer to her than to most of the other relatives on my dad's side, including Rahim's parents. She kept Mom updated on the Indiana happenings, which is a polite way of saying she gossiped. Rahim was graduating from college soon, and his mother had been spending a lot of time visiting friends with daughters. They were hoping to find a match for him. Rahim was older than me, but not by so much that I could wrap my head around the word *marriage* in the same sentence as his name.

But instead of Rahim's mom planning his wedding, Rahim's dad ended up arranging his funeral.

I pull into the parking lot of the strip mall where Yusuf works. Crescendo is on the corner, on the second floor. My friends and I sometimes study at Room, on the other end of the strip. I park the car and text my mom that I've made it here. She gets nervous when I drive, more nervous than she gets when Yusuf drives. She told me once that it was because she feels like *I'm* nervous when I drive, so I'm not quite sure where her feelings end and mine begin.

Yusuf, Chris, and Liam are in the studio practicing for their big night at WhereHouse. Yusuf isn't nervous. That's not his brand. When Yusuf has a show coming up or a song he's working on, he gets intense. These days, WhereHouse is consuming his attention. At home, he doesn't even notice me watching him tap his feet, practice his finger work even without a guitar in his hands, hum while he's doing homework. And with the Battle of the Bands heavy on his mind, he's been a little forgetful about other things—like the potluck holiday party at the studio today.

About an hour ago, Yusuf walked into the break room at the music studio, saw foil-wrapped trays on the counter, and called Mom, our personal 911 operator, to report his emergency.

Mom's love language is food, which is why the restaurant is a passion project for her. She has spent so much time behind our kitchen island, the fridge and stove within arm's reach, preparing for the moment Yusuf and I would inevitably become hungry. In the restaurant, she will always bring a free dessert to customers who have returned for more of her recipes. She also gives a free dessert to new customers because she wants them to have the experience of a complete Afghan meal. She loves bringing steaming palau and sautéed butternut squash to the Afghans who have found themselves so far from home and everything they knew.

I open the passenger-side door of the car and pull out the aluminum tray of bolani, which Mom predicted everyone would love. The mashed, seasoned potatoes were already in the restaurant fridge. Dad quickly fork-smashed the mix onto flattened dough, then folded and fried it.

I get out of the car and am almost to the steps when I spot something out of the corner of my eye. It's a fox, darting between two cars and running into the miniature forest behind the building. His long, bushy tail disappears and I'm trying to shake the feeling that I've just experienced a close call. I tell myself the fox probably feels the same way.

I walk up the concrete steps, passing a nail salon and a vacant shop with a "For Lease" sign in the window. This strip mall is one of the oldest in town and a few of the shops have had to close in the past three years, so people are wondering if it's time to tear it down and start fresh or if it can be revived with some paint and new stores. I think swapping out the vape shop for just about anything else would be a great start.

Crescendo is the end unit on the second floor. The concrete walkway wraps around the end, but the entrance to the studio is a few feet away from that. I open the door and see Beto, the manager, talking on the phone from behind the front desk. A small Christmas tree stands in the corner of the sitting area, decorated with a hundred tiny drum ornaments, the kind that come ten for a dollar. He smiles when he sees me and signals for me to go on through to the back while he reschedules a lesson. There are posters of bands and flyers for concerts on the walls, pictures of instruments and students performing on small stages.

On either side of the hallway are soundproof rooms. In the first room on my right, a woman is flipping through pages of a music book while a tween warms up on a violin. Chris comes out of a room down the hall.

"Hey, Yalda," he says. "Saving Yusuf again?"

"If he tells you he made these, throw a guitar at him," I reply. Chris laughs. He's the kind of person whose feelings

34

float close to the surface. Last month, the guys were at our house rewatching a Marvel movie. Yusuf had asked Dad to pick up some ice cream on the way home, and, of course, Dad obliged. I helped my dad take a tray of bowls and spoons into the living room, since Yusuf and his friends could not tear their eyes from the television screen. Yusuf and Liam said a quick hello and thanks, but Chris was different. He watched Dad put a hand on Yusuf's shoulder and then looked into the bowl of ice cream in his hands, like it was a wishing well. Chris lost his dad to some kind of cancer when he was seven. He reminds me of the people who stick around at the airport after they drop off a mom or brother to watch the plane take off. He has that look always—a permanent state of missing someone.

"You can put it in the break room," he says, pointing to the end of the hall. Yusuf and Liam are in the room just before the break room. Liam's sitting at a drum set that looks like the grown-up version of the Christmas ornaments on the tree. He's wearing a flannel shirt with a white T-shirt underneath. Yusuf's got his back to me. Looking over his shoulder, I can see him texting someone. He's been more guarded with his phone lately. He turns slightly so I can't see his screen and switches apps when I get close to him.

I called him out on it once but he just laughed and invited me to hand over my phone so he could go through my messages. That was the end of that conversation.

I set the bolani on the small round table, moving foil-covered bowls, a basket of white plastic forks, and a bag of tortilla chips to make room. If I'd known tortilla chips were an option, I would have told Yusuf to go to the gas station across the street and saved myself a trip.

"Yalda came through," I hear Chris say in the hallway. I join him and the guys in the room they use to play together, the biggest of the six rooms in the studio.

"Hey," Liam says. I wave at him. Liam is so quiet he makes me look chattier than an online gamer looking to entertain followers. Yusuf says he's got a classic drummer personality, reserved but steady and persistent. He and Yusuf have been friends since middle school, when Liam shared his earbuds with Yusuf and introduced him to some older rock bands.

I take a seat on a swiveling stool.

"Did you guys decide what you're playing yet?" I ask.

Liam scoffs. I think I've hit a sore spot.

Yusuf takes in Liam's reaction and shrugs.

"Not yet," Chris fills in. "Trying to decide between Yusuf's new song or something we've done before. Liam says the crowd likes stuff that's familiar."

"What do you think, Chris?" Yusuf asks, his arms folded across his chest.

"He's going to agree with you," Liam grumbles. "He always does."

"That's bull," Chris says. "And you know it."

Liam starts tapping his drumsticks at the edge of the drum.

"Name a band you like that plays other band's songs," Yusuf says. "I'll wait."

36

"Bro, are you serious right now?" Liam shakes his head, exasperated. As much as I know that feeling, I'm also prickled. Siblings have a solid standing when they're annoyed with each other. Others are on shaky ground. "This is not some school talent show. WhereHouse is a real gig and it wasn't easy to get."

"Thanks for the reminder because we almost forgot that you know the manager there," Chris jokes. Liam is not amused.

"I know it's a real gig. That's why I'm taking it seriously. I don't want to be a cover band. They should know we're not just mimics," Yusuf says.

"Fine," Liam says with a shrug. "We'll do your song."

"You want to do it? Or do you just want me to shut up?" Yusuf asks, trying to sound lighthearted.

"Does it matter?" Liam responds. The room is tense, definitely not holiday-party energy.

"It does to me," Yusuf says.

"Look, WhereHouse is two weeks away," I say, trying to defuse the situation. These guys never argue, but they've also never had a show this big before. "You have time to decide."

The guys don't look at me, probably because I sound like a kindergarten teacher trying to negotiate peace in the sandbox. Something buzzes. Chris digs his phone out of his backpack and answers it as he walks out of the room.

"Hey, Mom. Everything okay?" he says, then goes quiet. "Come on. Why can't *you* pick me up? He's always late."

Yusuf shakes his head and goes into the hallway. I watch him through the glass window.

"I'll drop you off," he tells Chris, who nods. It is a slight and subtle acknowledgment.

"I better get going," I tell Liam, who still looks frustrated. "And I don't think it matters which song you guys pick. You'll sound great."

"Yeah, maybe it doesn't matter," he says in a way that tells me his opinion hasn't changed much but his willingness to argue has.

I say goodbye to Yusuf and Chris and slip out of Crescendo. I drive back to the restaurant, forgetting to turn the radio on until I've parked the car. My mind has been elsewhere and the sky is heavy with clouds, the early evening darker than it has any right to be.

# 4

"No one beats this guy," Keith says as we stand with our backs against the moss-green hallway wall. His shoulder presses against mine as he holds out his phone so we can both see the screen, and his head is tilted toward mine. "After I watched this video, I thought, this is what I want to do with my life— make obstacle courses for squirrels in my backyard."

I recognize the guy instantly and laugh. He managed to turn his fenced backyard and his neighborhood squirrels into a moneymaking machine by building complex mazes and using nuts as bait.

"Oh, this was good, but it's gotten even better since then. Did you see the casino he built for these guys?" I ask. "The level of detail . . . I mean, he had blueprints and tiny tools inside the little squirrel houses."

"Yes! That trapdoor was sick," Keith says. "I'm impressed. I wouldn't have guessed you were the squirrel obstacle course type."

"You only really know someone when you've seen their streaming history."

Keith laughs. "Ah, well then, let me know when you're ready to reveal yours," he teases, and I gulp because this is almost definitely not just friendly chatting and now I feel like I've got my shoes on the wrong feet.

It's in that pause that I feel someone's gaze on me.

Her name is Nahal and she's a junior so we don't share any classes. The first time I saw her, it almost felt like invisible hands had turned my head to look in her direction. Her headscarf was pretty, a much prettier green than the locker she was staring at. She had a black backpack on her shoulder, so crisp that it looked like it had just been plucked off a store rack. She wore a flannel shirt that fell a couple inches past the back pockets of her dark jeans. Her sneakers looked new too, plain white and crisp, just like her backpack. They looked like the ones my mother had purchased off a refugee family's wish list. What made me freeze, though, was the sweatshirt she carried in her hands, an olive-green hoodie with a flowering cactus image on the back.

Not too long ago, that sweatshirt had been hanging in my closet.

I'd walked past Nahal without stopping to say anything or to introduce myself. I had my reasons. I would have been late to class and I didn't know what to say. It was entirely possible she wouldn't understand my broken Dari and actually maybe she'd prefer not to be approached by strangers. Once I'd slid into my seat, it occurred to me that the line between reasons and excuses is fine enough to cut skin, and that Nahal hadn't been turning the dial on her lock or doing much of anything beyond staring at her locker.

I wanted to do better but I didn't really know what to do. I thought about asking my mom if the family needed any more supplies but then felt like that could backfire. Mom has a way of turning a small ask into a major project. As an example, when I told Mom it would be cool to grow tomatoes, she came home with seeds and soil and declared the grand opening of our family garden. The seven tomatoes and two miniature carrots we grew that summer cost me hours of my life.

A week after I first spotted Nahal, we crossed paths in the hallway and our eyes locked. I half smiled and then looked away when Nahal didn't smile back.

Since then, I've kept my eyeballs on a tight leash to avoid another awkward exchange. I felt I had proof that she didn't want my attention, and I didn't want to come off like I was pitying her or looking to be thanked for whatever my mom has done for the family.

But the universe plays its own pranks, so of course Nahal happens to be walking past us, and suddenly Keith's face feels way too close and my skin prickles where his shoulder and hips graze mine. Nahal looks at me for a long beat even as she continues to glide swiftly through the hallway, her books close to her chest. Instantly, I put distance between myself and Keith. I straighten my back and my smile has evaporated, but Nahal is already gone.

"Are you okay?" Keith asks.

I feel like Nahal caught us doing much more than standing next to each other.

"Yes. I mean, yeah," I say, trying to sound more casual and less startled on my second try. "I just realized I have an essay due for government and I need to get a book out of the library for an art assignment. I'll catch up with you later?"

"Sure," he says, sliding his phone back into his pocket and nodding. "See you after school."

As I turn the corner and make my way to the library, something electric runs through me, a mix of anticipation and fear because I don't know what's brewing between Keith and me. I wonder how other couples became couples. Is there a certain number of hours that automatically turns two people into a *thing*? Will he ask me? Am I being incredibly archaic to even think that's how things work? Rumors of crushes and *feelings* have floated around my classmates since first grade, but things are different now that most, though maybe not all, of us know the truth about the tooth fairy.

"So," Mona says, throwing an arm around me. I didn't see her coming, which means I'm more distracted than I thought because Mona is a gold medalist in making an entrance. There's a dangerous twinkle in her eye. "Is he officially your boyfriend or what?"

"Ugh," I groan. "Please don't do this to me."

"What am I doing to you?" she asks, feigning indignation. "I'm simply asking my bestie for clarification of her status so I can best support her as she begins her first relationship."

*Relationship.* My stomach knots at the word, which suddenly sounds as massive and intimidating as a whale beside a rowboat.

"God, Mona. You're so wrong. We were just talking about *squirrels.*" I emphasize *squirrels* as if that should make it very clear to Mona that this was not a romantic conversation. "Anyway, just drop the labels because seriously, it's not that . . . serious."

"Yalda, it's me. I'm not your mom or some judgmental auntie. And it's also not the Middle Ages. You like him, right? I mean, I don't see it. I think he needed a haircut ten Tuesdays ago and I'm proactively resentful of him for taking my BFF away from me."

"Mona."

"We've always spent so much time together, Yalda. Today might be the last of the good ol' days. You'll miss me too, won't you?" Mona asks, batting her eyes at me.

"I'll need some time to think about this," I say, and pull her into the library with me. We sit at one of the round tables tucked between two fiction stacks. I need to talk to someone about this, and of my two friends, I feel like I can have a more open conversation with Mona. I don't know how Asma would react, and part of me is afraid that she would be disappointed in me for dating Keith. If I were to date Keith, that is. If that's what going to WhereHouse together means. I think back to our conversation about rats jumping in and out of a dumpster and question my sanity.

"What's going on with you?" Mona asks, drawing out the sentence as she eyes me suspiciously. "Something's up. Say it or we can't be friends."

"Well, now I'm torn."

"Yalda!"

"Fine. Next week Yusuf's going to be playing at Where-House—"

"Seriously? That's a real place! Your parents are cool with that?"

I shake my head.

"He doesn't want to ask them because he thinks they're going to say no."

"High probability," she confirms.

"They won't like the idea, but Yusuf and the guys are really excited for this gig and I want to go see them play. And . . . Keith wants to go too. He asked if I wanted to go with him."

Mona drums her fingers on the table in amusement.

"I knew this was juicy. Okay, let's review. You want to— without your parents finding out—go on a first date with a guy you're not supposed to be dating to watch your brother secretly play at a bar he's not supposed to be playing at."

Mona's summary has me groaning with confusion.

"I don't know. Never mind. It's a bad idea."

"What's a bad idea?"

Mona and I whip our heads around at the same time and see Asma wanting to be in on the conversation.

"No wonder you guys didn't see me wave from the hall-way," she says, nodding at the glass wall. "What's going on?"

Mona gives me a second so I can explain, but when my hesitation tests her patience, she turns to Asma.

"Keith asked Yalda to go on a secret date to a secret gig that Yusuf is playing at WhereHouse."

"Oh," Asma says, then blinks a couple of times. This is a key difference between my friends. Mona doesn't think before she speaks, which makes it easy to know exactly how she feels. Asma, on the other hand, *over*thinks before she speaks, but in this case, it doesn't matter. I can read her face enough to see she has serious reservations about my plan.

I cover my face with my hands.

"We could go with you," Mona says.

I part my fingers and look to see if this is really Mona talking.

"Hear me out," she says, with fingers splayed on the table. "We can tell our parents there's something going on at school that night, like homecoming or something."

"Continue," I say, intrigued.

"Listen, they have no issue with us going to the mall or a

school game. So? This is 'a feel-good music competition' and I bet a bunch of people from school will be there. We can all go to cheer Yusuf on."

"I wouldn't mind going," Asma says. Now it's Mona's turn to look at Asma like she's grown fairy wings.

"What does that mean?" I ask. "Is that the same as you want to go?"

Asma shrugs. "I hadn't really thought about it before, but yeah. We should be there for Yusuf. And the other guys. It's a big deal for them to play there. I'm in."

Mona and I look at each other. We're not even close to being the kind of girls who get into trouble, but Asma is on another level. She's a literal moral compass guiding us in the right direction. If she wants to go, then going is the upstanding thing to do.

"Then it's settled," Mona declares, sealing the decision as she rises from her seat. "We're all going. What did Yusuf tell your parents?"

"He told them the band's playing at a community center. Like a talent show or something."

"Oh, that's good. That's very good. Let's go with that," Mona approves. "I mean, it *is* a center for music. And it's in the community."

Asma is pensive. She wiggles her head, the needle of the compass seeking true north.

"I think that's okay. It's not like it's a bar. You don't even have to be eighteen to go or anything like that, so it *is* pretty much just a performance hall," she decides, and I let out the breath I didn't realize I've been holding.

"Like Carnegie Hall. Or the Kennedy Center. Or . . . Broadway!" Mona adds.

"Yes!" I say, bursting into laughter. I feel lighter with this plan out in the open, even if it is just with my friends. "It's going to be good. Yusuf's been to WhereHouse a couple of times to check it out."

I tell them about the wall with postcards from all over the world, the photos of the bands who played there before they moved on to bigger stages. Mona's eyes go wide, sparks flying in her head.

"What if Yusuf and the guys blow up after this performance?" she asks, eternally obsessed with what-ifs. "Yalda, have you considered what it would be like to have a famous brother? Imagine people pushing through crowds to get closer to him. Paparazzi trying to snap pictures and reveal who his latest girlfriend is. Oh my God. Music videos. A duet with Billie Eilish. He could be a hashtag!"

Asma laughs. "Is that a goal? To be a hashtag? Maybe just let them play at WhereHouse and see where it goes," she suggests.

"You guys are giving me second thoughts about the whole thing. I don't want to be a hashtag's sister. All right. We have seven minutes left to grab lunch," I say, and push my chair back from the table. I should eat something before my next class. Whether it's anxiety or excitement, this strange energy has pooled in my stomach, and I hope a few bites of food will help tame my nerves. I don't know how this plan we've hatched is going to go, but I am very certain that our night at Where-House is going to be like no other night in my life.

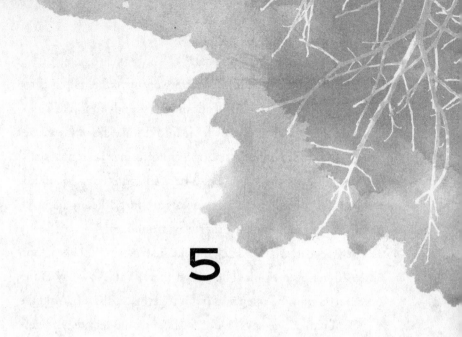

# 5

"We destroy everything, everywhere, and in so many ways," Mona says. "How am I supposed to get all of that onto one page?"

The substitute teacher has written the assignment on the whiteboard—describe the impact of humans on natural resources. He's maybe in his thirties and the level of enthusiasm with which he wields that dry erase marker makes it obvious he's new to this job. Hearing Mona, he walks over to where we sit.

"Is there a question?" he asks, so hopefully that I wonder if he has his fingers crossed behind his back. "Sorry, I don't know your names yet. You are . . . ?"

"Yalda," I say. "And no questions. I'm good."

"Yal— How do you spell that?"

I spell it out for him, all five letters of my name. He tries to pronounce it but what comes out of him sounds first like Yale-Duh. He then tucks a third syllable into the middle of my name and says Yalida. Mona looks from him to me. Like me, she's confused by how this could be so hard for him. For a second, I feel bad. He looks like he's in true discomfort, like my name is torturing him and not the other way around.

"Just repeat what I say," Mona instructs. "Yal. No, not Yale. I don't even think she applied there. Yal. Now say Duh. Like Bart Simpson. Then you put it together. Yal-Duh. Yalda."

"Cool name," he says, and I wish he would let me get back to our depleted planet, but he's not done yet. "Are you Middle Eastern?"

I really dislike this question. Most people could answer with a simple yes or no, but it's not that easy for us. Afghans may practice the same religion as a lot of the Middle East and maybe we have some foods in common, but the country is in central Asia. But when I've told people I'm Asian before, they looked at me like I didn't understand the question.

"No, not really."

"Persian?" he asks with a squint.

"My family's from Afghanistan."

"Oh, wow! Interesting place. Have you been there?"

I shake my head.

"Yeah, you probably shouldn't go," he says with a smile. I don't need to tell him that my parents dreamed of taking us

50

for a visit someday, but when the United States withdrew from the country and told the Taliban they could come on back into town, that possibility went out the window.

"Mm-hmm," Mona hums. I know she's thoroughly entertained by this.

"Well, welcome," he says, and flashes me two thumbs up.

"Welcome to you too," I say, and show him I, too, have a pair of thumbs. He smiles like we've got a secret handshake now and returns to the desk at the front of the room. Mona leans in but I beat her to it.

"I know. As if I weren't born here. Or as if it's not my fourth year in this school and his first day."

"Exactly," Mona says.

After class, I spot Nahal in the hallway. I hope she doesn't end up in a classroom with him. If I got two thumbs up and I was born here, he might break-dance to hear her story.

School ends and I take the bus to the restaurant to help Dad out for a few hours. The evening is busier than expected for a Tuesday, and I worry that Dad is going to ask me to come in again this Friday night, when Yusuf is playing at WhereHouse.

We are both beat by the time Dad pulls the car into the garage. Mom is there, tossing a few empty jars into the recycling bin.

"Guys, did you bring the boxes?" she asks.

We meant to. We really meant to. My dad looks at me for help.

"Yalda?" Mom says, but by now she's in the garage peering

into the back of the car and looking from my dad to me in sheer disappointment. "I can't believe it."

We could explain to her that we got a last-minute take-out order for twelve people, which my dad probably should have declined because we were supposed to close in fifteen minutes, but we're not busy enough to have the luxury of turning down customers. Of course, just as we were filling aluminum tins with rice, chicken kebab, and fried eggplant, I realized that we didn't have enough yogurt for our signature sauce, so I had to run across the street to the grocery store and pick up a tub before the customers came by to pick up their order.

This delayed closing and made Mom's request for boxes slip both our minds. I brace myself for a guilt trip.

Mom's guilt trips have always been effective motivational tools, but they took on near force-of-nature powers when the Taliban once again took control of my parents' homeland. It was the end of a quiet summer, one without a family vacation because we didn't have enough staff to cover us for even a few days. We watched video clips and saw pictures, which bounced from phone to phone on messaging apps, of thousands of Afghans desperate to get into the airport in Kabul. Crammed masses in huge military planes without seats. People crossing a stream of sewage, knee-deep in the muck with children in their arms. Scraggly-looking men with rifles on their shoulders riding through deserted streets on trucks. I can't imagine what it must have been like to leave home with a backpack of stuff and to arrive in a totally new country. I would catch my parents staring at their phones, and sometimes they wouldn't even notice me walking in or out of the room. I looked over my dad's shoulder one day and saw a woman pass her baby over a high fence into the hands of an American soldier. I once spotted my father walking out of the living room to watch a video of people injured in a bombing at the airport without me seeing it. I didn't bother telling him I'd already seen it on Mom's phone. People were literally running for their lives.

A few weeks later, some of those very same people were on American soil—people like Nahal.

*We have the same story*, my mother said one day. *But when we arrived here, no one helped us. Things are different this time.*

She started calling around to see where help was needed. She translated for a few people over the phone, her eyes sometimes red by the time she ended the call. My dad did the same. People were brought to military bases, some within an hour's drive from our house. Mom gathered clothing and used luggage and we drove together one day to deliver them to a base. When we got there, all I could see was a white-and-red water tank cutting into the sky. We didn't actually go in. We were met outside by two people in uniforms and others with official-looking lanyards around their necks. I wondered what it might be like to stay on a military base. Mom told us people were upset. There were rumors that refugees had smuggled weapons into the country and were the cause of a shortage of diapers in the town. I googled the base's name after and read that people living nearby felt the government was lying to them about the whole operation at the base. On the other hand, there were also a lot of churches, synagogues, temples, and community groups that sprang into action to help.

A couple months later, we heard that Afghan families would be set up with apartments in our town and my mother really went to work. She joined forces with a local group of do-gooders led by a determined retired teacher named Linda and our house swirled with a new kind of energy. Yusuf and I went with Mom to an apartment complex where lots of Afghans were being resettled. We carried furniture into the elevators and up to the fourth floor to set up an apartment, passing people in the hallways who had recently moved into the apartments themselves. When Mom greeted people, nearly everyone invited us to come in for a cup of tea even though it was very possible they didn't yet have cups. Mom declined, and Yusuf and I watched the politest back-and-forth this world has ever seen.

Inside the apartment, we made beds, arranged a coffee table and mismatched armchairs in the living room, and assembled a desk. Linda stocked the fridge with a bag of groceries and arranged bottles of spices in an otherwise empty kitchen cabinet.

Mom told me the family moving in was a single mom and three kids, one girl around my age. I made up the bed for her with my old blue comforter, the one that had stars embroidered on the edges. It wasn't necessarily childish, but I had asked for a new one last year and gotten it. I hung a couple of my sweatshirts in the closet too, and put a new hairbrush and a packet of hair ties on the dresser. We stocked the bathroom with toothpaste, shampoo, bodywash, and a box of pads. I did not know Nahal would be moving into this room, wearing the sweatshirts, and sleeping under that starry comforter. I felt strange when I saw Nahal with my cactus sweatshirt in school, like I had trespassed into her private world.

Once again, Mom's trunk is full of clothing, some new and some used, including infant onesies, winter boots for a girl, ladies' sweaters, and a man's wool coat. When she rounds corners or makes turns, the pots and pans make clanging sounds. They would slide all around if it weren't for the big jugs of laundry detergent buffering their movements.

"Mom, I'm so sorry," I say, ready to launch into a detailed explanation, but she stops me.

"It's okay, Yalda. You must have been busy. I'll bring them tomorrow when I go in," she says. "Let me text Linda and make sure the family won't be here until next week."

That feeling in my stomach is my conscience curling up in shame.

"I can drive back and get them," Dad offers. He takes a step toward the car to demonstrate his willingness.

"No, no," Mom says, and beckons us to come into the house. "It's so cold. Get in so we can close the door."

We've messed things up enough, so Dad and I hurry into the house. Dad closes the garage door and we take our coats off. I have one hand on my doorknob, eager to get to my extra-plush fleece pajamas, when Yusuf pops his head out of his room.

"Hey!" he whispers, then glances past me to confirm the hallway is empty. "I want to talk to you."

"Um, should I be nervous?"

"You really shouldn't. You're going to need to stay cool."

I love the flavors of our food, but I don't love the way cumin, garlic, and onions cling to my clothes and hair. I nod at Yusuf's door to signal we can talk in his room, then throw my bag onto my bed. Yusuf better make this quick so I can get to my shower and stop smelling like an entrée.

I fall into Yusuf's desk chair and lean back. Both our rooms have windows that look out onto the front yard, but Yusuf has the corner room, so he also has a window on the side of the house. The perk of having more daylight in his room comes at a cost, though—the family next door has two little children who use their binoculars to stare straight into Yusuf's window.

"So?" I prompt.

"About the show. Did you decide if you want to go?" Yusuf asks. He's perched on the edge of his bed, his elbows on his knees.

I nod.

"Actually, a bunch of people from school are going—Mona and Asma and Keith," I count off.

"Really?" Yusuf says, his head tilted in surprise. I prepare myself for questions about Keith going, but Yusuf just nods. I'm not going to tell him about Keith suggesting we go together because I don't really need to be teased about this. "That's cool. We've never played for this many people. But we've been practicing a lot. It'll be good."

I can hear a younger version of Yusuf in there, the Yusuf who always wanted me to go to the bathroom with him to brush our teeth at bedtime because he saw the shower curtain moving when he was in there alone.

"Are you sure you're happy about people coming?" I ask.

"Yeah, of course," he insists, but sighs when I raise an eyebrow. Because we've spent the majority of our lives talking to each other, we can hear things even when they're not said out loud.

"Here's the thing. Playing for strangers is easier. If they like you, great. If they don't, who cares because you don't know their names and you probably won't ever see them again and maybe they're jerks. But it's different playing for people you know. Friends, I mean. If they say you're good, maybe they're just being polite. And if they say you sucked, you must have really sucked."

I'm surprised to hear Yusuf say this. I didn't imagine there were holes in his armor of self-confidence.

"You guys always sound really good, and that's without a real venue and all the acoustics or whatever. And some people are telling their parents that the show is at school instead of WhereHouse," I add.

"Even Asma and Mona?"

"Yes, especially them," I confirm.

My mother appears in Yusuf's doorway.

"Everything okay?" she asks.

Yusuf puts his hands behind his head.

"Yeah, we were just talking about going with you this weekend when you deliver the stuff for the refugees."

Yusuf is a goddamned ninja when it comes to throwing a distraction grenade and staying undetected by Mom's hawk eyes. I am taking notes.

"Is it harsh to call them refugees?" I ask, genuinely unsure. "Feels a little . . . disempowering. Like, isn't it better to say *survivors* than *victims*?"

"I'm pretty sure these folks aren't feeling very empowered. And there's truth to it, even if it's not pretty. They're not Afghan Americans," Yusuf replies, curling two fingers on each hand to make air quotes.

"Yet," I add.

"Oh, don't worry so much about the names. Call them this, don't call them that. People are thinking too much. You know, before they came here, these families were at a military base for two months. Over there, the Americans were calling them 'guests,'" Mom says.

"Guests? That makes no sense," I reply. "Guests are supposed to go back home."

"Maybe it was to remind people to treat them nicely," Mom says with a shrug. "I don't know which is worse or which is better, and anyway, that's not the point. These families are just like us. Simple. And after forty years of fighting, 'Afghan' and

58

'refugee' is almost the same thing."

And the truth of that hits me hard—that so many Afghans across decades have been running. Away from violence, away from their homes, away from people they loved. I know I have something in common with these people who are moving into town right now. I know they're probably eating the same foods we serve at the restaurant, and the same words and music float through our homes.

At the same time, I've been living a comfortable, hyphen-ated life as an Afghan-American. Or is it Afghan American? I've never been a refugee or even seen anyone in my family in need of clothing donations, but I know the story of our people has always been one of loss. Maybe that's why I've kept my dis-tance from Nahal—because I can't decide if being around her makes me feel more or less like myself, if the hyphen sometimes used in my label means a connection between two worlds or if one side is being taken away from the other and leaving me as something less than whole.

6

I take another look in the mirror and debate changing my clothes.

"It's not like you're going to prom," I mumble to myself.

If I change, will that be taken as a sign that tonight is a special occasion? And is that occasion a forbidden night at WhereHouse or is it going to WhereHouse with Keith? I don't want to wear what I would put on any other day of the week, but I also don't want to look like I dressed up for this.

I check the time on my phone. Yusuf's already gone. He took the car so he could take some of the band's gear over and set up in time. Since my parents are at work, I've told them Mona, Asma, and I are going to watch the show, which is true. We are all going.

We're just not going *together*.

Then there's the part about where the show is happening. My parents didn't even question us when Yusuf said the event would be at a community center. It's frustrating when they go full investigative journalist mode when there's nothing going on and yet even worse to see them not ask anything besides what time to expect us home after the show on the one night that we're bending the rules.

For a ninth-grade English assignment, we had to submit a list of ten euphemisms. Bending the rules could have been my number eleven.

"This doesn't have to be so hard," I tell myself.

I put on a pair of distressed jeans, ones that made my father shake his head and wonder aloud if he should buy a lopsided coffee table to replace the solid four-legged one we have now. I pair the jeans with a blush-pink sweater that probably (definitely) shrank in the dryer. After I lace up my black ankle boots, I trace my eyelids with a thin line of liquid eyeliner and step in front of my full-length mirror.

The sweater hugs me as tight as my mom does. I tug at it and turn sideways to see what I look like from another angle. I either look ridiculous or . . . not ridiculous.

I go back to my closet and start poking between hangers, praying that the perfect top is hiding somewhere among these pieces I'm currently regretting buying. My phone dings. It's a message from Keith, whose number I have not yet saved in my contact list because I don't want anyone to look over my shoulder and see his name.

At the same second that I text back a thumbs-up and declare that everything is perfectly fine, the rod in my closet buckles and everything I own falls into a massive heap on the floor. It looks like the aftermath of an earthquake. Looking for another outfit will involve crawling, so I take a deep breath, shut the closet door, and commit to the clingy pink sweater I'm wearing. I can always keep my coat on, I figure.

Because I have a feeling in the pit of my stomach that something's going to go wrong, I make sure the stove is off and the windows are locked before I leave. The temperature's dropped so I stuff my hands into my pockets and hope my nose doesn't start running as I walk down the street. My mom's bought me plenty of those mini packs of tissues, but because I never actually carry them around, I end up stealing toilet paper from the nearest restroom, and bathroom chic is definitely not the look I'm going for tonight.

Keith is standing outside his house. His brother, Danny, and his mother are with him. She's adjusting his brother's coat, like he's younger than Keith instead of a full decade older. Danny served in Afghanistan but came home with a leg injury years ago. He moved back in with his family and has been doing all kinds of odd jobs—dropping off take-out meals and painting houses.

Keith waves and I wave back, smiling as if I'm glad his whole family is standing outside with him because Mona and Asma tell me my thoughts are always plastered on my face.

"Hey there," Keith calls once I'm close enough that he doesn't have to yell.

"Hi!" I reply, making eye contact with his mother and brother. His mother's smile is tight-lipped, like the kind my mother gives to anyone showing up on our front porch trying to tell us we need a new roof.

"This should be a fun night," she says to me. "Lots of students going, I hear?"

"Yes, a couple of my friends and a bunch of others."

"That's nice. Plenty of people to hang out with," she says, sounding awfully chipper.

Is she saying we should hang out with other people? I'm suddenly embarrassed, like I've been stalking Keith and she's calling me out on it.

Keith bites his lip and looks at Danny.

"Let's get going," Danny says, nodding in the direction of the car. Keith turns to me to explain.

"My brother's coming, too," he says. "He always wanted to be in a high school band, but Mom gave away his drum set three months into his freshman year."

"It was either the drums or me," Keith's mother calls out as she walks back toward their front door. Both Keith and Danny shoot each other knowing looks.

I feel the night shifting around me, making me a spectator. Maybe this was a bad idea.

"It's better than walking in the cold," Keith says, as if he's heard my thoughts.

"Yeah," I agree. "I mean, that's fine. And it is pretty brutal out here tonight."

Danny starts the car. I slide into the back seat and pray my mother doesn't call me now. Later, when she asks me how tonight went, I'll leave this part out. A benign omission. I don't see a way around it. We'll be at the venue in just a couple minutes anyway.

Keith opens the back door on the opposite side of the car. His brother swivels in his seat and shoots him a pointed look.

"So, what am I? Your Uber driver?" he asks with a laugh.

"Bro, if I could afford Uber . . . ," Keith says as he climbs out of the back seat.

"Get a job," Danny chuckles as he fastens his seat belt.

Keith slides into the passenger seat next to Danny. He sits almost sideways so that he's looking over the headrest at me.

"You good?" he asks.

"Fabulous!" I say with a little too much energy.

Danny reverses out of the driveway. The radio is on low but loud enough that I can make out the singer's auto-tuned voice, her repeated offer to do wild things all night long. I am glad to be in the back seat where no one can spot my face flushing.

"Sick of this canned music," Danny says, silencing the radio with a quick turn of the dial. He settles into his seat. "Remember the concert we went to in Virginia Beach that summer, Keith? I convinced Mom and Dad to let you go with me. I think you were the youngest kid there."

"How could I forget? Three people told me it was cool that my dad brought me to the show."

"It wasn't 'cause I looked old. You had that baby face going on. Looked like I should have had you in a booster seat on the drive over."

Although I feel like a third wheel, I like seeing Keith and his brother play the game that I've seen my parents play with my uncles and aunts. Yusuf and I play, too. It starts with a name, a song, a holiday. We jump from one memory to another, hopscotching through time. If we drive past a pond in town, my mom and dad will inevitably return to the day Yusuf and I had our biscuits nabbed out of our toddler hands by an especially hungry goose.

Keith is trying to make me feel part of the conversation, though. "I don't think we need to bore Yalda with your inaccurate memories," he chides.

Danny smiles and glances at me in the rearview.

"Yalda, your family's from Afghanistan, right?"

"Yup," I answer, and wait to see what will come next. Generally, this is when people comment about how tragic it is that the Taliban are back in power. Danny served in Afghanistan so I'm sure he knows how ugly things have gotten there. I wouldn't blame him for being resentful of all Afghans, even if we had nothing to do with him being sent over there. Then again, maybe he's thinking about the refugees landing in this town.

But Danny doesn't speak. He also doesn't slow down at the

stop sign, and the driver of a gray SUV leans hard into the horn after swerving to miss us. Danny slams on the brakes and I lurch forward in my seat, held back only by the seat belt.

The driver of the SUV pauses on the other side of the intersection, rolls down his window, and shouts something, but my head hasn't quite found its equilibrium yet. Keith leans over his seat to check on me.

"You all right?" he asks.

"Most likely," I reply.

"Shit," Danny mutters as he slowly rolls out of the intersection. "Looked like he was doing at least fifty."

My pulse is banging away at three times that.

I want to say that he should have been doing zero at a stop sign, but judging from the tension in Danny's jaw, I don't think he's going to find my feedback all that helpful.

"You good, Danny?" Keith asks.

"Yeah. Hell yeah," Danny replies, shifting in his seat as if to reset himself. He's driving again. I'm breathing again, thankful that we didn't end up in an accident because I would have had to explain to my parents why I was in this car in the first place.

The ride is quiet, the silence broken only by Danny clearing his throat and the buzzing of texts coming through our phones. I've gotten a steady flow of messages from Mona at thirty-second intervals.

Need directions? Mona writes.

I respond with an eye roll emoji.

Almost there, I add.

"Now this is a real hole in the wall," Danny remarks as he pulls into a parking lot lit up by three long-necked streetlamps. Just next door is a bar called Cedars. There's a faded mural painted on the front of what I'm guessing are cedar trees. I wouldn't know one if a branch fell on my head. There are two people standing outside, one talking on a cell phone and the other holding a skinny beer bottle.

Danny takes a spot near the WhereHouse entrance and locks the car behind us. We cross the lot, hands in pockets and shoulders curled in the chilly air. From the parking lot, we can hear someone warming up on a guitar. I'm half expecting to be turned away at the entrance, but no one even seems to notice us enter through the double doors. It's dimly lit inside, mostly by track lights on the ceiling that are aimed at the stage. There are posters of musicians on the walls and a few high-top tables toward the back of the room with stools and a handful of benches around the perimeter of the room.

This place is really living up to its name; it's an empty warehouse that is only passing for a venue because they keep it too dark for people to see what's making the floor so sticky. Three spotlights shine on a stage that's empty except for a drum set.

Keith takes off his coat, and despite the chill in the space, I do the same, hooking it over my elbow. He doesn't seem to notice my outfit, which is both a relief and a tiny bit disappointing too. I feel a little shiver run through me. There aren't enough people in the room to warm the space and the door keeps opening as people float in and out.

"Yalda!"

Mona calls me from the far side of the room. She's standing and waving at me. On the bench behind her sits Asma, bundled in her coat and offering an uneasy smile.

My friends' eyes are on me like hot lasers as I stand with Keith and Danny. Since I told the girls I was coming with Keith, Mona has regressed into a third grader. She coos and bats her eyelashes and once asked how serious we are on a scale of one through Jasmine and Aladdin. I'm hoping she'll recover some of her dignity soon. Asma, on the other hand, said Keith seemed like a good guy and that she hoped we would have fun hanging out together. It felt like there was more she wanted to say, but she held back and I didn't press her on it—probably because I didn't want to hear any words of caution.

"I think I spotted your girls. Did you want to hang out with them?" Keith asks, noticing Mona's arms flailing in the air like she's directing traffic. She's still got her burgundy puffer on. I'm not sure if Keith meant for us to part ways here. I don't want to assume too much. Actually, it's probably best I don't assume anything at all.

"I don't have to," I say. "Unless, do you want to?"

Keith looks at Danny, who is standing a couple of feet back. He has one hand stuffed into his pocket and his cell phone in the other hand, the screen illuminating his face and furrowed brow. I turn to Keith. "I guess I wasn't sure if we were just coming here together or if we were going to watch the show . . . together."

68

"Like a date?" Keith asks, cocking his head so his hair falls away from his eyes.

"No, that's not what I meant," I say quickly, maybe too quickly.

Keith lets out a long sigh.

"Here's the thing," he says, and I think maybe a head-on collision at the intersection wouldn't have been so bad. My face is hot enough to melt a crayon. I instantly flash back to our conversations and I can see it all clearly now. The watermelon in winter, Asma's chastising look, and the smell of cumin on my black jeans—I'm a curiosity, not a crush.

# 7

"I didn't know my brother would be coming with me," Keith says with a conflicted look. "Maybe we can hang out some other time . . . without everyone else. Also, my brother aside, I have serious concerns about Mona."

I follow his gaze and almost die to see Mona staring at us.

"Oh my God," I say.

Mona shrugs and shakes her head in a "what gives" gesture. Asma, the patron saint of subtlety, tugs on the sleeve of Mona's coat, but Mona hardly seems to notice.

"So, another time. What do you think?" he asks. At this critical moment and without warning, someone flips a switch and a rock song blares through two large speakers in the back of the hall. I feel the vibration through the soles of my shoes.

"Yeah, that sounds like a very good idea," I agree.

"What?" Keith asks, because it's hard to hear anything now that the music is on.

"Good idea!" I say, and give him a goofy thumbs-up. I'm partly disappointed and partly relieved. Maybe this evening is a sign from the universe. Maybe Keith has just had a what-was-I-thinking moment and is saving us both from a very awkward second half of senior year.

Keith bites his lip but doesn't say anything more. He nods in the direction of his brother before we part ways. He walks back to Danny and I cross the room to join my friends. When I reach the bench, Mona cuts her smoky eyes at me. She's been experimenting with her mother's kohl eyeliner lately and she's gotten really good at smudging it, not smearing it.

"Fears!" she says.

I blink. Am I that transparent?

"You look fierce!" she repeats, adding a snap of her fingers for effect, and my shoulders loosen with relief. Words are toying with my head these days. "Holding nothing back tonight, I see. Isn't he going to sit with us? I've shooed at least five people away from this bench so you two could fit with us."

"She told those two people over there that our friend's in the bathroom," Asma says, shaking her head. "People are going to think you have a bad case of food poisoning or something."

Asma's always more sensitive to what people think. This has been especially problematic since her parents didn't bother to think through how kids would pronounce her name. While her name means *supreme* or *beautiful*, people butcher it. They turn her into a respiratory ailment in need of an emergency inhaler. Or they put all their energies into the first two letters of her name and turn her into the literal butt of their jokes.

"He's going to sit with his brother," I reply, and wonder if Keith is watching me. I lean back and twist my hair over one shoulder to look casual and not like I'm bursting from the conversation we just had. "It's not a big deal."

Mona's eyes go soft with sympathy. She reads my no big deal as a very big deal. Her voice drops with the weight of the situation.

"Oh, he brought his brother, too. So this wasn't really a—"

"No, actually it wasn't like that. He wasn't expecting his brother to come so he said we should hang out some other time . . . without everyone else," I say, repeating his words.

"As in, he wants you guys to hang out alone, just the two of you," she confirms. Why does her version sound so different? But come to think of it, that *is* what Keith said. I'm suddenly fizzy inside, effervescent.

"Oh my hot bod. What did you say?" Mona asks.

"I said sure."

"I bet you did!" Mona squeals. "Now all you have to do is pull it off without your parents losing their minds. Actually, your parents are cool so they probably wouldn't."

"*Your* parents are cool," Asma says, then shakes her head. "Mine, not so much, but that's mostly because my grandmother is a legendary matchmaker, and all marriages are supposedly

72

doomed if she doesn't handpick the people."

"It's just hanging out," I say, cringing at the mention of marriage and matchmaking. How did that even come up? I'm so glad Keith isn't hearing this conversation. "Hanging out is no big deal. It's nothing serious."

My parents have never explicitly told me that I cannot date. That would require them to put the words *date* and *boys* in unacceptable proximity to my name, and I think they fear the power of suggestion.

My mom, who seems to be in charge of addressing all taboo topics with us, finds oblique ways to talk about dating. And there are some conversations she seems to have only with me. Watching a movie, she'll shake her head and say it's impossible for guys to see girls as only friends. She'll throw in an oh-so-casual mention about the boy-crazy daughter of so-and-so who neglected her schoolwork and will be selling hair accessories in the mall and eating fast food for the rest of her life because she didn't listen to her parents. Even these sideways mentions of relationships seem to give my dad severe heartburn. He pretends he hears his phone ringing in the next room or feels an urgent need to bring in more paper towels from the garage.

But it's not just that dating will kill my chances of having a career or a salad. I remember my mom's older sister warning us against dating because of a different set of consequences too terrible to name.

*The boys see the girls and they are one day with this one, another day with that one. Like a cheap thing. For the boys, nobody says anything. But for the girls, forget it. She's this and that. Anyway, now is the time for thinking about school. Everything else can come later.*

And that sums up the discussions we've had in the family about dating or relationships. If this had been an English assignment, Ms. Deroche would have failed my mom and my aunt for lack of detail, no citation of sources, excessive use of hyperbole, poor structure, and failure to address the topic.

My father would have been marked absent.

A guy in acid-washed jeans and a black T-shirt appears on the stage. Someone in the crowd lets out a whoop and others follow. In the last ten minutes, the crowd has grown to where I can't see the other side of the room, and if I look for Keith, Mona will start teasing me for craning my neck.

"Well, look at who crawled in tonight," the guy says with a laugh. "You guys here for a show or what?"

The room hollers back. Asma lets out a whoop, much to our surprise. Mona claps, more for Asma than for the performances that are to come.

"For those of you lucky enough not to know me, I'm Jace, and I'm glad you didn't have anything better to do tonight." There are more cheers. Jace grins at the crowd, then turns and waves to someone offstage. He checks his watch. "All right, we've got a great lineup tonight. We're going to have some fresh talent on the stage. Who knows? Maybe we'll be hearing from a group that'll end up on our wall of fame."

Someone appears at the corner of the stage and kneels beside the speaker. Suddenly, a brain-piercing screech erupts. We cover our ears and groan.

"Whoa, man. Late for a sound check, isn't it? Sorry about that," Jace says, then shoots the guy a grim look and pivots to the crowd. He turns a shade more formal, more like a manager. "So, for real, though. Thank you all for coming out tonight. I'm ready to hear these bands rock the house. What about you?"

Another round of cheers, laughter. Jace introduces the first band. I don't know the group. Their lead singer is a woman with chunky blond highlights. She looks from the crowd to her bandmates, standing in front of the drummer as she sings.

The last time I stood on a stage was for a fourth-grade play. I was a spider. My costume had eight legs that we'd made too long and floppy. Every time I took a step, I was whacked in the face by one of my own hairy limbs, much to the delight of the audience. Yusuf might like the stage, but I prefer to keep eyeballs, lights, and cameras off me.

"Do you know this song?" Asma asks me.

"Nope," I say, shaking my head.

Mona nods. "My brother listens to this stuff all the time," she says. "I think it's kind of depressing."

The second band comes onstage. Jace introduces the lead singer, Larson. I'm straining to see if I'll recognize them, but when they step into the light, I realize they're a few years older than us.

"We're going to do an oldie tonight," Larson says. He looks

to be in his late twenties and is wearing a brick-red flannel shirt over dark jeans. He nods at the drummer and turns his attention to his own guitar. I don't recognize it until they hit the chorus and repeatedly refuse to take *it*. At this point, I can even sing along. I don't know what *it* is, but none of us are going to take *it* anymore.

I look around and see people nodding and cheering, a fed-up consensus.

"I like this," Mona laughs. "Who sings this?"

Asma has her phone out.

"I should know this. I'm way too weak in music references," she groans. Asma dreams of one day winning at least five days straight on *Jeopardy!*, so in preparation she leaves no question unanswered. She even has the game show's music as her ringtone. "Twisted Sister!"

"Don't you mean, 'Who is Twisted Sister'?" I say. Asma grins, like I've just spoken her language.

"That's such a weird name," Mona reflects. "What's it supposed to mean?"

"If the internet knows, I'll find out," Asma says, scrolling on her phone.

At the end of the song, Larson riffs on his guitar for a few seconds, then shouts into the crowd.

"Sounds like you can't take it anymore either," he tells the crowd. Encouraged by the cheers, he laughs. "I'm with ya. I've had enough of people telling me I need to love *everybody*. No offense, but I've had enough of people who feel *offended*."

There's laughter in the crowd.

"If you feel me, say enough!" he commands.

"Enough!" the crowd echoes, half laughing. Asma doesn't yell and isn't about to start just because this guy said to, and I'm always a second too late to join any cheer, but Mona whoops loudly enough for the three of us. I spot Yusuf on the stage wings, mostly hidden by the curtain. They were scheduled to be onstage five minutes ago, but Larson is clinging to the spotlight.

"I think I saw an *everybody* in the grocery store trying to figure out how to make a bomb out of cornflakes. Eff that. Say enough!" He leans into the mic this time. His voice rattles the speakers. I am having a hard time believing what I'm hearing.

"Enough!" the crowd echoes. Larson throws a fired-up fist in the air. Mona snaps her arm back to her side and whips around to look at me.

"What the hell?" Mona shouts, but she's a whisper against this crowd.

That flutter in my chest, the pit in my stomach—my body knew before I did that tonight could go so very wrong.

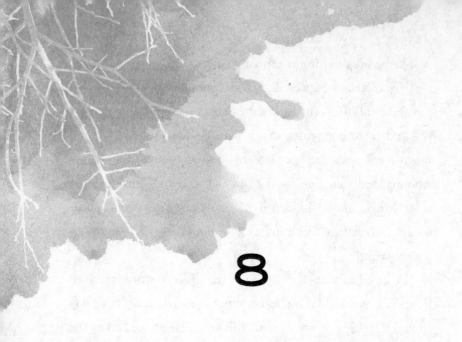

# 8

Groans and laughter, applause and protest ripple through the audience like warm and cool currents in the ocean. I know the town has been tense because of refugees being resettled here. That cranky vibe has seeped into our school too, but I did not expect to hear that bitterness onstage at the WhereHouse. I look around the room and suddenly feel like I'm on another planet.

Mona and Asma look as stunned as I feel. A guy standing near the front shouts something at the stage before making his way out of the auditorium. I don't know exactly what he said, but he's got the same olive skin and thick hair, so I know we're made of similar ingredients.

The band clears off the stage and Jace returns, looking more perplexed than when the mic screeched.

"Hey, hey. Can everyone settle down for a moment here? Remember, we're here for the music. Let's keep all that other stuff out of here. I think it's time to bring out the next band," he says, giving Yusuf a nod.

"That's it?" I say. "Is he serious?"

"How dare he? You can't say things like that," Asma says, shaking her head.

"Apparently you can, and everyone looks pretty happy to ignore it," Mona declares. "That guy is such a piece of—"

"Trash. Such trash," I say. His grocery store comment has me fuming. I spotted an Afghan family at a grocery store a few days ago. A father and two teenagers had divided up the bags from the shopping cart, each carrying two bags. They left on foot, maybe for the apartment buildings down the road. I watched them walk away and wondered if my parents looked like those kids when they first landed in this country. "He should have been booed off the stage."

It occurs to me, as soon as I say this, that I did not stand up to boo him off the stage. I didn't even boo from my seat on the bench. Where did my voice go?

"Without further ado, I give you The Hipper Campus," Jace says, then leaps off the front of the stage like it's burning his feet.

Yusuf and his bandmates drift into their positions. Liam takes his seat at the drums and taps a cymbal gently, then stills it with two fingers. Christopher takes one mic and Yusuf the other. They plug their guitars into the sound system and Yusuf turns to Liam, who gives him a nod. Yusuf leans into the mic.

"Talk about a tough act to follow. Let me start by saying therapy works and maybe some people should try it," he says, and the crowd reacts with noise I don't know how to interpret. There's definitely some laughter in the mix. "Anyway, it's a dream to play for a hyped crowd and you guys seem pretty lit. We have a different vibe, though. Ready for it?"

People applaud. Yusuf grins and begins plucking at the strings of his guitar, the one he bought from Crescendo with a few months' worth of paychecks, and that was with the employee discount. The studio manager, Beto, lets them practice there since both Chris and Yusuf give lessons to kids.

"This one's an original," he says, then shoots a look at his bandmates. Standing in the crowd, I am second-guessing Yusuf's decision to play something unfamiliar to the audience. I'm nervous for them. "Here goes."

The song kicks off with a spiral of notes, climbing a scale and then sliding back down. It's haunting, especially in the darkened auditorium. Then Yusuf adds his voice. Christopher steps up to his mic and adds the harmony.

"His pitch is gold," Asma adds with an air of musical authority. "They're going to be the favorites tonight. No question."

"And I can't believe he wrote this song," Mona says. She looks like she wants to say more but doesn't because she'll miss it.

*A chemical burn, you never learn*

*Don't reveal too much too soon*

Everyone in this room can hear it. His voice isn't strained or boring. It's sometimes gentle, sometimes edgy, but always smooth. Of course, I say none of this to anyone because I don't want to brag about my brother, and I certainly don't say it to Yusuf because his ego needs no inflation.

Keith and his brother have moved toward the front of the room. They're a few feet away from the stage and easy to spot because Danny is bigger than most people here. Keith leans toward his brother and says something to him, his hand cupped over his mouth to funnel the sound. Danny nods, his eyes on the stage. Maybe Keith feels my gaze because he looks in my direction and smiles. He points at the stage and gives me a thumbs-up. I nod, return the smile, and turn my attention back to the stage.

"I see him looking at you!" Mona teases.

"Mona," I say, my voice deep with warning.

"What? It's an observation," she replies.

"Observe something else, please," I suggest.

"Looks like Keith likes your whole family," Mona says, unable to contain herself. Does he? I don't know what to make of his brother asking me where my family was from. I don't know how they feel about the new folks in town, especially given what Danny's been through.

"Mona, drop it," Asma chides. The room bursts into applause and we join in. "Can we just listen to the music? They're on their second song already."

81

Yusuf takes a swig of water and returns to the mic.

"Can you guys show my buddy Chris some love?" Yusuf shouts. Chris closes his eyes and strums on his electric guitar. "And a little appreciation for Liam!"

Liam adjusts his black-rimmed glasses and raps out a rhythm on the drums, then rumbles into the beat for the next song. I've been on the other side of the wall listening to Yusuf practice this song he wrote over the past year. Yusuf walks across the stage as he sings.

I've told Yusuf the song is really good, but the truth is the lyrics rock me and they nail the song, slowing down the final lines to let them fill the room. He repeats them and it may be the best he's ever sounded:

*If we stay or not, all the battles we fought*
*They cannot steal this*
*They take us apart, but we're a work of art.*
*And they'll never unsee this.*
*I come in peace,*
*Breathe with me or*
*I'll leave in pieces.*

Chris looks back at Liam, drumsticks raised as part of the finale. Yusuf beckons the crowd, inviting us all to join him. The line gets louder as voices lift, converge, and blur together.

*I'll leave in pieces.*

I sing it too.

"Hey, we sound pretty good together! Let's change it up a little," Yusuf calls into the crowd, some people still singing that last line. He starts to vocalize. "*La la la la . . .*"

He points his mic to the audience.

"*La la la la . . . ,*" they repeat. I sigh. Yusuf must really think he's some kind of star now. He is going to be impossible to live with if The Hipper Campus wins tonight.

"*La la la la hey lee la!*" Yusuf moves with the notes, gets up on his tiptoes for the high of the *hey*. Liam's holding his sticks, watching Yusuf with an expression on his face that probably mirrors mine. Christopher looks a little confused but strums a few notes, trying to give the chant a melody.

The crowd repeats. I've never seen Yusuf croon like this. It doesn't even sound like the song. He does a third round, going higher in pitch and then ending low. By this point, it sounds like the entire audience has joined in.

"Hey now, people," Yusuf says to a captivated room. "What would you say if I told you you've all just recited the beginning of the Shahadah? Say it three times and you're officially converted, so al-salaam alaykum, everybody, and peace and cornflakes be upon you, my friends."

"Oh my God," Asma says.

I gasp and sit frozen in my seat. I can't believe he just said that. The room bubbles over with noise. In the dim light, I see mouths opened, eyes narrowed, shadows deepened. People are on their feet. Chairs squeak against the sticky floor. Angry shouts break through the rumble.

Something catches my eye in the periphery. Danny is pointing at the stage and shaking his head, his face flushed. He says something to Keith, who nods and runs his fingers through his hair. He glances in my direction and when our eyes lock, I try to read what he's thinking but can't. There's no message in his expression, just something simmering under the surface.

"Yusuf!" I shout. I want my brother off the stage and away from this crowd. Their performance got a wave of love but now I can also feel the pull of a dark countercurrent here, too.

Liam and Christopher look from each other to Yusuf and the crowd. Liam is seething, and I wouldn't be surprised if he threw his drumsticks at Yusuf's head. Jace reaches center stage in three long strides.

"All right, all right," he says, trying to signal the crowd to settle down by waving his hands, but this is not an orchestra he can conduct. Everyone who was sitting is now standing and people who were standing are now shoving. "This has been quite a night. I'm going to—"

When Jace tries to take the mic from Yusuf, my brother raises a finger to ask for a moment. Jace shakes his head and leans in to take the mic from him, but Yusuf takes two steps back and shakes his head.

I hold my breath, afraid to hear what comes out of my brother's mouth next.

"I promise—that wasn't actually the Shahadah. No one's been converted," Yusuf says. I can see his nerves through his sheepish grin. He didn't expect this reaction.

Someone in a black T-shirt rushes to Jace from behind the stage, shouting something into his ear. Jace listens, his eyes on the crowd. He signals to someone in the back of the room, a larger guy with a denim jacket, a goatee, and the wide-legged stance of a security guard.

"Larson served up some straight-up retrograde racism tonight and where was this outrage then?" Yusuf asks, then re-purposes Larson's performance in a singsong voice that makes it sound like playground banter. "Well, guess what? *I'm not going to take it!*"

Jace grabs the mic this time and Yusuf doesn't resist. He puts his hands up as if to say he's finished. The auditorium devours his response, but I can feel in my bones it's only because everybody loves a good clapback. Jace brings the mic to his face a couple of times but waits for the room to go from a roar to a simmer before he asks everyone to chill out.

"Delete your band!" someone calls out. It's hard to keep up with what people are shouting. It's even harder to figure out who people want to delete—Yusuf or Larson.

"Take out the trash!" someone calls out.

"Settle down!" Jace shouts, his face flushed. He looks like a parent who is beyond fed up with fighting siblings. "And as of this minute, I want both bands out of here. Find the door you came through and get the hell out."

Larson stands at the side of the stage. He points at Yusuf and says something I can't make out. Yusuf beckons to him to come on over. Chris pushes Yusuf in the opposite direction, trying to get him offstage. Liam is already gone.

I look back at the security guard, who is shouldering his

way through the crowd to get to the stage. Without thinking, I rush to the stage too, but halfway there, my foot catches on someone or something and down I go, into the belly of this angry beast.

Asma pulls me up.

"You okay?" she asks. Mona is beside her, elbows out to keep people from jostling us. I look to the stage and see that everyone, Jace included, is gone.

"Let's go find Yusuf," Asma says, and I nod. We wind our way through the crowd and spill out the entrance. I breathe deeply, hungry for air. I've never been so relieved to be out of any building but there's no time to celebrate because I spot Yusuf and Chris by the car. Yusuf kicks the ground and Chris shakes his head.

"What the hell," I say, breathless.

"Exactly," Chris mutters. Yusuf looks from me to my friends, then shakes his head just as Liam pulls up in his hatchback. He nods at Chris, who walks around to the passenger side, throws his guitar case into the back seat, and gets in without saying goodbye. Yusuf exhales through pursed lips. He looks drained, nothing like the defiant figure he was onstage a few moments ago.

"Let's get out of here," he says.

"Yeah," I agree. Mona nods and says she's going to drop Asma off at home. She's borrowed her mom's car for tonight and parked it, as she usually does, as far away from other cars as possible to avoid any dings.

"Give me a sec," I say. My head is spinning but I haven't forgotten that I came here with Keith. Danny's car is still parked in the same spot. I look for them among the people hovering around the entrance but they're not there. I don't want to go back inside so I take out my phone to text him that I'm leaving with Yusuf. I am about to hit send when I think I hear Keith's voice.

"Danny, let's just go." That's definitely Keith, sounding very much like an impatient younger brother. I walk to the corner of the building, closer to the dumpsters, and my stomach drops.

Keith and Danny are standing with their backs to me. They're not alone and there's no mistaking the shaggy-haired person they're talking to. After tonight, Larson's face is one I don't think I'll ever forget.

# 9

"So you think I should have just let him talk that nonsense? That was true hate speech, Yalda."

Yusuf and I are sitting in our driveway. Neither of us said a word on the ride home but now we're parked outside our house and this is our last chance to talk without our parents hearing all about tonight.

"You couldn't come up with anything else to say? You had to tell the crowd you'd just converted them? There are other ways to address the problem."

"What happened after those dudes drew that garbage in the boys' locker room? Two coats of paint and a few words about good citizenship from the principal. You call that addressing the problem?"

"No, it definitely wasn't, but now they're going to look at you as the problem instead of Larson," I say.

"I wanted to make a point," he says. "I wanted them to hear me. I'm not going to shove everything I'm thinking into a drawer."

"That's a cheap shot," I snap. I rub my ankle, which is sore from bending at an unholy angle when I tripped on my way to the stage.

Yusuf lets go of the steering wheel, which he's been clutching even though he's parked the car. He shakes his head.

"Yalda, I didn't mean . . . ," he says softly. He stares out the window, looking torn. "Seriously, I'm sorry. Maybe I do need to shut up."

I know he didn't imagine the evening ending the way it did. "Well, someone needed to say something. Jace was useless," I add.

"What a clown," Yusuf scoffs. "Kicking us out like what I said was the same as what Larson said."

Yusuf stares at our garage doors, looking at something I cannot see.

"Maybe I should have done nothing," he says quietly.

"Yusuf, you—"

"I screwed up everyone's night. Yalda, people showed up for us. Asma and Mona, Keith, his brother . . ."

"You guys were really good," I said, my mind flashing back to seeing Keith and his brother with Larson. They had looked like three guys chatting outside, as if not a thing was wrong in the world. But I don't want to tell Yusuf about that now. "Asma and Mona thought so too. They were glad they came out."

Yusuf lets his head fall to the steering wheel and sighs. I feel a chill on my face when I see his forehead touch the cold leather. I'm about to suggest we go in when the porch light comes on.

Yusuf sits up quickly. We unbuckle our seat belts just as Mom opens the front door and waves at us to come in. She gives us expectant looks and pulls me in for a squeeze as we slide past her. I try to give her a quick hug back and slip out of her grasp because my mom employs all five senses to keep our home in order and I'm pretty sure my coat stinks of fries and deception.

"Do you want to get sick? You're sitting in a cold car instead of coming in to tell me some good news," she chides. She's holding her phone and shows us the screen, which is bright with a picture of her sister's face. "How did it go? Your khala says hi. Say salaam to her."

The extended family used to think Yusuf's music was a useless hobby or distraction from his schoolwork. Even our cousins thought he had strange taste in music. But last year, when Yusuf started finding obscure college scholarships for musicians, everyone's attitude changed. All my cousins started catching heat for not finding creative ways to feed the tuition monsters.

"Salaam, Khala!" Yusuf calls out in the direction of Mom's phone, and I do the same, our voices overlapping and messy but present. My mom loves to put us on the spot like this, inserting us into her phone conversations with little warning and zero permission. My aunt shouts back a cheerful greeting, then she and Mom start their goodbye process.

My father steps out of the kitchen holding a mug. His eyes look heavy, too heavy for the story of what went down tonight.

"Did you win?" Dad asks.

"No, we didn't," Yusuf replies.

"They picked another band?" Mom asks, a hint of how-dare-they in her voice.

"Not really," Yusuf replies. "They didn't pick anyone."

"Oh, so everybody won," Mom says.

"Everybody wins a competition?" Dad says, raising an unimpressed eyebrow. He had the same look on his face the day Mom explained gender reveal parties to him.

"It wasn't a competition," I say, because someone needs to shut this conversation down. "Anyway, it's late and I was ready to go to sleep an hour ago."

Yusuf mumbles some kind of agreement and we both head to our bedrooms. Any further conversation with our parents is only going to require telling more half-truths and I'm carrying enough guilt on my shoulders. I brush my teeth and open the bathroom door to find Yusuf standing in the hallway.

"Thanks for . . ." He nods in the direction of the living room.

"You don't have to thank me. You're right. Tonight totally sucked. Larson was a pile of donkey diarrhea," I declare. Yusuf laughs at one of the insults I used to sling as a child. "He shouldn't get a free pass."

"Exactly. It was wrong and dangerous."

*Dangerous.* His last word echoes in my mind as I pull my comforter over my shoulders and let my eyelids close.

Something tells me the danger isn't behind us yet.

# 10

I make every effort to sleep in the next morning, doing my best to ignore the creak of floorboards under my mother's feet. I know as soon as I step out of my bedroom, she'll try to rope me into whatever fatal deficiency she has detected in our home, and I'm not in the mood to vacuum under the living room furniture today.

I check my phone, my eyes still blurry with sleep. I have a ton of messages from Asma, Mona, and Keith. Each asks me if I've seen what people are saying about last night. I groan and switch over to Pic-Up to see what's happening.

WhereHouse is all anyone is talking about on Pic-Up. I scroll through the posts and see pictures of Yusuf with the mic in his hand. Most people didn't think to start recording until after

Jace took the stage. There were a couple of clips of Larson and his band performing, a few of Yusuf and the guys, and some reactions in the parking lot. But the most popular clip posted is one that's been spliced together. In it, someone's started with a few seconds of Yusuf's fake Shahadah and then they jump to him saying: *Say it three times and you're officially converted, so al-salaam alaykum, everybody, and peace and cornflakes be upon you, my friends.*

#Cornflakes is one of the hashtags.

New comments appear even as I'm scrolling, ranging from defending freedom of speech to asking which grocery store to avoid. Someone's offered to egg Larson's house but made sure to walk that back when others pointed out that he would be a prime suspect if something were to happen to Larson and this post could be admissible in court as evidence.

Some people say Yusuf should consider dropping out of school, and one person suggests Yusuf and Larson should settle their differences like real men, whatever that's supposed to mean. Two people say they heard that the new people in our town didn't even get a background check. Then I see someone share a post in which a string of hashtags includes one that makes my stomach lurch: #Yusuftheterrorist.

*No, no, no, no, no!*

A new message from Keith breaks through my internal screams.

Everything okay with your bro? He's not answering my texts.

I start to text Keith back because I really want to know why he looked so cozy chatting with Larson after Yusuf and the guys got kicked out last night, but then I think about Yusuf scrolling through the same comments and posts I've just seen.

"Yusuf!" I yell. I jump out of bed as my mother pops into my room. She must have been in the hallway.

"What is it?" she asks.

I set my phone on my nightstand facedown.

"Nothing, I just wanted to see if he's up yet," I say.

"Did you . . . ?" She points a finger in the direction of the wall that separates my bedroom from Yusuf's.

"Yup. No answer," I say. Wanting to get to him first, I slip past her and go to Yusuf's door. "I need to ask him about our math homework."

Mom heads to the kitchen, where I can already smell her coffee brewing.

Per our mutually agreed upon protocol, I knock and wait ten seconds before entering Yusuf's room. He's got his back to me and is staring at his computer screen with headphones on. It takes him much longer than usual to notice I've entered his sacred space. When he sees me, he closes out the tab and shuts his laptop.

Yusuf frees one ear from his headphones, which means he's open to an interruption, but not a conversation.

"Have you seen it?" I ask.

"Yeah," he says. His shoulders are stiff, betraying the calm in his voice.

"It's going to be over soon. They just need something new to talk about," I say, realizing quickly that I cannot freak out right now.

"I know," he says.

"Keith said he texted you."

"I'll text him back later," Yusuf says, and then there's a long pause while I try to figure out if I should stick around or leave him be. He doesn't even question why Keith messaged me.

"Have you talked to Chris or Liam?" I ask. It feels important to keep him talking, to hear the timbre of his voice.

Yusuf winces and rubs his eye with the heel of his hand. I could kick myself. This was probably a dumb question to ask.

"I've got a few things I need to finish, Yal," he says, and puts his headphones back on to signal the conversation is closed.

I go back to my room intending to make my bed but pick up my phone and text Keith instead.

He's in the shower.

This is my attempt at protecting Yusuf's privacy. Three dots appear. I wait for Keith's reply.

It'll cool down before Monday. Put your phone on airplane mode for a while.

Good idea.

Actually not a good idea. Don't want you to ignore my texts too.

I wouldn't, I reply.

He sends a smiley face.

I want to smile back. There is a smile somewhere inside

me. I like Keith and I like that whatever is happening between us is my own. It's the most normal thing since the beginning of time—two people being interested in each other. It's also totally abnormal and bizarre because I've never been one of those two people before. I wish I could feel free to enjoy it without wondering about the judgment and the consequences and the doubts. And I need Keith to clear up at least one part of that night for me.

But why am I even thinking about Keith right now? I take a deep breath and remind myself that on the other side of this wall, my brother is suffering. On the posts, people were talking about him as if he wouldn't see their comments. I wish I could do something to make him feel better, something to lift him out of his feelings. But I know him and I know he needs time on his own.

Normally, I would get together with Mona and Asma to hang out or maybe study, but I don't know if I can handle Mona's questions right now, and Asma is babysitting her highly energetic younger cousins who live next door. I've helped her out with them more times than I can count, but I've since realized that there are about fifty things I'd rather do than try to negotiate peace between two small humans who are willing to go to war over a fidget spinner. This time, I didn't even offer to go over to her house. The introvert in me needs some recharging, and it's rare that I get a few hours to myself.

The lockers clanging and swirling voices at school, the honking on the roads, and the sound of bad news spilling from the talk radio station sometimes make me want to put the world on mute. I take my sketchbook out of my nightstand drawer and sit at my desk. My ink pens stand at attention in a warped ceramic mug I made in middle school art class. I stare out the window to the street outside. Our neighbor is pulling his trash can to the curb.

I pluck a pen from the cluster. Sometimes I plan my drawings, starting with pencil and then moving to ink when the image comes into focus. I am unscripted right now, drawing the faint silhouette I see in my mind, a figure in the shadows with his back turned to me. I close my eyes to focus and when my eyes adjust to the dark, I can make out more details. I start off linear, outlining shoulders and legs with marks that look like sheets of rain. He's wearing a jacket two sizes too big for his frame and, by the slouch of his back, too heavy to carry. Then I'm crosshatching shadows and his jacket starts to take on movement, dimension. It goes from cardboard to leather. I switch to a thicker pen. His hair is a riot of musical notes that come together to create a chorus, a wild mane. In his hands is a microphone engulfed in flames. I switch pens again. He is staring into a mirror. I give the mirror a frame, the overly ornate kind that matches all the furniture in my aunt's home. There's a crack in the mirror, a jagged line that runs from the top right corner of the mirror to the bottom left, the center obscured by the figure.

I set my pen down and look at the drawing. Am I drawing Yusuf? I didn't mean to but there he is, emanating defeat. I steal a glance at the wall between our rooms and then look back at

98

my drawing. What does this guy see in the mirror? I can't move the figure in my mind to see his expression or reflection.

That feels tragically accurate.

At eleven o'clock, I change into black jeans and a black button-down top. This is the unofficial uniform for the restaurant. I head to the kitchen before Mom can complain that I'm making her late. Yusuf is at the breakfast table working on his math homework. He's got an elbow on the table, his hand tented over his brows so I can't see his eyes. An untouched sandwich sits on a small plate a few inches from his book.

"You all right?" I ask.

"I'm fine," he says. "Mom's waiting for you in the car."

Yusuf must have put on a good song and dance for Mom or she would be probing his emotional well-being instead of honking for me to hurry.

"Are you going anywhere?" I ask.

He shakes his head.

"Don't really feel like it," he says. "And it's cold out."

"What about Liam and Christopher?"

Yusuf takes his hands off the keys of his laptop and unfolds himself. He leans back in his chair.

"If you really want to know, Christopher's gone dark. Hasn't replied to me. And I talked to Liam but I can't say it went very well."

"They need some time," I say. "It'll die down."

"Yeah." Yusuf sighs, though he sounds unconvinced. Something makes me reluctant to leave him. I don't like the idea of him on his own, in the hollow of an empty house.

"If you want, you could come to the restaurant today. You could take all the high-maintenance tables," I offer in an attempt to lighten the mood.

The car horn bleats again.

"Yeah, I've got some work to catch up on," Yusuf says, then adds an afterthought, "But Yal, don't forget the extra bread."

"Always," I reply. Two years ago, Yusuf showed me a video of a social experiment that showed offering extra bread resulted in higher tips to waiters and waitresses. He has often suggested that he deserves a cut from my tips for bringing this to my attention. I take a step toward the garage but halt when Yusuf calls after me.

"Yeah?"

He looks at the floor but I think I see him grimace.

"Thanks for being cool about this," he says. "I hope I didn't . . . I dunno. I hope I didn't embarrass you or something. I wouldn't ever want to do that."

I did not see that coming.

"Well, I usually embarrass myself. Maybe it's good to switch things up sometimes," I say.

Yusuf smiles and looks away before I can tell if his eyes have gone dewy, too. Maybe the blowback has gotten to him more than he let on.

"And actually, I wasn't embarrassed. I was a little nervous. The vibe there was not good," I admit. I don't want to say I was scared, but I was definitely not feeling at home in WhereHouse.

"Yeah, it was pretty toxic," Yusuf agrees. "Anyway, just wanted to say that. See you tonight."

I spend the car ride staring out the window and thinking Yusuf and I haven't had a conversation that felt so heavy since the last time we talked about Rahim.

"Yalda, why are you so quiet?" my mother asks. "Something bothering you?"

"No, I just . . . I think I'm getting a headache."

"You don't sleep enough," she declares. She picks up her water canteen from the holder between us and offers it to me. "Drink some water. You're probably dehydrated, too."

To hear how often my mom worries I'm dried up, one would think I spend my days crossing a desert. I unscrew the cap and take a sip so my mom can't say I never listen to her. To her credit, Mom doesn't push me to talk after that. She just exhales heavily and glances at me out of the corner of her eye, waiting for the water to cure me.

In the restaurant, I plop my backpack onto the table closest to the kitchen doors. I've gotten good at using the downtime to get some homework done. My dad, who has already been here setting up for a couple of hours, gives me a hug and returns to the kitchen before the lunch crowd comes in.

I seat two women who look like they just came from a yoga class. An hour later, I seat an older couple who share two appetizers and an entrée.

"The food was delicious," the man tells me when I bring them their check.

"I'm glad you liked it," I say.

"It's so terrible everything that's happened there. Your family must be so glad to be here," his wife says, nodding in the direction of the woven map of Afghanistan on the wall as she wipes her hands on her napkin.

"We sure are," I say brightly, and clear their plates from the table.

My father comes out of the kitchen and surveys the room. I can feel him counting the empty tables, and his brows knit together with concern. I look at the clock. The sign outside advertising a free appetizer with the purchase of two entrées isn't exactly drawing people in. I wonder if our online appetizer coupon is getting seen at all and wish I understood the algorithms better. There must be a way to bump it into people's feeds.

I take a seat at the table closest to the kitchen, pull my phone out of my backpack, and go to the neighborhood app. As I scroll through, my mouth goes dry. The top post is about "the incident" at WhereHouse, though the place isn't named.

A Middle Eastern man took the stage at a music venue on Clover Street and started converting people to Islam. I know for a fact there were some minors in the crowd. Does anyone know if there's a law against trying to convert people against their will? I think it's a huge violation of our rights.

The responses are all over the place.

> WhereHouse used to bring great bands but I was there last year and the bands all sucked.

> Media! That's the only way to get attention. My cousin is a weatherman at WQVP and I'm going to share this with him right now.

> Please tell me you have some proof to back up these accusations because I'm so damned tired of people blaming every little thing on immigrants.

> I wonder if the people who decided we should let all these people in are going to keep an eye on the mosques? That's where these people get radicalized.

> Yeah, doesn't he know you can only convert people on Saturday mornings on their porches?

> Actually he's on this app and look what he posted. Guess who wants to convert us at his restaurant.

Below the comment is a screenshot of Yusuf's bare-bones profile on this app, a profile I didn't know he had. It's a picture of our free-appetizer coupon, a photo that has prompted three people to call for a boycott of our restaurant, as well as a full investigation. They seem to think Yusuf is a full-grown adult and owner of this restaurant.

If they did investigate, they would find out just how wrong they've got it.

"What is it, Yalda?"

I drop my phone in surprise. I am so immersed in these comments that I didn't see my dad walk over to me.

"What is what?" I reply. I hate playing dumb.

"What are you looking at?" he asks, nodding at my phone.

"Nothing, just some school stuff," I reply. My dad slides into the chair opposite me and moves the chutney tray aside so nothing sits between us. He looks directly at me, which is the parental equivalent of a hundred police flashlights in my face. My dad doesn't waste his time with small talk, not at home and most certainly not at the restaurant, so I know that he wants a real response now.

"Tell me," he says. I'm struck by the injustice of this moment. Why isn't Yusuf here to answer for himself?

He deserves a response. More than that, he deserves the truth, but still I hesitate. Against the empty tables and the melancholic song playing in the background, my dad looks oddly fragile, and I don't want to be the one to break him.

# 11

"What were you thinking? Why . . . how could you . . . ," Dad asks, so baffled he can't get the question out. Yusuf is slumped in his chair, his arms folded across his chest.

"Am I supposed to keep quiet when someone says stuff like that?" my brother asks.

"Yusuf," Mom says, her eyes pink. "People say so many stupid things. Don't let every little thing bother you."

"Little thing?" Yusuf repeats, as if to confirm he's heard Mom correctly. "Mom, you can't be serious."

Yusuf doesn't look at me. I hope he realizes our parents would have found out what happened the night of the show even if I hadn't been the one to tell them. Dad made me repeat the whole story to Mom, who went from standing to sitting and back again. She seemed conflicted, unsure if she should be more upset about us lying about where we were or about the way Yusuf responded to Larson's taunts. Sitting in our home, just the four of us, it almost felt like this wasn't as big or as bad as I had thought, but then Mom's phone started to ding with notifications. People following the digital trail had found their way to our restaurant's profile on the app. The comments were growing on the free-appetizer post. Mom thought it was good news at first, expecting all these people would soon fill the tables at the restaurant. But then she read through the calls for a patriotic boycott and an investigation. There were supportive comments in the mix too, but the harsh ones stood out as if they'd been written in neon lights.

"I don't understand," Dad says. He rubs his eyes with his hands. He looks more exhausted than yesterday, which I wouldn't have thought possible. "One month of Ramazan and you only fasted on weekends. Now you are some kind of mullah for the school?"

"So I'm not allowed to call out hate speech because I'm not a perfect Muslim?" Yusuf asks, a tinge of outrage in his voice.

"No one is a perfect Muslim. That's why we call it practicing," Mom says, then lets out a tortured sigh. She turns to my dad. "But what now? Should we reply to all these people? Or put up a sign outside the restaurant?"

Dad rejects the idea with a tight-lipped shake of his head. "Everyone wants to get attention now. There's too much talking about who hates who instead of just doing your work and minding your own business. This is a good country. No one bothers us and we're happy. You know why? When people come to our restaurant, they get good food, not signs or shouting."

I think of the forms Dad had me fill out to sponsor a Little League team and the annual lunch he caters for the firefighters and police department. When the local paper ran a story about it, Dad framed the article and hung it just behind the register next to three certificates from the state that say we have permission to operate as a restaurant and a thank-you note from a couple who enjoyed the free dessert Dad threw in when he learned it was their anniversary. That little wall of frames is evidence that he is accepted. And acceptable. Would he need those pieces to be so prominent if we weren't an Afghan restaurant?

"I'm sorry," Yusuf says. "I just . . . no one was saying anything. I had to call them out."

"You also have to think," Dad says. "Seven years we work on this restaurant. This is how we pay for this house, for your clothes, for your car. One stupid kid says something. You want us to lose everything?"

Mom shoots Dad a warning look.

"God forbid," she says in Dari, then switches back to English. "We're not going to lose everything. We will be fine."

Dad walks out of the kitchen without announcing a plan or issuing any kind of punishment on Yusuf. Mom follows him, probably to remind him how delicate Yusuf and I are and to warn him against being too harsh on us. The family meeting dissolves, and although nothing was taken away from Yusuf, he doesn't look relieved.

"I'm sorry," I say. "I didn't want to be the one who told them."

"It's not your fault," Yusuf mumbles, pushing away from the table. He leaves me alone in the kitchen with a sink full of dirty dishes. I rinse them and put them in the dishwasher so that there's one less thing for my mother to worry about. I check my phone and see a message from Asma, wanting to see how my parents are taking the news. She's clearly seen the neighborhood posts because she adds that she thinks we'll have a lot of understanding people show up to support the restaurant. I text back thanks and tell her that Yusuf shut himself in his room without saying much to me. I stare at the phone and wait for her reply.

Damn. That is really horrible, she writes back, and I grow heavy with disappointment. I was hoping for reassurance, not confirmation.

Mom's phone is on the counter. I click on the neighborhood app and see there are now eleven new comments under the picture of our restaurant. My chest tightens as I scan them.

I miss the days when restaurants just served food.

Where is this place? I have been looking for good falafel.

And this is why we can't have nice things. #closetheborder

> My sister and I ate there last month and the owners are lovely. Let's not judge before we know everything.

> If you convert, do you get to eat for free?

> Has anyone driven past the mosque lately? I saw five guys carrying big boxes into the back door last week. A little suspicion never killed anyone.

> So you're the shoot first ask questions later type. Sure, never killed anyone. #TrayvonMartin #BreonnaTaylor

The conversation has splintered off into divergent threads. The comments make my head spin faster than the blades of Mom's blender. I decide for her that she doesn't need this in her life and delete the app from her phone so I don't end up smashing it against the counter.

On Sunday, Dad calls and tells Mom that he can manage the restaurant on his own. He's giving us the day off.

"Are you sure?" she asks, glancing at me from the corner of her eye.

"Yes," I hear Dad say. "Tell Yalda she can work on homework or whatever she needs to do."

I doubt I can think clearly enough to put two sentences together at this point. In my head I'm picturing my dad wiping down empty tables and organizing menus. I wish I could delete every comment on that neighborhood discussion and hate thinking that all this angry attention traces back to Yusuf.

Mom has two ways of burning nervous energy—she either banishes every speck of dust from the house or laces up and goes for a run. I've tried both and neither seems to bring me the relief they give my mother. I end up worrying if the all-purpose cleaner is carcinogenic or if running on concrete will predispose me to early arthritis. I retreat to my room to see if the book I checked out from the library can help me get out of my head.

That afternoon, my phone buzzes with a text from Keith. A dog with perky ears and inky eyes is staring straight at me.

Hi. My name's Fisher, Keith writes.

Hey, Fisher, I reply.

Maybe you can tell me what Keith was doing with Larson that night? I type, then delete without sending.

Keith sends me a picture of two chewed-up women's shoes.

Off to a strong start, he captions.

"What am I supposed to do with this?" I mutter.

My mother pokes her head into my room right then. I know our house isn't the biggest, but it seems like she's always one step away from my door, which I have to leave open so she won't freak out and barge in.

"What are you doing with what?" she asks, her eyes wide. Her anxiety has leveled up and I'm sure not the only one who can feel it.

"Oh, Mona was supposed to send me our AP Government

110

homework, but . . ." I trail off, shaking my head. "I don't think this is the right one."

She looks over at my phone and I can see the effort it must take for her to resist the urge to pluck it out of my hands and check for herself. Instead, she just nods, tells me to call her if I need anything, and taps the doorframe a couple of times before she retreats.

Another text comes in from Keith.

Hello?

I put my phone facedown in frustration. I once splurged on an indigo sweater with a big-eyed llama embroidered on the front in cream and fuchsia threads. But for as much as I'd paid for it, the sweater still snagged on every little thing—the bristles of my hairbrush, a clothes hanger, a belt buckle—and unraveled a bit every time. That's how I've felt lately, like even my best days get snagged on big and little things that I don't see coming. I like talking to Keith but I can't unsee him talking to Larson and I certainly can't coo over his new dog without addressing the elephant in the parking lot.

Why were you talking to Larson?

I've typed and sent the question before I can delete it again. It takes a minute for those three dots to appear.

Can I call you? he writes, but I tell him I can't talk now. I want an answer, not a conversation.

Danny worked with him over the
summer mowing lawns and stuff.
Tried to talk some sense into him.

111

I don't know what explanation I was expecting, but this certainly wasn't it. I feel a bit guilty for assuming the worst. I hated the way it felt to think that Keith might have found what Larson said to be funny or justified.

Appreciate him doing that, I reply.

But I can't say it worked, Keith added.

Of course it didn't. I doubt Larson would have heard anything said to him, and not just because all our ears were buzzing from the volume of the music that night. In science talk, Larson was on the other side of an impermeable membrane.

Effort counts, I reply, then tell Keith I've got to go. I look at my sketchbook and feel too exhausted to even pick up a pen. I tuck my phone into my nightstand because I need the world to hush, to let me hear myself through the noise.


By Monday morning, I wonder if I was too insistent on quiet. The house is thick with silence. There's no race to the bathroom, and I couldn't say the word *prank* much less plan one. Yusuf and I move through our morning rituals and join Mom in the kitchen. With her supernatural optimism, she's made strawberry-banana-kale smoothies with her new nutritional find, some kind of immune-boosting mushroom that has a tragically shrimpy taste.

"Come on, guys. Not everything has to taste like apple juice," she says, slurping a spoonful from the blender to prove us wrong. She turns, but not in time to hide her puckered face.

112

I see candles on the counter and remember that today is Yalda, and I bet she's hoping tonight's celebration of the winter solstice will reset everything.

Coats zipped, my brother and I leave the house, our smoothies barely touched. Our feet move in and out of synchrony as we head down the sidewalk. I'm glad I cleared things up with Keith before this morning. Yusuf and I have brought this gray cloud from our house out with us and I am hoping Keith will change the mood.

The door swings open and Keith steps outside. Even from the sidewalk, we hear Keith's mother call his name inside their house.

"Did you hear me?" she calls after him. "This is not the time."

He lets the screen door clang shut behind him and walks across the lawn with his hands in his pockets. I wonder what his mother is worked up about. By the weight of his sigh, I can tell he's not thrilled.

"How's it going?" Yusuf asks, throwing Keith a nod.

We hear barking from Keith's house and spy a dog's face in the bay window. Keith closes his eyes briefly, then shakes his head and grins.

"Hey, you got a dog?" Yusuf asks.

"Yeah," Keith confirms. "Yalda didn't tell you? That's Fisher. Picked him up from the shelter over the weekend."

"That's cool. I didn't know you wanted a dog," Yusuf says.

He looks at me and I see in his eyes the surprise at hearing I've already heard the news. I look away to hide the flush creeping up my neck.

Keith looks back at the window, which Fisher has now partly fogged up with his panting.

"He's technically my brother's dog but I think he likes me better," he says, and as if to agree from inside the house, Fisher barks. His bark becomes more urgent seeing Keith with us, un-sniffed strangers. "My mom isn't too happy about the barking but she says it'll make people think twice about breaking into our house."

"Think that would work with Dad?" Yusuf asks me.

I just laugh. Yusuf and I begged for a dog when we were in elementary school but Dad said he would only consider it if we did all the yard work for a whole summer. After twelve minutes of weeding in the front yard, we decided we were probably allergic anyway and didn't really need a dog.

We fall into our usual formation on the sidewalk. Fisher's barking fades as we grow the distance between us and Keith's house. I keep my feet close to the grass so Keith can have more room. Today, Keith seems to edge a little closer to Yusuf, and I get the sense he's trying to make more space for me.

Maybe I'm reading too much into things.

We don't talk about the night at WhereHouse or the horrible comments people have made about Yusuf since then. We don't talk about it but we're all thinking about it. Keith fills the space with more details about their visit to the animal shelter and Fisher's first night with the family. Things almost feel normal by the time we get to the entrance, where we part ways. I find Asma and Mona waiting for me at my locker. Mona looks relieved that I've finally appeared, while Asma seems rattled.

"What is it?" I ask.

"It's bad is what it is," Mona says.

# 12

"Someone drew a bunch of hate stuff and wrote 'terrorist' on Yusuf's locker," Mona says.

"No. Oh, *please* no," I say, as if I can beg this news away. Asma links her arm with mine.

"I'm so sorry, Yal, but it's true. People can be such shits," Mona declares.

"It's so awful. He was just trying to do the right thing," Asma says. "How are your parents reacting?"

"I don't really know how to describe it," I say. My parents were upset, but it was unclear who they were upset with. Yusuf hasn't been grounded or had his driving privileges taken away, though the heavy look on Dad's face and Mom's fidgeting are punishment enough.

The bell rings and forces me to move with the routine of the day. In class, I struggle to follow my teachers. I keep rereading the minefield of comments on the appetizer post and remembering all that happened at WhereHouse. I wonder what will happen to Yusuf. What will this do to my parents? Every time a teacher or a student or even the custodian looks my way, I wonder what they've heard and what they think of my family. Did Ms. Martin really need to check the time on her watch or was she avoiding me? Was Leonna giggling because she's read some of the trolling comments online about Yusuf? Between classes, I search the halls for Yusuf but I don't see him. Maybe he's avoiding everyone.

It's not until I'm on my way to history that I pass Yusuf's locker and see for myself what Asma and Mona were talking about. There's a large sheet of white paper taped over his locker to hide the graffiti but I can see right through it. It's even worse than my friends let on. Someone's also drawn a pig's face above two letters in thick black marker—*F* and *U*. Asma comes down the hall from the opposite direction and finds me paused in the middle of the hallway looking at the locker.

"Don't look at it," Asma says.

But I can't take my eyes off the pig's face. It's cartoonish and almost cute, which infuriates me because nothing about this is goofy or charming. Asma takes me by the elbow and leads me into our AP Government class.

Graffiti. "Was this Wyatt again?" I ask. "How stupid could he be?"

"I don't know, but that's what I heard some other people wondering, too."

"Eff him," she whispers in my ear, which is out of character for her but matches my mood. I slide into my chair feeling like the day is upside-down. Mr. Dempsey stands at the front of the class, watching us enter and open our notebooks. He's wearing a beige sweater with leather elbow patches. The plaid collar of his shirt pokes out from the neck. If he ever got tired of talking about voting laws and the separation of powers, he could teach a class on how to dress like a history teacher.

"Welcome back," Mr. Dempsey says once the fidgeting dies down and the last notebook has been opened on the last desk.

I look at Asma, who's staring into the open mouth of her pencil case. We're not supposed to bring our phones into the classroom but mostly that means we keep our phones out of sight. I touch my back pocket and realize I've left my phone in my locker. She pulls a pen out of her case before she zips it up and looks over at me. She offers a sympathy smile.

"*Plessy v. Ferguson*," Mr. Dempsey says. "Let's start where we left off. Asma, can you give us a summary of the incident?"

I breathe a sigh of relief that Mr. Dempsey didn't call on me. I can't get the word *terrorist* out of my head and have the sudden urge to look around the classroom to see if the person who drew the pig is sitting somewhere near me. I look at my hands, which always reveal whether I've been drawing lately. Mine have not a hint of ink. Does the person who drew the graffiti have smudges on his hands? Does *she* have smudges on *her* hands? The handwriting isn't very distinctive. It could be anyone.

"... but when Homer Plessy refused to sit in a car for Black people he was arrested," Asma says.

"Good. Now, I'm going to pull up the Fourteenth Amendment so we can have that for reference as you summarize the implications of the seven-to-one ruling in this case."

I did read ahead to prepare for today's class but it seems I've retained nothing. I flip open my book to an ink depiction of a Black man wearing a suit and a top hat sitting on the tufted seat of a train. Plessy looks like he's on his way to a wedding, the chain of a pocket watch hanging between the buttons of his vest. He has his hand over his bags and looks unamused and unfazed by the white man standing over him, a representation of the person who tried to get Homer Plessy to leave the train car. The artist used linear strokes, short and vertical for the most part. There are some curves—Plessy's eyes and the round head of the baby in the arms of a white woman looking at Plessy with interest to see if he'll comply. I trace over the drawing without letting my pen touch the page, reimagining the sketch in my own lines. I wonder if I could draw something like this but with more curves. I am fascinated by the pocket watch that is just out of view, counting the moments Plessy remains fixed in place. In my mind, an image flashes—a dozen watches and clockfaces floating into a sky like balloons light with helium.

But Plessy's sense of style and floating clocks won't be on the test, so I write today's date in the top corner of my notebook and try to bring my attention back to this assignment. Something in the hallway catches my eye and I look up to see Yusuf walking past our open classroom door. Where is he going now that we're five minutes into the period? I want to jump out of my seat and ask him, but Mr. Dempsey clears his throat in a way that convinces me I should stay where I am and keep my eyes toward the front of the room.

By the time the bell rings I have written only a single paragraph on the Fourteenth Amendment and the separate-but-equal doctrine. Asma must have noticed because she shoots me a concerned look as we close our notebooks and rise from our seats.

"Girl, are you okay? You usually run out of ink on these assignments," Asma says.

"Just didn't know what to write," I say. I look up and down the hallway, hoping to spot Yusuf and check in with him, but he's nowhere to be seen.

"Can I borrow your phone?" I ask Asma. "I want to call Yusuf."

Asma frowns.

"Sorry, I left mine in my locker," she says. I could have sworn she snuck a look at her phone while we were in class. Was she just staring into her pencil case? Maybe I was wrong. "I'll walk with you to yours if you want. We can make it if we hurry."

"Then we'll both be late," I say. "Can you tell Ms. Kupfer that I had to use the bathroom?"

"Yeah, sure," Asma says. She looks relieved to be able to do something for me. I'm glad to have Asma in most of my classes. I don't know where my classmates stand on what happened at WhereHouse the other night, and I can't tell if I'm imagining the charged air around me.

I double my pace. My locker is at the other end of the school, which means I have to go past the main entrance. There's a bathroom a couple doors down from Ms. Kupfer's class so if I take too long, she might not be all that forgiving.

I lengthen my stride, turning my shoulders to slip between the students filling the hallway. I pass by the school's main office and am sure someone will notice I'm walking away from where I'm supposed to be right now, as if the staff have memorized my schedule and can spot me in the swirl of students walking between classes. If I ever committed an actual crime, I would probably turn myself in so I could stop panicking about being caught.

I steal a quick glance into the principal's office, which is attached to the administrative office. Thankfully, the principal is busy talking to a couple of students. I get just past the office when I halt mid-step. Is that Wyatt in there? I hope so.

Someone steps on my heel, and I yelp.

"Whoa, sorry!" the girl says, and stoops to pick up the book she's dropped.

"My fault," I say, stepping closer to the wall to get out of the way of traffic. She shakes her head and hurries off down the hall.

I take two steps back and peek through the glass window.

Principal Tordoff is leaning against the front of his desk with his arms folded. Yusuf, Chris, and Liam are sitting in three chairs across from him, their backs to the door. The guys are arranged the way they would be onstage, with Liam in the middle, his seat a few inches behind the two others'. Chris sits on his right, closest to the door.

I spend the next two minutes trying to look like I'm not eavesdropping. My eyes scan the hallway while I stand with my shoulder to the wall, trying to catch any part of their conversation, but the stragglers are still filling the hallway with their chatter. When the bell signals that class has started, I know I should get going. Walking into the classroom late will mean all eyes on me. But I can make out a few words and am too curious to walk away.

"Irresponsible . . . music doesn't . . . disappointed."

I move in closer and focus all my energies on listening.

"What about my locker? Have you even talked to Wyatt?" Yusuf's voice is clear. He's upset, which automatically dials his volume up.

". . . a separate matter . . . assumptions . . . middle school . . . wrong influence."

"That's not fair!"

I know how much Yusuf loves teaching those kids. I want to go in there, to tell Mr. Tordoff that this is all one huge mess but Yusuf wasn't the one to start it.

While I'm wondering if I should, the door opens. I spin,

turning my back to the office and trying not to look like I wasn't just eavesdropping.

Chris comes out first. He looks at me, his face unreadable.

"I'd hate for this to mark your senior year. Yusuf, we can talk more tomorrow." The principal's voice floats into the hallway as Yusuf emerges. He's jostled by Liam, who storms out behind him, his jaw set and his lips pressed into a thin, grim line.

"Liam," Yusuf says. But Liam doesn't turn around. He's down the hallway and around the corner without a word. Yusuf turns to Chris, who shifts his backpack onto his shoulder.

"Not now," Chris says to Yusuf before he can get out another word. "Just . . . not now."

When Chris has rounded the corner too, Yusuf turns to me. He looks defeated.

"What happened?" I ask, my voice low. "What did he say?"

Yusuf purses his lips.

"That actions have consequences. And that I should apologize in the school paper."

"And about the middle school lessons?"

"This was a warning. The middle school music teacher doesn't want upset parents calling in."

"That's ridiculous. They love you as a teacher. And Where-House became hostile because of that guy Larson. Did he even hear about what Larson said?" I ask.

Yusuf nods.

"And?"

"He told me it's poor citizenship to blame others for our own actions. And he also said, 'Sometimes cornflakes are just cornflakes' or something like that."

"Wow, deep thoughts. What about Liam and Chris?" I ask.

"Pissed to be having this conversation but they're in the clear. They weren't on the mic that night."

"Okay," I say, trying to sound reassuring. "If they're not in trouble, then they'll get over this in a couple of days. It's not the end of the world."

"Yeah, I don't know about that. The manager of Where-House called Liam and told him we're not welcome back there."

Liam's anger makes more sense now. Playing at Where-House wasn't the endgame. It was supposed to help them book spots there and elsewhere as real, paying gigs, which is nearly impossible for high schoolers to get.

"And what about your locker?"

"My locker," he sighs. "He said they're going to give me a new locker down the hall and paint over this one. Could have happened anytime this weekend so they have no idea. Wyatt denied it and he was three hours away at his grandfather's house all weekend."

"Mom is going to sit Tordoff down for an epic lecture."

"There's no reason to tell her, Yalda."

I stare hard at Yusuf. "But won't they—"

"They're upset enough as it is. They don't need to hear that someone's got it out for me at school too. It's already too much."

I hear so much hurt in Yusuf's voice. Maybe he is starting to regret what he did. I want to hug him but I'm afraid it'll make things worse.

"C'mon, Yusuf. You heard her. She said everything was going to work out fine. They didn't freak out. And she's already got all those candles out for tonight so she's already over it."

Yusuf toe-kicks the floor with his scuffed sneaker. The laces on his left sneakers have come undone. I want to tell him to tie them so he doesn't trip and fall but that seems like the least of his worries right now.

"I don't know if I'm in the mood for all that right now."

"But it's—"

"I'm late for English. You should get to class," he says before he turns his back and starts to walk away. It's not until I'm in my seat and trying to wrangle my attention back to my teacher that it occurs to me Yusuf was walking in the wrong direction.

# 13

"Yalda!"

I turn around, surprised to hear Keith calling my name. Aside from my friends, it's felt like everyone at school has tried to steer clear of me, and since Yusuf is supposed to be at Crescendo this afternoon, he's left ahead of me. He's routinely late for other stuff but doesn't want to disappoint the kids he teaches there. I think he likes the way they look up to him because he's got enough years on them to be cool but not enough years to be old.

"Oh, hey," I say, waiting for Keith to catch up to where I am on the sidewalk. I haven't gotten too far. I probably slept a total of two hours last night. Somewhere around three in the morning, I was so desperate that I went online for hacks. I counted backward by sevens, repeated the word *relax* to myself until it didn't sound like a real word anymore, and tried to imagine each of my limbs as weightless. Today, in revenge, my arms and legs are making themselves feel twice as heavy. It feels like I'm walking through water.

"Are you okay?" he asks.

"Yeah," I lie. "I . . . I thought you might have left already."

Keith nods and doesn't push it any further, which is a small act of kindness.

"Saw Yusuf's locker."

I nod.

"I'm sorry that happened. Everyone thinks it was Wyatt."

"Sounds like it wasn't him, though," I say. "This was the last thing Yusuf needed."

There was an announcement on the loudspeaker just before the final bell rang today, but only to remind everyone that defacing school property carries severe consequences and that hateful words have no place in our school community.

"Yeah, I heard Wyatt say he wasn't around this weekend. I just can't understand why someone would do something so horrible. People need to chill out. Everyone knows Yusuf's not like that."

"Like what?" I ask.

"Like radical or something," he says, as if that should be obvious. "You guys don't even look . . . religious."

"Um, okay. What do we *look* like?"

Keith lets out an uncomfortable laugh, then bites his lip, like he's considering his words before responding.

"Normal, regular. I mean . . ."

The front door of Keith's house swings open and his mom steps onto the porch without a jacket. She's got Fisher on a leash. He's tugging hard, ready to tear away and jump at our legs. She smiles and waves at me and I wave back, unsure what to make of her. Sometimes she's friendly but other times I get the sense she wishes I wasn't around. I want to ask Keith how she feels about me but don't want to come off as overly sensitive either.

Fisher, on the other hand, is not hard to read. He's overjoyed to see Keith.

"Normal doesn't have a dress code. Anyway, looks like someone's been waiting for you," I say.

"That's the truth," Keith says, and I'm not sure if he's talking about normal not having a dress code or Fisher waiting for him. "So, talk to you later?"

"Yeah, later," I say. I pull my shoulders in and pick up my pace to put some distance between us. Did something just change? I replay the scene in my head and see Keith's face. Maybe I was too harsh. He is not the enemy. I don't think I've ever been so relieved to step into my house. Inside, I'm greeted by the crisp smell of pomegranates.

"Yalda? Is that you?"

"Yes, Mom," I call back. She sounds closer to her usual self, which surely has everything to do with the holiday. When I was little, I thought the night was named for me and not the other way around. I would imagine families like mine gathering around candles and decorating tables in my honor. Even now, knowing that on this night I'm just as anonymous as any other person, it still feels kind of special.

"How was school?" my mother asks. She's standing in the kitchen doorway wearing jeans and a burgundy sweater. She has her hair tied back in a knot, loose curls framing her forehead. Her eyes dart to my left, so I take the hint and look into the living room to check out her setup. A red tablecloth with a faint gold pattern is draped over the coffee table. On top of the tablecloth, a half dozen tapered candles of varied height form a circle around a carved wooden bookstand. On the stand is her book of poems by the long-gone Sufi poet Hafiz, the verses on each page framed by intricate drawings of vines and tulips in mid-bloom. I use some of those patterns in my drawings sometimes. I once drew a girl standing on a tree stump, flowering vines swirling in the palm of her hand like a small tornado. Mom has also set out a bowl of pomegranates, ruby pearls glistening in the slant of afternoon sun falling through the window.

"School was fine," I say. The arrangement tells me she's been busy, and I'm glad she's been doing this and not reading comments on social media or talking to Principal Tordoff about hateful graffiti on lockers.

"Fine?" my mom repeats. She's always hoping for more, but today she's got reason to be extra curious.

"Yeah. This looks really nice, Mom. Where did you get

those candlestick holders?" I ask to keep the conversation on safe ground.

"Aren't they nice? Thrift store next to the restaurant," she says, planting a kiss on my forehead. "It's hard to believe next year you'll both be in college. I hope you'll come home for Yalda."

Yusuf and I applied to the same state university, but we also each applied to five different private schools. His farthest is in California and mine is in Rhode Island. On any given day, I'm not sure where I'm hoping I'll end up. I've never been apart from my family for months at a time, but I've also never had the chance to turn my art into something real. I've only applied to schools with strong arts programs, even though I told my parents I wanted to major in psychology. The combination makes sense to me, but I knew it might not to them, so I slipped into the conversation that therapy can cost up to $200 per hour, which caused my father to nearly choke on the walnuts and raisins he'd been snacking on.

*For listening to people talk about their problems? Your mother could become a millionaire off your aunts*, he'd said before suggesting for the hundredth time that I would make a great doctor and then going straight into a mini lecture on mortgages, health insurance premiums, and taxes. Yusuf, on the other hand, has only applied where there are strong music programs. Having dealt with immigration attorneys and real estate lawyers, my parents were hoping Yusuf might go down the law path. It's been helpful to remind our parents that spending four years taking classes in subjects we don't like will be an expensive mistake, but only temporarily.

"We'll be home for winter break. Or maybe one of us will end up staying here," I say, not wanting to look too eager to be out of this town. Truthfully, I applied out of state not because I wanted to *leave* my parents or this town, but because I wanted to *go* somewhere.

"I know, I know. As long as you're happy. That's all that matters," she says wistfully. She's in full melancholy mode, and after everything that's happened today, it's rubbing off on me too. Yusuf looked miserable at school. I haven't seen him like that since . . . actually, I don't think I've ever seen him like that. I wonder how long it'll take for his mood to turn around.

"Yalda, are you—"

"I'll eat something later, Mom. Not hungry now," I say before she can even ask.

In my room, I let my book bag fall to the floor and flop onto my bed. I wonder if Keith is done walking Fisher now. Maybe he's back in his house getting questions from his mom about his day and maybe even about me.

It's a fair question and I'm curious how he'd answer it. I'm also nervous to hear the answer.

And what did he mean when he said we don't look religious? Would he still feel that way if he saw me in a headscarf at the masjid?

Just thinking about this, my stomach starts to swirl and knot. I don't know why I've done this to myself. Keith is just a boy who lives down the street. We only walk to and from school together because he's friends with Yusuf and we live on the same block. In June, we'll be graduating, and in the fall we'll be starting college in different places and I'll probably never see Keith again.

No big deal, I tell myself.

I smash my pillow over my face to stifle a groan.

# 14

I tap my pen against my notebook as headlights brighten my room and the garage door rumbles open. Yusuf is home. Finally. I stand and look out the window only to realize I'm wrong. My father pulls his car into the garage as I look at the clock. He must be letting someone else close the restaurant for him tonight, which isn't a good sign.

Yusuf should have known better. It's one thing to pull pranks at home and a whole other thing to stir up boycott-level trouble. Did he really do it for the cause or was he just trying to be the center of attention? He's always been the kid who could make his lunch table crack up. He makes me look about as lively as a scarecrow in comparison. Then again, Keith says I have a dry sense of humor, which sounds more refined and mature.

133

Keith again. I have to stop thinking about him.

Yusuf was not wrong. What was said that night was hateful and mean and didn't come out of nowhere. There were some grouchy yard signs around before, mostly because there were people who didn't like immigrants coming across the border from Mexico. But when refugees from Afghanistan moved to our town, the signs seemed to multiply. And it's not just signs. Last week, Mom and I made a Target run to buy some candles for tonight. I was grabbing coffee creamer for Dad when I overheard a lady grumbling to someone on the phone that the store was running low on baby formula. *Now they've got us looking like some third world country, too. Open the doors and this is what happens.*

My feet are cold so I put on a pair of fuzzy socks and walk into the living room. My father is admiring the arrangements. The lights are off and the living room is aglow with the light from candles of every size and shape. What I saw earlier was only the beginning. Now there are tea lights and long tapered candles. There are thick candles with bamboo wicks and the stout candles in round tins that I picked out. They're scattered across the living room like stars across the night sky.

"Salaam," I say to my father. He looks up from the table and holds his arm out for a hug. I give him a squeeze and smell the cumin, sautéed onions, and smoky grill from a long day in the kitchen.

"Noor-e-chashm," he says. Light of my eyes.

"I thought you were Yusuf," I say.

He looks at his chest and arms. He touches his face.

"I look young today?" he says, joking. As if Yusuf never caused a moment of trouble. But I can see him remember and his smile fades quickly, the way a small wave erases a heart drawn in sand.

"Your mother made a beautiful table," my father says. Besides the pomegranates and Hafiz's poetry book, the table now holds a platter of skinny watermelon slices and a small bowl of pistachios.

Dad opens the book to a random page and reads a few lines. The language is too floral, too embellished for me to understand.

"Translation, please," I ask, and my dad smiles.

"Translation will only destroy it," he says.

"Please."

Dad obliges, as he's known to do.

"'Do not speak to me of candy and sugar

When still I have the sweet taste of your lips on mine—'"

Dad stops abruptly and closes the book.

"I think that's enough," Dad says, and Mom laughs. She's standing at the edge of the living room, a glass of water in her hand.

"Hafiz was a romantic," she says.

"I thought Beloved was supposed to be God?" I ask. I think I'd prefer that because I am squirming listening to my dad talk about ruby-red lips.

"Usually. But sometimes, maybe one of God's beautiful

creatures," she says playfully. "Is there a difference? It depends on the reader."

Words don't have a gender in Dari the way they do in some other languages. We don't even differentiate between *he* and *she*, so there's lots of room for interpretation. How very progressive, I think.

On a small pedestal serving dish are almond cookies dusted with powdered sugar and cardamom. Two small vases with red roses are perched like bookends on either side of the sweets.

Against our eggshell sofas and ottomans and our silent white walls, the Yalda table stands out like a drop of blood on fresh snow. A chill runs down my spine and I look outside. The start of winter is cold but dry.

"Yusuf isn't home yet?" Dad asks.

"I'm going to text him. He will come soon, inshallah," my mother predicts, emerging from the kitchen. She's drying her hands on a kitchen towel. She tacks *God willing* onto every statement because the Almighty could have other plans, and arrogance can be dangerous.

My father looks at the clock on the wall, checks his phone, and sighs.

"I'm going to shower and change. If I had ever done this, my own father, God rest his soul . . . ," he mutters as he walks away. Yusuf needs to come through the front door now or my dad is going to deliver the most epic lecture of our lives. The angrier he gets, the further back in time he reaches to make his point. When I stayed up overnight to binge-watch a season of

*Criminal Minds*, he went back to how many games they had bought for me as a baby so that I wouldn't rot my brain with television. When Yusuf fell asleep and left Dad alone at the restaurant for a busy evening shift, Dad traveled generations back, to the story of our great-grandfather apprenticing under a carpenter as an eight-year-old so he could start supporting his family. He will dig up stories of the ancestors' ancestors to help him make a point tonight.

The kettle whistles. As if summoned, my mother and I walk into the kitchen. I get the glasses out of the cabinet while she spoons tea leaves into a thermos and then fills it with boiling water. I don't normally drink tea but I might need some to stay awake tonight.

"It was better when he was at the restaurant with us," my mother says, shaking her head. Mom's forgotten how much Yusuf disliked being in the restaurant. The day my parents said he was free to look for other part-time jobs, he looked happy enough to float.

I take my phone out of my back pocket and text my brother. I can understand him not being in the mood for pomegranates, but coming home late tonight is only going to make our parents more frustrated.

You better be on your way.

I'm getting angry too. Logically, one would expect that when Yusuf does something that lands him in hot water, he should be alone in that water. But that's not even close to what happens. As if we're the kind of twins who are literally attached,

I end up simmering in that water with him. My parents get tougher on me so I don't make the same mistake.

Yusuf's job at Crescendo is just one example. Yusuf and I both wanted to get part-time jobs somewhere other than the restaurant. The music studio seemed like a great fit and everyone was happy until he started getting really serious about his music and even started talking about majoring in it in college. When I told them I had signed up for dog-walking jobs on an app, they acted like I'd just agreed to sell my left kidney on the black market.

I stare at the screen of my phone. Yusuf still hasn't texted back.

"Did you finish your homework, Yalda?" my mother asks, sealing the thermos. "You've been staying up so late all week. You need sleep, you know."

Has she been spying on me?

"I thought you wanted me to stay up late with you and get drunk on poetry."

"Don't say drunk," she chides.

"But that's what Hafiz calls it," I tease.

"Yalda! You know in the poetry it means happy, bold. Don't make it so terrible," she insists. Truly, in English the word *drunk* sounds like car crashes and the clanging of cans and bottles.

"Tonight is different," she says, leaning against the counter. Behind her, the dinner dishes are drying on the rack. One of the benefits of having a restaurant is that we can bring food home and the pots and pans don't end up in our kitchen sink. At the restaurant, Dad has a couple of people helping him in the kitchen. If they're cooking for forty customers, it doesn't make sense to cook another meal for four at home.

Mom slips into Dari, rubbing lotion on her hands. "These were the sweetest nights for me when I was a girl. The little toys my uncle would bring me, all of us cousins sitting at my grandmother's feet while she told stories, and the smell of a slow-burning fire. What nights those were. If only we knew . . ."

Mom shakes her head as the end of her sentence floats away from her.

My phone lights up and I grab it to see how close Yusuf is to home, but it's not from him. The message is from Mona to me and Asma on our group chat.

> SOS. If I spontaneously combust during the chem test will I automatically pass?
> And if so how can I create the right conditions for spontaneous combustion?
> Pretty sure I know nothing.

Mona's lowest grade in her entire life has probably been an A-. Still, she sounds the alarm before every exam, which would be irritating if she weren't amusing and if we didn't know that intensity is her brand. Studying with her is a little like boot camp. Asma and I feel obligated to balance her out, so we make sure we have plenty of snack breaks and music interruptions. We are the jelly to her peanut butter. I type out a reply.

> Study sesh this weekend?

139

When and where? Don't say library, **Mona replies.** I have been there so much, they offered to name a chair after me. Like I'm a founding father or something.

How about Room? **I suggest.**

Mona responds with a relieved emoji and a brown thumbs-up sign. I can't settle on exactly which shade best represents me so for now I'm still the color of an egg yolk.

Saturday @ 4? **Mona adds.**

Asma joins the conversation then.

I think home would be better, **she types,** much to my surprise. Since when is home better than being out in a coffee shop? Asma was the first of us to visit Room.

I could go for a lemon ball though, **Mona says.**

Home is less distracting, **Asma adds.**

"Yalda, call your brother, please. He should have been home by now," my mother says.

"I just texted him," I reply.

"Call him, Yalda," she says, exasperation in her voice. To my mother, texts are the absolute lowest form of communication, and often she denies they even count at all.

I dial my brother and listen to the ringing, ready to hear him tell me he got my message and is on his way—but he doesn't answer. It is late and this is unlike him. I tell myself not to picture a car crash. He's fine—just not in any rush to get home and face any questions about WhereHouse or school.

"He's probably driving," I say. Mom nods but she looks unsure. We head to the living room and I curl up on the sofa, my legs tucked under me. My mother sits beside me with the Divan-e-Hafiz on her lap. She flips open to a page and starts reading. My father joins us, dressed in a sweatshirt and sweatpants that make him look like a soccer coach for a junior league.

"Still not here?" he says. He goes to the closet and takes his phone out of his jacket pocket. He taps on the screen and I can hear his call go to voice mail, too. "Is he with his friends again? God knows what these boys are doing at this time of night. This is too much. Yalda, really, you don't know where he is?"

"No," I reply, and the look on my dad's face makes me feel like I've failed in some sisterly duty. "He's not answering my texts or calls either."

My father pours himself a cup of tea and walks over to the window. He has a hand on his hip. I can almost hear the lecture swirling in his head. My mother traces the lines of a poem, reading the verse under her breath. I don't know if it's the poetry or Yusuf or the candlelight making her eyes glisten.

"Do you want to read me something while we're waiting?" I ask my mom. We need to work out some of this tension.

She glances at her watch and shakes her head.

"Your brother is not here," she says.

"But I am," I say. Sometimes it feels like our home revolves around Yusuf. Maybe every family's universe is arranged this way and that's why boys are called sons.

"Let me call him one more time," she says, reaching for her phone.

I head back to my room, feeling antsy. Everyone's tense and annoyed in the house and I can't fix any of it. Instead of showing up tonight, Yusuf has ghosted us.

I lie down on my bed and stare at the last message I sent Yusuf, still unanswered.

# 15

It takes me a minute to figure out I've fallen asleep on top of my blanket. It's as dark as a dungeon outside but the light is on in the hallway and I can hear voices. Groggy, I step into the living room to see what's happening.

My father is pacing the living room; one hand holds his phone to his ear while his other hand rubs the back of his neck. My mother is standing near the fireplace, arms folded and her forehead grooved with worry. The taller candles are still aflame, but a fraction of their original height. The bowls of fruit and nuts are untouched.

"I want to report a missing child," my father says. "They transfer me two times. Yes, I am the father."

Yusuf's still not home. Dad's calling the police. My stomach drops. My mother looks at me and blinks.

"What's going on?" I ask her. I look between her and my father.

"Yusuf didn't come home," Mom says, her voice breaking.

My mind races. I dash back to my room and check my phone. Yusuf still hasn't replied, which makes my stomach drop. I dial his number and walk back to the living room. It goes straight to voice mail. He was at work. Why isn't he responding?

"Yes, I can hold," my father says, his hand falling against his thigh in frustration. He puts the phone on speaker and looks straight at me.

"Dad, let's go to the studio," I say, touching his arm. Why are we sitting here? We should go out and look for him.

"Wait, wait," he says to me, shaking his head.

"Mom," I say, turning my attention to her. "Let's just go there. We can check for his car."

She lets out a jagged breath. Her usual optimism is nowhere to be found.

"Your father went already. His car is in the parking lot. Yalda, can you call him again? Maybe he'll answer you."

My skin prickles. If Yusuf's car is in the parking lot, where is Yusuf?

"My name or my son's name?" Dad says. He starts to spell his own name but shakes his head and tells the person on the line that he's going to start again. He repeats himself, his accent a little heavier than usual in the midnight hour.

I can't imagine Yusuf taking off with friends and not saying a word. Maybe he had a gig somewhere tonight with his band? No, he would have told me.

"Seventeen," my father says. "No, not seven. Seventeen years old."

"Okay, sir," says the voice on the phone, drawing out the *sir* so it sounds like a small growl.

"He is a child," my father argues. "Not that kind of teenager."

Yusuf is fine, I tell myself. Or at least he will be until my parents get their hands on him. But I can't reassure myself, especially not while I'm watching my parents. My dad bracing his neck, my mom with her arms wrapped around her chest—they look like they're literally trying to hold themselves together.

I scroll through my contact list on my phone, looking for any of Yusuf's friends. I don't have anyone's number, not even his bandmates'. I've never needed to call them. I tap on the icon for the Pic-Up app and bring up my brother's profile. His last post was about thirty minutes after he was supposed to get off work. It was right around the time my dad got home.

It's a picture of a flyer. A guy with a ukulele will be playing live music Saturday night.

Signing off tonight with this. Life ain't life without music.

I tell myself this is a good sign. He took a picture and wrote a post. He's fine.

145

"No, we have no fight. Nothing like that," my father says. His frustration has him tongue-tangled.

"Sir, do you have someone there who can help translate for you?"

My dad squints, like he's trying to see through fog.

"Translate? You don't understand me?" His volume is rising as well.

"Sir, maybe someone else in the house could help?"

My father looks like he's going to protest but then shakes his head and hands me the phone. Suddenly, I'm talking to the police. I picture someone with a badge and a gun on the other end, which frazzles me for no good reason. Does Yusuf want me talking to the police about him? He doesn't need to be on their radar.

"Hello?" I say.

"Hello. What's your name?"

"Yalda. I'm his daughter. I mean, you were talking to my dad about my brother."

"Got it. Thanks for helping, sweetheart. How old are you?"

"Seventeen."

"I thought your brother was seventeen?"

"We're twins."

"I see. Now, I just want to make sure I understood what your father was trying to say . . ."

She recaps what my father told her, down to the name of the music shop where Yusuf was working tonight. I decide not to congratulate her on getting it all despite the nonexistent

146

language barrier because the sass won't help me now.

"Does your brother have any medical issues?"

"No, nothing."

"Any mental health issues? Depression?"

"No, nothing. He was a little upset today, but he's not . . . depressed or anything."

"I see. And does he take any medications?"

"No," I reply. "He doesn't take anything."

"Okay, I see," she says. Hang on. What does she see? I want to rewind our conversation in case I said the wrong thing.

"We'll send an officer to check out the strip mall. Do you know what your brother was wearing tonight?"

"Jeans and . . . maybe a gray hoodie. Actually, I don't remember," I say.

"That's fine. Here's what I suggest you all do in the meantime. Call his friends and use social media to tell people you're looking for him. You can keep trying your brother's phone too, though it's possible his battery is dead if it's going to voice mail."

She says we can expect someone to swing by the house at some point tonight. I picture Yusuf walking in and finding a police officer standing in our living room. My brother, the king of shenanigans, is going to laugh so hard, and I'm going to kick him in the shins for thinking this is funny.

"Sure, I can do that," I say.

She tells me I've done a good job and I resist the urge to correct her. She doesn't know I was just sleeping while my parents were trying to find my missing brother. I hang up and turn to my parents. They look at me like I'm about to announce where Yusuf is.

"I'm going to try his friends," I say, and they nod.

I take out my phone to post about Yusuf. I write a couple lines asking people to hit me up if they've heard from him. Then I tag Chris and Liam in my post so they'll see it. Since I don't have their phone numbers, this is the best I can do. I look through my contact list. A couple of our classmates are online right now, including Keith. My cousin on the West Coast, where it's only nine o'clock, comments that she'll be praying for his safety and adds an emoji of steepled hands. Most of my family isn't all that religious, but she's different. She started wearing a hijab when she was fourteen despite her parents' worries that she would attract the wrong kind of attention, which is oddly the same thing my parents say to me when I wear a dress that falls a couple inches above my knees. I don't know if there's a "right" kind of attention, but if there is, I'd bet it's almost impossible to dress for it.

My screen goes black and I'm left staring at my reflection. What else can I do?

My mother starts clearing the table she'd set up for Yalda. She puts the bowl of pomegranate seeds straight into the fridge—no cover or plastic wrap. She does the same with the watermelon, moving with a resignation that makes me anxious.

I wish my parents would just sit down. I can't think straight with them moving around, and maybe if I could just break

148

through the noise in my head, I could be helpful. Yusuf posted his last update over three and a half hours ago. I think back to when my mother chided me for saying we'd get drunk on poetry tonight, when our living room looked like a scene from a cheesy romance novel. Why does it feel like that was a year ago?

I take my sketchbook out and stare at the pages. I keep checking my phone to see if any messages have come in but find nothing. My mom is calling Yusuf's cell again. She leaves another message, her voice breaking as she tells him to call her back. She tells him Dad loves him and is worried about him, which is really her way of telling him Dad isn't mad.

"We're waiting for you. So call me right away, okay?" she asks the hollow line.

Another hour passes—painfully. My parents tell me to go to sleep but say nothing when I don't move. My phone's battery is running low. I thought I had the charger in the kitchen but it's not there. I come back to the living room to see if I left it by the couch again. I'm always losing this stupid thing.

It's then that I remember the phone tracking app. All four of us are on a family plan and I think there's a way to see where a phone is. I bring my laptop from my room.

"Dad, I want to log into the phone account," I say.

He looks at me and then takes two quick steps to join me at the computer. I type in his phone number to access the account.

"What's the password?" I ask. He looks at my mom.

"Kabul1999," she says. Of course it is. That's the year Dad's family fled Afghanistan.

I'm in the account and clicking on all the tabs, trying to figure out how to track Yusuf's phone. My parents look over my shoulder at the screen.

A map appears. There's a flashing blue circle. The names of the streets start to load and I see the outline of the strip mall where both Crescendo and A Room with a Brew are located.

"See, his phone is there. Maybe in the car. Why would he leave his phone in the car?" my dad wonders aloud.

But the blue dot is surrounded by a big blue circle. The app doesn't give us exact coordinates, just a general area.

"Maybe it's not in the car," I say. I would have felt a lot better if the flashing light had shown up at one of his friends' houses.

My father's already swinging his jacket on. He grabs his keys from the hook by the door. I throw on my boots and put on the first jacket my hand finds in the closet. He starts the car and is about to pull out of the garage when my mother bursts out of the house.

"I'm coming with you," she shouts.

My dad doesn't look happy about us all going but he doesn't protest either. It's a fifteen-minute ride to the strip mall but we're there in ten. My dad pulls into the parking lot and parks next to the car Yusuf and I share. The car looks the same as always—a midnight-blue sedan with scratched-up bumpers and a guitar decal on the rear window.

Dad brought the extra set of keys this time and clicks open the doors. He opens the driver's-side door and I open the

150

passenger side. There's no sign of Yusuf or his phone. There's a paper bag from a burrito place in the back seat, but the car is otherwise empty. We look under the seats and then at each other, but only briefly.

My mother shuts the trunk softly and takes a step back. A shudder ripples down my spine. Something flutters in the thick of trees that surround the strip mall. Shadows move across a sky of spilled ink. Birds or bats? I cannot tell. I've never seen a night so dark.

I search the dark for clues, for answers. I blink hard, like I'm trying to wake myself from this nightmare. The air feels heavy moving in and out of my lungs.

I hate the silence.

"Where are you, Yusuf?" I say, my voice trembling.

We start walking in three different directions, a small search party. My mother breaks the quiet, calling out my brother's name. A cool wind stirs the chimes outside the coffee shop, releasing tinny notes into the night. I stuff my hands into my pockets to keep my fingers from freezing.

I should know where he is. Why don't I know where he is?

"Yusuf?" I call out. My voice is timid at first, but then I remember Yusuf turning away from me earlier today, the sullen look on his face. My mother climbs the cement steps to the second-floor shops; her hand hovers over the metal railing as if she's afraid she might lose her footing. She peers into each darkened window on her way to the music shop on the corner. There are only three cars in the lot right now. I walk over to look inside each of them, although I can't exactly say I'm hoping to find Yusuf in any of them.

My father walks to the corner of the building, just below the music shop. There are no stairs on that end of the shops. Why would Yusuf have wandered back there?

I see the light of my father's cell phone swinging left and right. I feel something drop within me. I walk toward my father, my feet moving of their own accord.

"Yusuf!" my father yells, and my breath catches in my throat because there's no lift at the end of my brother's name. It is not a question. It is a declaration.

"Yusuf!" he calls again, and I run toward my father's voice as the light of his phone drops to the ground on the longest, darkest night of the year.

# 16

I'm on the phone with the 911 operator, trying to keep straight in my head what the person on the phone is saying and what I've already said and relaying everything to my parents. All the while, I want to grab Yusuf by the shoulders and make him open his eyes.

Yusuf's face is smeared with dirt and his hands are icy. One eyelid looks dark and swollen. Yusuf hasn't even moaned. I've never seen him this silent.

Dad slides one arm under Yusuf's neck and another under his knees and grunts, but Yusuf doesn't budge—like he doesn't want to be pulled away from the asphalt. Mom kisses his forehead and calls his name. When my father's eyes meet hers, she points at Yusuf's leg. Dad lets out a whimper that terrifies me.

"What is it?" I demand.

"His leg," Mom says. "Tell them to hurry."

I notice the unnatural angle. I look up again and see the height from which Yusuf fell.

"Please hurry. He's badly hurt. We need help to carry him," I tell the operator. Her voice is so calm that even as she tells me an ambulance is on the way, I wonder if she doesn't comprehend that Yusuf's not talking or moving or doing any of the things my brother should be doing right now.

"Please don't try to move him," she says. "In case he has any injuries to his spinal cord, it's best not to move him, especially his neck. The EMTs will be able to stabilize him."

"Don't move him!" I shout at my parents. My father stops trying to get Yusuf's head onto his lap but keeps his hands on my brother's arms. "Don't touch his neck. You might hurt his spine."

My mother pulls her hands away and I see them shaking.

"I'm sorry, I'm sorry," she says.

She puts her hands on either side of his face, though, because she needs to touch him. She leans in, her body in a prayer pose, and presses her cheek to his. Maybe she's trying to warm him. She's talking to him but I can't make out what she's saying because the 911 operator is asking me more questions. Three voices are coming at me while I'm trying to listen for Yusuf's, and my head feels like it's glitching.

I look up. We're below the music studio, where the walkway goes past the door and wraps around the side. One end of the handrail has come away from the building, jutting out into the air. Mom was headed that way but didn't make it around the corner. Dad's yelling brought her back down the stairs.

The second story looks so far up that Yusuf might as well have fallen from the sky.

My dad presses an ear to Yusuf's chest again. He keeps checking, then searching the road for a sign of help. One car passes by with music blaring. Another set of headlights goes past and my heart sinks.

I don't know why it's taking the ambulance so long to get here.

The 911 operator stays on the line with me. She promises the EMTs are almost there. She tells me I'm doing all the right things, but all I'm doing is holding my brother's hand, which I probably haven't done since we were in pre-K.

The parking lot lights up with swirling red and blue lights. I run over to flag the ambulance down. Everything happens so fast but not fast enough. We give up our places at my brother's side so the EMTs can listen to his chest and lift him onto a stretcher. My mother clambers into the back of the ambulance with Yusuf. Once she's under the lights, I see a streak of dried blood on her cheek, like she's wounded too.

My father and I hurry back to our car to follow them to the hospital. There aren't many cars on the road and he follows close behind the ambulance, running through red lights. The piercing wail of the sirens is the only thing that makes any sense at all right now.

We pull into the hospital parking lot, in a spot closest to the red awning of the emergency department. I've only gone through these sliding doors with my grandmother. She suffered a small stroke first, then another stroke that was a little bigger. After that, she had a new diagnosis every other month. Hip fracture. Pneumonia. Urinary tract infection. I hated to watch my grandmother wincing as a needle slid through her papery skin. My mother would always sit with her and squeeze Bibi Jan's free hand, though I wondered if she was doing it to comfort Bibi Jan or if it was the other way around.

We burst into the waiting room; people watching the television in the corner look up. I walk up to the clerk at the registration desk and give him my brother's name. I tell him they came by ambulance. He nods and looks from me to his computer screen.

My brother is in a trauma bay. People are working on him while a doctor talks to us outside the room. We recap what we know about what happened to Yusuf tonight, which is close to nothing. My mother shakes her head when the doctor asks if Yusuf has any medical problems or if he's taking any medications.

"No, no, no. He's very healthy," she insists, even as he lies unconscious a few feet away.

"Does he smoke or drink or use any drugs? As far as you know?"

My father shakes his head.

"No, no. He's a good boy," he says.

156

The doctor nods and smiles politely. Does she not believe us?

We're ushered to the waiting room. They're stabilizing Yusuf. They're taking him for scans. He may need surgery. My parents blink back tears and sign papers.

They let my mother go back to be with Yusuf but warn her that they need space to work and that there's going to be a lot happening.

"Okay, I promise. Yes, I promise," she says, as if she's afraid she might be pulled away from him again. My dad and I are left alone in the waiting room. People watch us from the corner of their eyes. Curious? Concerned? When I look at them, their gazes slip away.

We slump into chairs, eyes opening and closing. Moments later, my mother returns, followed by a grim-faced surgeon who tells us he's going to take Yusuf to surgery to remove a blood clot that's compressing his brain. My mother's face goes pale. She's murmuring something I can't understand. My father bites his lip. We nod and remain standing for a long time after the doctor is gone. At some point, he returns and tells us that the surgery went well but it will be a long time before we know if Yusuf will be okay or what kind of damage the blood clot caused.

I want to ask him why Yusuf wouldn't be okay if the surgery went well, but he's explaining to my father where the intensive care unit is. My father doesn't bother telling him that we already know. He just nods and thanks the surgeon.

Two police officers arrive and pull us aside. They take turns asking questions and jotting down notes. We tell them every-thing was normal today. Yusuf and I walked to school. He came home and picked up his car to go to the music shop.

"And around what time was that?" the officer asks each step of the way. They ask about his friends and if there was anyone he didn't get along with. They ask about his mood and if he was seeing a therapist. We're asked again if Yusuf was using any drugs or drinking or staying out late.

"Late?" my father asks, sliding an arm around my mother's shoulders. Sure, there were nights Yusuf was playing with his band. Or practicing with them. "He's studying and working. His grades are all A. He is thinking about law school."

Whether or not Yusuf wants to be a lawyer doesn't matter right now.

"What are you getting at?" I ask the police officers because I'm really not sure where this conversation is going.

The younger officer straightens his shoulders while the older officer directs his reply to my father.

"We're trying to get an idea of when this accident might have happened. That side of the building isn't easy to see, so it's possible no one saw your son fall."

"Toba khoda," my mother mumbles, repenting for whatever she might have done to bring on this calamity.

"Where are you all from?" the younger officer asks.

"Afghanistan," my father answers.

"Oh, interesting," says the police officer, as if this detail has shed fresh light on the situation. He makes one final note

158

before sliding his pen into his pocket. They'll be in touch, they say. One officer nods in the direction of the doors behind us and tells us Yusuf is in good hands.

"This is not an accident. Somebody hurt my son," my mom says with conviction.

"Ma'am, we're taking a good look around to see what we can figure out. That railing was rusted pretty bad."

"But how could he—"

"We'll take a close look and see what we can figure out. With young people, there are always surprises. And if you hear anything, let us know. Right now, we're going to let you focus on your son and his medical care."

My mom blinks quickly, then looks over her shoulder to the doors and hallways that lead to Yusuf. My dad runs his hands through his hair and stares at the floor. The officers slip away and I feel curious eyes on us.

My mouth feels dry and sticky. I fish a dollar from my mother's wallet and get myself a cold bottle of water from the vending machine. The water soothes my hot throat. A mother comes through the doors and walks up to the clerk. She has one baby in her arms and is holding a coughing toddler by the hand. We've watched people come and go without realizing that it's morning now. I am trying to stifle a yawn when I feel my phone vibrate in my pocket.

It's a text message from Asma.

Hey where are you?

I take a deep breath.

159

Hospital. Yusuf just had surgery.

Typing it out makes it suddenly more real.

Three dots appear on my screen, then disappear. Asma can't figure out what to say to this, I'm sure. She's the type who whispers words like *cancer* or *racist*. I don't blame her for being speechless now.

> Is he okay? Surgery for what??

I've already answered a lot of questions tonight, but this is my best friend asking. This is someone I *want* to talk to.

> Blood clot on his brain. He just got out of
> surgery.

> OMG. Is he okay? What happened?

> He didn't come home last night. We found
> him outside Crescendo. He fell from the
> second-floor balcony.

I look at what I've typed. The letters form words but the text is so wrong. It looks like a made-up story and still I hit send.

Did he fall? Was he pushed? That building is in terrible shape. Could the railing have given way? Why would Yusuf have been leaning on that corner of the balcony anyway? He should have been walking in the opposite direction to get to his car.

> But he's going to be okay?

I don't know how to answer. What had the surgeon said?

> The surgery went well.

I look over at my parents. My mother's resting her head against my dad's shoulder. Her eyes are closed but I can tell she's not asleep. They've moved so that their backs are turned toward the television. Like me, she's probably just sick of watching infomercials for garden hoses or staring at the dust balls in the corner of the room. Maybe she won't open her eyes again until the nurse tells her we can see Yusuf.

I check my phone. Three little dots appear and disappear. Of course. Who would know what to say in a situation like this? I sit in an empty chair and stare at the screen. I'm sick of this room too.

It's another two minutes before Asma replies. It's a sad face emoji followed by prayer hands.

I press the button and my phone goes dark. I lean back in the chair and spy my father speaking softly to my mother. He squeezes her hand and touches his lips to her temple. She leans into him.

Maybe my mother's right. Maybe texts shouldn't count as true communication.

# 17

"And do I have it right that you're Yusuf's sister?" the nurse asks. He's wearing pale blue scrubs and white sneakers. He has a gentle smile, the kind that comes more from the eyes than the lips. I nod. "I'm William. What's your name?"

"Yalda," I say, and remembering my manners, I add, "Nice to meet you, William."

"Under happier circumstances would have been preferable, but likewise. Yalda. That's a pretty name. I bet it means something nice. Am I right?"

"It's the winter solstice," I say. My voice sounds automated. I leave out the parts I loved hearing as a child—that Yalda marked the birth of the sun goddess, Mithra, in a religion that gives us some of our traditions. Mom would tell us about nights sweetened by rock candy and stories, one about a little girl named Yalda who convinced a frightened town that the witch they feared was a lonely, kind woman.

"Oh, I love that," he says, because he hasn't connected that the winter solstice was when Yusuf was rushed into the operating room. "And Yusuf is a great name, too. Pretty legendary."

"Yeah, he kind of is," I say, and I feel suddenly grateful for this stranger's warmth. My brother is in good hands, I'm sure of it.

"Tell me something about Yusuf," William says while he enters information into a computer on wheels.

What should I say? I look at Yusuf, half expecting him to speak for himself.

"My mom named him after a prophet," I say. "Yusuf. Joseph. Same guy. When we were little, my mom would tell him he was just as handsome as Joseph."

Yusuf had to do some digging to learn about his namesake. He had shouted for me to come to his room, where he sat at his computer grinning like he'd just gotten an invite to open for Coldplay at their next concert. He tapped on the screen and waited for me to take in the discovery. I stood behind him and read over his shoulder about the Prophet Yusuf being so ravishingly good-looking that his master's wife could not keep her hands off him. The guy's wife needed her girlfriends to see for themselves so she invited them over for apples, and when Yusuf walked through the room, the hungry-eyed women lost their minds and sliced through their palms with paring knives. The tale made me wonder what other juicy scenarios were in these holy stories and why we didn't talk about this more.

For a full week, Yusuf acted as if he could cause women to melt for him. It was a long, hard week of eye rolling for me. We were young then, and any mention of people lusting after each other called for an enthusiastic demonstration of disgust, even if I did secretly wonder what it would be like to be the object of someone's affection.

"He learned about his namesake in the holy texts?" William asks.

"Wikipedia, actually." I smile despite myself. It almost hurts to do so.

"Ah, the other sacred texts," William replies. Mom steps back into the room then, looking from my smile to Yusuf to see if something's changed for the better. I bite my lip as William, who noticed me stiffening, leans in slightly to offer a few words of advice. "My two cents? It's important to keep your spirits up. It's good for everyone, including Yusuf."

Yusuf had been . . . *extra* that day. He'd spun out of his chair and run off to ask her. *Mom, did you know this story?* I didn't follow him because while Yusuf stopped reading after the second paragraph, my eyes stayed on the screen. I closed out the website before I walked away and never did tell my brother what else happened to his namesake—that he was thrown into a well by his envious brothers and left to die.

I hadn't dwelled on that part of the story because I couldn't even have imagined anything more than a paper cut happening to my brother.

I squeeze Yusuf's hand and see him grimace.

William notices and calls it "really great progress," which causes my mom to tilt her head back and say a prayer. I've never seen my parents pray so much.

William checks the bag of clear fluids hanging over Yusuf's bed, following the clear tubing as it leads into the back of his right hand. He moves to the computer in the corner of the room and stares at the screen. *Click. Click click click.* He rolls the computer aside and turns his attention to my mother.

"We usually allow only two visitors at a time, but I know how important it is for you all to be here with Yusuf right now. Mrs. Jamali, if you need water or a blanket, just let me know." There's a soothing drawl to his voice, like a warm mug to cold hands. Mom thanks him, her voice hoarse and her eyes on my brother.

Yusuf's head is wrapped up, like a gauze turban. Another square of gauze covers his left eyebrow. His face is pale and swollen, with a breathing tube going down into his mouth. There's tape on his face to hold it all together. The fluorescent hospital lights exaggerate every bruise, each place Yusuf's skin has been rubbed away. All that had been concealed in the dark is now brutally exposed, and I can't look away. A white sheet covers Yusuf's bottom half, except for his right leg, which has been casted. Yusuf's spinal cord wasn't injured in the fall,

165

which seems like a miracle. He has two rib fractures and a broken bone in his left arm, but it's been casted as well. I want to get closer to Yusuf but I'm afraid I'll dislodge something vital.

"We're going to be watching him closely," William tells us as he lifts the edge of the sheet near the foot of the bed. There's a plastic bag with measurement markings on it. It's filled with amber fluid, which I quickly realize is Yusuf's urine. I look away, feeling like I've trespassed. His hand is a little warmer than it was in the woods, but not by much.

He doesn't look like my brother. He looks disassembled. I turn away and try to take some deep breaths without my parents noticing. The air in the room is thin, like all the oxygen is being drawn into the machine that's breathing for my brother.

Visitors walking into this unit look nervous. If they've brought flowers, they hold them tight to their chests like a shield.

I know ICU stands for intensive care unit. In my head, it's a whisper.

*I see you.*

Do they? They see only what their machines can read. They see only what they can dress with gauze or reposition with tape.

*They don't see the real you, Yusuf.*

My head gets light and the room seems to wobble around me.

"Honey, are you okay?" William asks. He's at my side, pulling me into a chair. I don't know how he crossed the room so fast.

A few minutes later, I'm back in the car. My father is driving me home so I can get some sleep. My mother stays with Yusuf. The car ride passes in silence, my head bumping against the cool window. Drivers stop their cars at red lights and I spot a woman checking her lipstick in her rearview mirror. An elderly man walks a terrier on the sidewalk. All these people are under the impression today is a normal day, like last night was just another moonless night.

I walk into the house and glance into the living room. The Yalda table, which Mom had cleared before we'd tracked Yusuf, has only the tablecloth and half-melted candles on it. My dad hangs his keys on the hook by the door and asks me if I'm hungry. I shake my head and go straight to my room. I leave my socks on, put my phone on the charger, and slide under my comforter. I've slept about four hours over the past two nights and it's hitting me now. Dad pokes his head in my doorway just as my eyes shut.

"I'm going to take a shower and go back. You okay?" he asks.

I nod again. I don't know how I am but I'm a lot more okay than Yusuf right now.

My father lingers in the doorway for another minute, and I wonder if he's going to say something, but he doesn't. He pads down the hallway toward their bedroom and I hear the distant whisper of water as he turns on the shower.

I could use a shower too. I feel the night on my skin, buried under my nails. I can smell the hospital on my clothes and in my hair. But there is no way I can get myself to peel this cover off so I stay where I am and bury my nose in my bedsheet. I am asleep before my father is out of the bathroom.

Hours later, I'm awakened by the bright light of day. My mouth feels sticky and my clothes stale. I've gotten some rest but don't feel very rested. Images flash in my head, recalling me to this moment. Gauze wrapped around Yusuf's head. Mom leaning into Dad's shoulder. The broken metal railing. Dad walking across a deserted parking lot.

My eyelids open. I hear footsteps in the living room.

My stomach drops at the thought that I might not be safe. What if someone went after Yusuf and is now coming after me, too?

I look at my window and for a fleeting second wonder how likely I am to break a leg if I jump from the second story of a house.

I hear drawers open and close. A phone rings and I recognize my mother's ringtone. I exhale.

"Khairyat ast?" she asks in Dari. There's her eternal optimism asking if everything is all right when I can hear in the tone of her voice that she's almost certain something's wrong.

"Okay, I'll bring it. No, I haven't called your sister. What can they do from there? We have enough to deal with. If you want to call them, you can. I can't talk to them now. I just can't."

We flew to Indiana to be present for Rahim's funeral. When

we boarded the flight, I already felt like my insides were in a knot. I loosened my seat belt and fidgeted a lot but couldn't seem to get comfortable. About forty minutes into the flight, things got worse. The pilot announced there was going to be some turbulence ahead and turned on the seat belt light. I was not prepared for the rattling that followed. I kept expecting the oxygen masks to drop or alarms to go off. Seeing me lock my elbow with my mom's, Dad had leaned over to tell me that there was nothing to worry about. He didn't look totally convinced himself and hadn't even known where to plug in the headphones, so it was hard to think his opinion was backed up by any kind of aviation knowledge. I kept my eyes on the flight attendants, looking for any hint that they were bracing for impact or making farewell phone calls to loved ones at home. I sat, white-knuckled and ready to throw up, watching those unperturbed faces until we hit smoother skies.

My parents have not pushed for reunions lately. Our gatherings were loud, messy, and fun before Rahim died. Even talking on the phone with my aunts feels forced now, with vague promises to make time for a visit in the summer or the fall, when things at work slow down, when school lets out, when basketball season ends.

Or when we don't remind each other of freshly turned dirt wreathed with white roses.

I wish I had more pictures of Rahim, but he wasn't the type, so I'm stuck with remembering how he looked when I saw him last. I kept expecting him to open his eyes, to give a sly smile and tear off the white cloth he was cocooned in. But he didn't move. He was terrifyingly motionless. I was shaking at the burial. I hadn't eaten anything and thought I might pass out when they lowered his casket into the hollowed plot of earth that Rahim's father had purchased for himself. It looked like a mistake. There were low, broken moans and sniffles around me as Rahim's father cast the first shovelful of dirt over the casket. My dad and Yusuf did the same, as did the other men in the family and a couple of Rahim's classmates.

The funeral was the quietest family gathering I've ever been to. A cloak of silence descended upon us and got heavier the closer we got to Rahim's home. Every whisper felt like a violation.

Uncle Zahir was the one who found him in his room and has hardly been able to speak since. I don't blame him. The details were whispered to me by another cousin. When my parents did speak, it was mostly to pray for Rahim's parents. Most of their sentences went unfinished, as did our plates of food. Yusuf and I spent the next two days having aunts melt into tears at the sight of us, while we mumbled rehearsed condolences and stared at our feet.

Ama Leeda, my dad's sister, had been a withering mess the entire time. Uncle Zahir had been statue-like. He kept his head bowed and seemed to be in quiet prayer at all times. On a few occasions I saw him lift his head with great effort, as if he were losing a fight against gravity.

Weeks after we'd flown back home to Virginia, the silence

lingered. When it finally lifted, it had left its mark on our home, like a handprint on wet cement. Mom insisted that we keep our bedroom doors open. Yusuf and I still keep closing them when we go to bed, but plenty of mornings, I wake up to find the door open again. When Mom asks us how we're doing, she stares at us like she's trying to see through our answers into the hidden spaces of our minds. My dad, who would rather get a root canal than go to the mall, made a habit of coming home with stuff we don't necessarily need or want, like plain white socks. A dozen doughnuts. Pokémon cards, which we stopped collecting years ago.

I wished they would just come out and say what they were really worried about, but I wasn't brave enough to put it into words. Some thoughts feel too dark for daylight. I once said Rahim's name and my mom looked like I was summoning a djinn. And I was pretty sure that if I tried to talk to Dad, he would come home with roller skates or pistachio frozen yogurt.

A week after the funeral, I found Yusuf lying on his bed with his hands folded behind his head, his eyes on the blank ceiling.

*You thinking about him?* I'd asked from the doorway.

Yusuf nodded but didn't look in my direction.

*Me too*, I'd said. When Yusuf remained silent, I inched further. *I just . . . I just wonder how . . . I mean, why . . .*

*We didn't really know him, Yal. We can't make guesses now.*

*Do you ever wonder what would have happened if you would have called him that morning?* I asked.

171

*If ever means all the time, then yes,* Yusuf replied, his voice so full of regret, a mirror of my own feelings, that I wished I'd never asked.

*I didn't mean* you *should have. I was talking about me . . . but he wasn't even on Pic-Up. I don't think he wanted to be around family.*

I didn't know that, of course. But Yusuf shouldn't have been carrying around a brick of guilt for failing to save Rahim when I hadn't done anything either. What if I had called him that morning? Or a month before?

I didn't bring up Rahim to Yusuf again because I didn't want to see the angst on my brother's face. I wondered what had hurt Rahim more—that we didn't hold on to him tighter when he was alive or that we seemed even more eager to let his name evaporate after he was gone.

# 18

I crawl out of bed. I don't feel rested, but I'm also not a zombie anymore. I lumber down the hallway and into my parents' bedroom. My mother tosses a phone charger into the gaping mouth of a tote bag on her bed, followed by a rattling bottle of ibuprofen.

"How's Yusuf?" I ask.

My mother must not have heard me coming. She turns and blinks a couple of times, startled from her thoughts. She wraps her arms around me and kisses my forehead. Her hair is pulled back in a knot, damp and smelling of shampoo.

"Same," she says, and exhales through pursed lips. "I'm going back now. I just came to change my clothes."

"I'll go with you," I blurt. She starts to protest, then stops herself. "I just need to shower. I'll be fast."

"Okay. And bring a book. Or some homework," she says, looking conflicted. "It is good to stay busy."

I shower quickly and throw a few things into a backpack. I meet her in the car and spot her tea thermos in a bag on the floor of the back seat. She hasn't really slept in over twenty-four hours and it doesn't look like she's planning on crawling into bed anytime soon.

We walk through the hospital to our posts in room five of the ICU, at Yusuf's bedside. My phone lights up and I realize I had mistakenly put it on mute when I connected it to the charger at home. There are dozens of messages from my friends. I scroll through messages from Mona, who was surely the first person Asma talked to.

> OMG, I heard about Yusuf. How is he?
>
> Where are you?
>
> Hey, everything okay?
>
> Text me when you can. I'm so sorry.
>
> And I'm texting you too much. I'm sorry if this is interrupting something. I'm going to stop but just call me or text or whatever when you can.

I can picture her chewing her lip. Probably praying for Yusuf. I feel bad that I haven't replied yet.

> Just got back to the hospital. I don't know much yet.

Her reply comes almost immediately, as if she had it ready to send the moment I answered.

Asma and I are coming. Leaving here now.

My eyes burn. As much as I don't want to be alone, I'm also already feeling overwhelmed and I don't know if I have the energy to answer their questions or to take my attention away from Yusuf.

Don't. Not yet. I'll let you know.

I tack a heart on to the end of my message so she knows I appreciate her willingness to walk out of class and be here with me.

Yusuf looks just like he did when I left, except the shadows under his eyes appear to be a shade darker. A doctor is leaning over him, listening to his chest. She glances at us when we enter and offers a fleeting smile. My father is standing on the opposite side of the bed, holding Yusuf's hand.

"It's going to take some time for the swelling of his brain to subside. But for now, his lungs sound clear, his heart rate is normal, his kidneys . . ." She continues to list Yusuf's many perfectly functioning organs while we stare at my bruised and broken brother. "Like I said, it's far too early to know what this means. We're doing all we can, but I also need to be realistic with you. His condition is very precarious right now."

My mother turns to me automatically, as she always does when she meets a word she doesn't know.

*Precarious.*

She looks away, having gotten the meaning from the expression on my face.

*Precarious. Pretty scary.*

Seeing my brother lying on his back with his eyes closed, my mind flashes to Rahim in his casket. I push the thought away angrily. My brother is not dead. He is alive.

"Can he hear us?" I ask. The doctor turns to me, a bit blindsided by my question. My parents wait for her to reply. I point to the monitor, to the undulating lines and the sawtooth line and the one that doesn't seem to alarm anyone even though it runs flat across the screen. I can read them just about as well as I can read palms. "Does anything here tell us if he can hear when we talk about him?"

The doctor's face softens. She speaks slowly, like she's choosing her words carefully.

"We can capture his breathing, heart rate, blood pressure, his oxygen level, and more, but there are some things we don't know. What I've seen happen in these rooms tells me that it would be helpful if you pulled up a chair and talked to your brother. Let him hear your voice and know you're near. Not everything vital is measured by these monitors."

My father, his hair mussed and his face shadowed with stubble, nods emphatically. He immediately slides a chair over to Yusuf's side as if he's been given a directive. He looks at me and points to the open seat.

My parents are waiting on me expectantly. The doctor goes back to examining Yusuf, lifting his right eyelid and swinging a penlight over his pupil. I take two slow steps across the room and slide into the chair. My brother smells like a Band-Aid, adhesive and dried blood and hurt. His hand rests at his side, a small sticker with a red light taped over the tip of his pointer finger, which makes me think of the finger protectors he used to use when he was first learning to play guitar.

When we were ten, I declared that I wanted to learn to play piano, and Mom chose to take advantage of the sibling discount and enroll Yusuf as well. Six months into lessons, I was still struggling with "Twinkle, Twinkle, Little Star." My fingers turned into Popsicle sticks when I sat on the bench. At the first recital, I saw children half my age doing twice what I could do and decided I shouldn't waste any more of my parents' money. But the lessons brought Yusuf to the behind the scenes of songs, and he fell hard and fast. He quickly became fluent in the language of music, the notes and the rhythms. After a year of piano, Yusuf wanted to try the guitar. When he picked it up, it was like a reunion, not an introduction. He didn't practice because he had to. He did it because it came as naturally to him as getting out of bed in the morning. It became the thing that made him Yusuf. Mom and Dad thought his passion was great until the day he said he wanted to be a musician. They looked like they were struggling to understand the words coming out of his mouth.

Freshman year, Chris, Liam, and Yusuf started to play music together on a regular basis. They began to cover songs from bands they liked. About a year later, they named their band

The Hipper Campus. When I asked him what The Hipper Campus meant, Yusuf said band names were meant to be intriguing to followers and an inside secret for the members of the band.

I stare at Yusuf's ear. I talk to my brother every single day of my life and somehow can't find any words right now.

"Hey, Yusuf," I say softly. "I just . . . please . . ."

My head drops. What am I supposed to say to him? It can't possibly be me Yusuf needs right now. Yusuf needs our parents to comfort him the way they did when he was little and fell off his bike or burned his finger on the stove or got upset because I took a stuffed animal from him. I stand up and grab my backpack.

"Dad, you should talk to him first. I'm going to be in the lobby for a bit. I don't . . . I don't want to be in the way," I say. My father gives me a hug and a twenty-dollar bill in case I get hungry.

I leave the precarious lines on the monitors, the dinging of the machines, and the slow drip of fluids behind me. My eyes well with tears, blurring the hallways. I keep my gaze lowered so the nurses don't notice. In the elevator, I jab at the button for the first floor seven times, and just when the doors are about to shut, a hand slides between them. A foot follows, then a clipboard.

"Ah, sorry to hold you up," says a woman in shapeless black pants and a button-down shirt with the sleeves rolled to her elbows. She smiles at me before checking the phone clipped to her belt.

*Precarious. Pretty scary.*

I stare at the floor and clear my throat in this impossibly quiet elevator. There's nothing more awkward than crying in front of a stranger in the confines of an elevator. Mercifully, we are transported to the first floor without any other stops. I spill out of the doors before they fully open and step into the lobby, where tiny red lights strung on a Christmas tree cast a red glow on the gift boxes arranged on the floor. There are tables set up near the tree with vendors selling last-minute holiday gifts. People are wandering through the rows of tables, which is surely better than staring at the television screen.

I head over to the café, which is just a corner kiosk. The salads look a little wilted and the only sandwiches left are tuna or ham and cheese. My parents should eat something. I order two cups of green tea and three blueberry muffins from the woman wearing a denim apron. She slides her hands into gloves and reaches into the pastry case to bag the blueberry muffins.

"Give me a few minutes for the tea, hon," she says as I swipe my mom's credit card. "Someone unplugged me so I've got a pot of cold water right now."

"Sure, okay," I say, and touch my back pocket, only to realize I've left my phone upstairs. I take a few steps away from the kiosk, which brings me closer to the tables.

A woman in a knit cap smiles at me. I smile back reflexively. There are green and red mittens on her table, the kind that are connected by a length of yarn so a child doesn't go home from school with only one. "Baby, It's Cold Outside" plays in the background.

"Didn't they try to ban this song?" a man asks, chuckling.

"They'd ban white bread if they could," a woman replies. "Taking things too far, if you ask me."

"Ain't that the truth. Glad my grandson graduated two years ago. Trying to teach all kinds of nonsense in schools these days and then wondering why kids are acting up instead of growing up."

"All I'm gonna say on that is merry Christmas, merry Christmas, merry Christmas," the woman says, enunciating each cheer.

"They're coming for you," he chuckles, and through their loaded holiday banter I'm reminded of how funny Larson thought he was, talking about cornflakes.

My cheeks burn. I turn to get a good look at them.

The woman has light brown hair and is wearing a sweater embroidered with flowers. The man is the same height as my father but heavier around the middle. He has spots of gray in his beard and is squinting like he should be wearing glasses.

"I don't have a problem saying merry Christmas," I say. "Do you have a problem saying happy Eid?"

The man turns around. He's still smiling. He hasn't really seen me yet but when he does, his jaw slides forward and he squints even harder. The woman behind him puts a hand on her hip.

"Happy what?" he asks.

"No one's coming for you," I tell him.

"Listen, sweetheart, I don't know—"

"Don't call me sweetheart," I say. "You don't know me. You don't know my brother or my family. You don't know anything."

My heart is thumping in my ears. I turn my back on them and start to walk away, half expecting to be grabbed from behind. I return to the kiosk, where there's a paper bag on the counter. The cashier points at it and gives me a wave. I take the bag while she wipes the counter. My hand is shaking hard enough to register on the Richter scale. I use both hands to hold the bag and walk back to the elevator, looking toward the tables out of the corner of my eye to see if anyone is pointing at me or staring. I don't see anything.

When the elevator doors close, I let out the breath I've kept trapped in my chest. What was I thinking? What good did that do? I'm trembling and messy and those people downstairs are probably laughing at me.

I lean against the wall because the last thing my parents need is to see me in this state. I take slow, jagged breaths to steady my nerves.

When I walk back into the room, I see my mother has fallen asleep with her chin in her hand. I set the paper bag next to her as quietly as I can. She needs sleep as much as she needs to eat.

181

I take one cup of tea and a muffin and hand it to my dad. He thanks me and opens the lid to let his tea cool.

I take a bite of my muffin, then slide into the chair next to my brother's bed. Yusuf's left hand has slid toward the edge of the bed. There's a bruise near his wrist from where he had an IV placed yesterday. I pick up his hand and position it closer to him; his fingers are colder than I expect. I take a hospital sheet off the shelf in his closet and spread it out over him. It's starting to sink in that Yusuf didn't just break an arm or leg. It's not lost on me that in discussing Yusuf's recovery, we hear more *ifs* than *whens*.

I think of the doctor listing Yusuf's uninjured organs. Do his kidneys know what's happened? Is his heart *rap rap rap*-ping a rhythm and waiting, still waiting, for a reply?

I look at my parents, the three of us without a single bruise or scrape but huddled around a broken Yusuf.

My brother's hand in my own, I tap on his wrist the way I would on the wall between our rooms.

*Tap. Tap-tap. Tap.*

*I'm here, Yusuf. Will you please wake up?*

# 19

"Yalda, where are you?" Mom asks. I am standing outside, in the hospital's serenity garden, a courtyard with a stone water fountain outside the hospital's chapel. Brick pathways weave between mulched flower beds. I take a seat on a wooden bench with a cross on the back. The fountain isn't running and the mums have succumbed to winter; their withered brown blooms look like heads bowed in prayer. Tall, wispy grasses have been trimmed and squared, stems standing at attention.

"What happened? Is he okay?" I ask.

"No, nothing happened. He's . . . the same," Mom replies, and I can't tell if she sounds disappointed or relieved. I'm a mix of the two myself. "The police officer wants to talk to you. Can you meet him in the lobby?"

I breathe a sigh of relief that Yusuf hasn't taken a turn for the worse and hurry back through the sliding glass doors into the hospital and into the mostly empty lobby. After a few minutes, I see a police officer coming toward me. He gives me a tight-lipped nod and points to two empty seats. He looks younger than my father but not by much. My eyes flit to the holstered gun on his hip.

"Yalda. Did I get that right?"

I nod.

"I'm Officer Song. I want to ask you a few questions," he says, taking out a small notepad. "When was the last time you spoke to your brother?"

I recount the evening for him. I am nervous as I catalog the events of my day, realizing there were huge chunks of time during which I had no knowledge of where my brother was or what he was doing. I see the countless missed opportunities to send a check-in text or even a call to remind him about Yalda. Why hadn't I felt in my bones that something was wrong? Mom has told us since we were little to watch out for each other at playgrounds or at school, or when the cousins got together and went into the woods behind Ama Leeda's house for a nature walk.

*Yusuf, anywhere you go, make sure no one bothers your sister. And Yalda, keep your eyes on Yusuf.*

They wanted Yusuf to make sure no boys crossed any lines with me. And they wanted me to make sure Yusuf didn't cross the line from mischief into trouble.

These were implied messages, of course. I could hear the sexism in there and brought it up once. Mom hid behind her vague language, but Dad doubled down.

*Yalda, come on. Sometimes brothers have to look out for their sisters. The world is not the same for girls and boys. You hear the news. I don't have to tell you what's happening out there.*

I didn't argue with him because I didn't want to wade into those swampy waters any more than he did and because I couldn't imagine a situation in which I had to watch out for Yusuf's safety. I was tragically wrong.

How much sooner could we have found him if I'd just realized that even if he were really upset about the WhereHouse fallout, Yusuf would never have stood us up like that?

"Are you all right? You need water?"

I shake my head.

"I'm fine," I mumble.

"Okay, good. I just wanted to see if you could help me with a few questions. Can you tell me anything about what Yusuf was doing last night? Anyone he might have been meeting up with?"

I shake my head.

"No, no one," I answer. "He was supposed to come home from work."

"And he works at the music studio?"

I nod.

"Yes, Crescendo. He gives lessons to kids there. His band practices there too."

185

"Chris and Liam, right? That's what your mom told me."

"Yes," I confirm. He asks for their last names, and I oblige.

"And he had lessons scheduled for that evening?"

"Yes," I say. My thoughts start running. "I mean, I think so. Beto's the manager. I . . . Do you think they have cameras in the studio? Maybe the cameras caught something?"

The police officer nods the way a teacher does when you give a good answer to the wrong question.

"We've talked to Beto. And we're looking into the cameras."

So the police are talking to people, which means they must not think this was some terrible accident. I wouldn't call it relief, but I feel better that they're asking questions.

"Please, you have to find out who did this to him," I say.

"You sound pretty certain someone did this to him," he says. "What makes you say that? Had Yusuf been arguing with anyone lately?"

How do I answer that question? Yes and no. I hadn't heard any yelling or fighting, but it had felt like the world had been pitted against Yusuf since the night at WhereHouse. Do the police already know about that?

"There was this other band playing at WhereHouse the same night my brother's band played, and the singer . . . ," I start. I tell him about Larson and the back-and-forth that night. I tell him about the online comments about our restaurant and the graffiti at school too.

"Outside the school or inside? There's been a lot of that going around. Swastikas and whatnot."

186

"It was on his locker," I explain. "It was meant for him."

He nods but doesn't react with any change in expression or even just a sympathetic sound. He is very hard to read.

"School have any idea who was behind it?"

"No. Or if they do, they didn't say anything about it." Why does it feel like there are secrets everywhere now?

"How often did your brother hang out at WhereHouse?"

"Never. I mean, just the once and it wasn't to hang out. He was performing. That's why we were there too. The guys were just really excited to get to play at a real venue."

"And how did the guys react to what went down that night at WhereHouse?"

"They were upset about it. I mean, they were upset about what Larson said and the way everyone reacted."

He taps the tip of his pen on the open notepad. His lips thin to a line as he considers what he's written down. In his silence, I think about what I've just shared with him.

Larson. The graffiti. The town. Us at WhereHouse, which he surely knows is next door to a bar. Yusuf has always been the guy with lots of friends, but he now sounds like he had a lot of enemies and hangs out in the wrong places.

"Well, thanks for this," he says, and moves to the edge of the chair and checks his notes.

"Look, I don't know what happened to Yusuf, but I know he wouldn't have fallen on his own. Somebody must know something." I remember the guy onstage who tried to take the mic from Yusuf. What was his name? "And you could talk to Jace!"

"Jace?" the officer confirms. "Jace who?"

"I don't know his last name. He's the manager of Where-House. Or maybe not the manager, but he works there. He was emceeing the show that night and he heard what Larson said, the whole thing. He can tell you more about Larson."

He adds Jace's name to the list, then asks me for my number as well. He clears his throat.

"Okay. And I understand your parents didn't know Yusuf was going to be playing at WhereHouse. Was there anything else your brother was keeping from your parents?" Officer Song asks.

"No, Yusuf isn't like that," I say, feeling a bit defensive. "He would have told me. I mean, I don't think he would keep something big from me."

"Of course. I have to ask. Look, I know this is a stressful time. You're worried about your brother and you want answers. I get it. I have a sister too, and she's had my back my whole life. But for now, just be there for your brother. I've got this. Here's my number," he says, handing me a card with his contact information. "Give me a call if you think there's anything we should know."

I watch him walk away, my head spinning with questions. I don't know what to make of our conversation. Why do I feel like Yusuf is in trouble? He doesn't have some secret life. Everything is really so much simpler than I just made it sound, and yet there's no denying that Yusuf's world has been a tangled, thorny mess too.

My chest and throat feel tight and I'm afraid I'll suffocate here. I call my mom and tell her I'm going to take the bus home. She's not thrilled with the idea, but driving me would mean leaving Yusuf's side, and no one wants to do that now. As I walk across the parking lot, I remember the times I've entered Yusuf's room and seen him slide his phone out of view. He and the guys do a lot of group texts. I figured they were talking about stuff he didn't want me to see, like girls or whatever. But was there more to it?

Every pothole we cross jostles and scatters my thoughts. By the time I get off at the bus stop, I've rehashed the conversation with Officer Song a dozen times. My mind is still going as I walk down the street to our house. Does he think I'm covering for Yusuf? Does he really care about what happened or did he ask a few questions because that's his job?

Mona messages me just as I walk through our front door.

How is he? Where are you?

Same, I reply. I'm home now.

I fall onto the sofa and kick off my shoes. They look so wrong in the middle of the floor that I drag myself off the couch and put them in the closet. I stare at the living room and wonder who the police officer might be talking to next. I should have asked him. How would he even know who to talk to?

I take out a notebook and pen. I don't know what the police are asking people and start to think I should be asking questions myself.

I start my own list and begin with the guys in the band—Christopher and Liam. I don't have their numbers but I can reach out to them on Pic-Up. I add Beto's name and all the names I ran through with the officer. What have I missed? Yusuf's been spending so much time with Chris and Liam lately that he hasn't been hanging out with his other friends as much. Still, I add their names to the list. Roman. Evan. Kareem. Nestor.

I almost forgot about Keith. Yusuf talks to him almost every day. Of course, I'm usually around for the conversation and don't think I've missed much, but I should still ask. He hasn't called or texted. I don't want to read into his silence too much because I don't have the space for it.

I open the Pic-Up app on my phone and send friend requests to all of Yusuf's contacts so I can get in touch with them or they can get in touch with me. I am not the type to reach out on social media, but it feels as important as breathing right now to be doing something useful. I call the studio and ask for Beto.

"He's not here and we're actually closed today. Can you call back some other time?"

"Chris?" I say, recognizing the voice. "It's Yalda."

"Oh, hey!" he says, clearly surprised to be talking to me. "I sent you a message. How's Yusuf doing?"

"He's still in the hospital. In the ICU," I say.

"Shit," Chris says. "I can't believe he fell . . . I mean, this is so crazy."

I nod, which is dumb because Chris can't see me.

190

"Is he going to be okay?"

I wish I knew.

"They said he's stabilizing but we have to give him time."

Chris lets out a sigh that fills the line.

"I'm trying to figure out . . . from last night. Do you know what time Yusuf left?"

"It was around eight o'clock, I think. I didn't get to talk to him much. We were both giving lessons last night. Mine went later but I saw him leave. He waved on his way out," Christopher adds. "I waved back. I mean, I think I waved back."

Chris sounds a bit raspy, like it's rough getting the words out.

"Did you say the studio is closed?"

I haven't even thought about what's happening at the studio.

"Yeah," Chris says. "We closed after . . . we heard. Beto's been here, but just for a couple lessons. With Yusuf in the hospital, we just couldn't. And Christmas Eve is tomorrow anyway. This place wasn't supposed to be open."

I think of those tiny little drums on the Christmas tree at Crescendo. Maybe Chris is looking at them now too.

"What are you doing at the studio?"

"I'm actually meeting a police officer. He wanted to ask me a few questions and asked me to meet him here. I don't know. It's so weird to come back here. It just didn't feel real. How did I not see . . ."

My dad has been wrecked about that too, about not looking hard enough for Yusuf or sensing that he was nearby and hurt.

"I know. It's a lot to think about. But can I ask you something? Did you notice anything wrong with the railing before this happened?" I ask.

"No, I didn't," he says. "Look, everyone knows this place is falling apart. We had water come through the ceiling of the break room last month so now there's just a bucket sitting there. It's bad, but I didn't think it was bad enough to get someone hurt. Someone's taped it off now."

I can picture the yellow tape, fluttering in the winter wind.

"What about when you left?"

"It was dark then. I don't know. I think I just closed the door and didn't look around the corner. I'm sorry, Yalda. I'm really sorry."

"I know. Thanks," I say. Yusuf, Liam, and Chris had been friendly before the band, but it wasn't till they started playing together that they became really tight, like the harmony they found through their instruments carried over into life. "One more thing. Does the studio have any security cameras?"

Chris is quiet for a moment.

"There are . . . ," Chris begins, then exhales. "But they haven't worked in forever. I don't even think they're plugged in. It sucks, Yalda. I'll see if I can think of anything else. And hey, Yusuf's going to be fine, right?"

"Yeah," I say, unsure if he's asking me or telling me.

After I hang up, I lean back and close my eyes. I heard disbelief in his voice, like he couldn't possibly fathom that his friend Yusuf could be hanging on to life by a thread.

192

About a month after Rahim's funeral, a couple of police officers came to our school with a golf cart, orange cones, and crates. They set up a driving course in the parking lot. It wouldn't have been a tough course, but they had a few seniors wear a pair of "drunk goggles" to simulate driving after a couple of beers. We watched them knock over crates, laughing when they realized they'd swerved too far and driven over a cone. Then they had us take a seat on the school lawn so one of the officers could talk to us about the purpose of the exercise.

*We do this year after year for a reason,* he'd said into a microphone attached to a speaker on wheels. His voice came out jagged and tinny. His sound system looked about as old as us. *Teenagers feel like they're invisible.*

I had looked up then, feeling suddenly very seen.

He'd looked out at us, pausing for effect.

*You're young and full of life. You can't imagine that anything could hurt you.*

He'd said invincible, not invisible.

I'd stolen a look at the classmates sitting around me then, wondering if what he said was true. If it was, that would make me an oddball. I think I feel defeated more days of the month than I care to admit.

*That's why far too often someone from this school makes a big mistake and a family ends up organizing a funeral instead of a graduation party. Impaired driving puts everyone on the road at risk. Sometimes others get hurt. Sometimes the driver.*

*Don't do that to your parents*, he'd warned, deepening his voice for impact.

At home that night, I'd wandered into Yusuf's room and flopped onto his bed.

*Can I ask you something?* I'd said.

*You just did*, he'd replied. I'm sure I rolled my eyes.

*Do you feel invincible?*

*Why do you ask?*

When I didn't reply, Yusuf had pushed his chair back from his desk and looked out his window.

*He had it wrong*, he'd said. *Kids aren't driving around drunk because they think they won't die. It's because we've figured out that everybody dies and if we don't live full throttle right now, we're wasting the chance to feel alive.*

I find myself back in Yusuf's room, staring at the faint lines of cracking paint on the ceiling. I can almost hear his toe tapping out the beat of whatever song was in his head.

Yusuf hadn't felt invincible. He'd been living urgently, writing songs and taking risks and inviting punishment—as if it wasn't the beat of a song he was tapping out on his carpet but the ticking of a clock.

# 20

*Hope is the thing with feathers* is what Emily Dickinson said. I don't know why I'm thinking about that poem while I'm watching the doctor examine Yusuf.

We wait for him to give us hope, but the air around him is heavy enough to ground even the most weightless of creatures.

"His scan today looks stable, which is good. Let's give him some more time."

He is careful with what he tells us, balancing the good against the bad. I want this doctor to linger, the same way I want every person in scrubs or a white coat to stay in this room a bit longer. It's so much worse to be left alone with only the beeping and whirring of the machines keeping Yusuf alive. I've never felt so antsy. It's a struggle to keep myself in this chair.

I've brought my notebook with me and sketch only when my parents can't see what I'm drawing. I have pages of meaningless lines, waves, and swirls. On today's page, I've drawn an elephant peeking out from behind a hospital curtain, his trunk holding the fabric back. Behind the elephant is a small child, sitting on the floor with his head tucked between his bent knees. The pen in my hand is the only thing I can control.

"Leeda called," my father says to my mother in a low voice.

My mom nods. She doesn't ask how Ama Leeda is doing. Talking to her always taxes Mom emotionally and she already looks depleted.

"She offered to come. To help," my dad adds.

"It's not necessary," Mom says in Dari, which brings me relief. I can't imagine having Rahim's mom around right now. Every time I think of her arranging a marriage for him, I feel a knot of anger inside.

Dad says nothing more.

There's a cheesy quote about today being a gift and that's why we call it the present. Being present is a gift too. I feel bad whenever I walk out of the hospital room, even if I can't figure out what being here does for Yusuf. I'm not even sure what it does for me. One minute, I want to hold his hand and talk into his ear, and then the next minute, I can't breathe seeing the tube in his throat. I want to pull it out so he can sit up and ask me if I've seen his phone charger.

I look at my phone. I've been getting a steady stream of text messages from people wanting to check in on Yusuf. Mona and Asma. Chris.

There's a new message from a number I don't have in my phone.

Hey I just heard. How's Yusuf doing?

Sorry this shit happened to him. By

the way, this is Liam.

He must have gotten my number from Chris. Where Chris is more transparent with his feelings, Liam is fogged glass, and I've always wondered if Yusuf really knows him as well as he thinks he does. As far as I know, though, they never had any friction between them before they had to choose a song for WhereHouse. It's too bad Yusuf had to be in a coma for Liam to get some perspective.

While I'm chewing on this, my phone buzzes with a text from Mona asking where I am.

In the ICU, I type.

My parents don't look up. It's strange how quickly we've become accustomed to the orchestra of sounds in this room: the beep of the electrode confirming my brother's pulse, the whirring of machines dripping clear liquids into his veins, the clunk of the bedrails being lowered so the nurses can turn his motionless body, and the crinkle of plastic and whoosh of a suction catheter clearing Yusuf's airway.

As loud as this room is, so much happens silently. Yusuf's blood filling rubber-capped tubes. The two edges of his scalp wound soldering together beneath staples. My brother fighting for his life.

But is he fighting?

As still as he is, it is hard to know.

I look at my phone.

We're in the lobby, comes Mona's reply.

I check on my parents. My father has positioned his chair so that he is as close to Yusuf's head as he can be. My mom is directly behind him, her eyelids closed but fluttering slightly. I quietly tuck my sketchbook and pens into my bag. Only my dad notices me stand and walk out of the room, but there's no objection on his face.

An elevator ride later, I spot Mona and Asma sitting on a lobby bench. The lobby is especially quiet today, and it dawns on me that it's Christmas. The days have lost meaning. They're both perched on the edges of their seats, as if they're afraid leaning back might commit them to these chairs forever. Asma is on her feet the second she spots me.

"Oh my God, Yalda. How is he?" she asks, her eyes glossy and her nose pink.

Before I can answer, Mona throws her arms around me and squeezes tight. She pulls back to look at me, though she's still holding me by my arms like an aunt might.

"This is so goddamn terrible. How's he doing? How are you doing?" she asks. "What happened to him?"

Her questions take my head in different directions so it's

hard for me to formulate a linear response. I lead them to a corner of the lobby away from the television, where only one gray-haired man is sitting reading a newspaper. The seats are connected and I take the middle seat. Mona and Asma each tuck a leg in and swivel toward me.

"They had to operate on him because of a blood clot pressing on his brain. They say everything went well, but he's still on a whole bunch of machines. He's hurt so bad," I say.

Asma brushes a tear from her cheek. Seeing her do that makes my own eyes well with tears. I did a lot of crying when we first found Yusuf. Since then, I've been doing quiet, out-of-sight crying.

"But how? Did somebody do this to him?" Mona asks.

"It was late and the studio's cameras don't work so we can't know for sure. Honestly, I think . . . I think . . . somebody pushed him over the railing outside the studio. The police are asking questions, but they haven't told us anything yet. Or maybe they don't know anything. I wish Yusuf could just tell us what happened."

"Oh my God," Mona says, shaking her head. "Who could do such a thing? And to Yusuf?"

"Is he talking yet?" Asma asks.

I shake my head because I don't want to say that my brother is being held together by safety pins and rubber bands.

I parrot the line I keep hearing. "They say he needs time."

"But he's going to be okay, right?" Asma asks her question

as she blinks. She's an empath and I love that about her, but right now I worry she's going to tip me over the edge, so I let out a long, slow breath.

"Okay," Mona jumps in so I don't have to answer. "How can we help? My mom's going to drop some food off at your house. Do you need anything?"

"And there's going to be a vigil at the masjid," Asma says. "My parents talked to the imam there and he felt like we should do something. I hope that's okay. People just want to help."

I don't know who "people" are, frankly. We only go to the masjid on holidays or for funerals. My parents are so busy with the restaurant and home that most of their socializing consists of video calls with siblings and cousins in different states or continents. But I've seen the masjid nearly bursting with people on holidays, and if all those people will say a prayer for my brother, then I should be nothing but grateful.

So why am I cringing inside?

"Thanks," I say, and Mona nods as if we've just agreed on a battle plan.

Asma puts a hand over mine.

"I just want him to wake up," I say.

"And he will," Mona says, her voice full of conviction. I want to believe her, but she hasn't seen the condition Yusuf's in, nor does she have any medical knowledge. "You'll see. Everyone's thinking about him. Liam asked me for your number too. Some people are probably afraid to bother you. People keep reaching out to me like I have all the info, but don't worry,

I'm just telling them I don't know anything because it's not my place to share."

"Yeah, Liam texted me," I say. Thinking of Liam reminds me that Chris hasn't gotten back to me about the security cameras. I've got to ask him.

"He must feel pretty stupid for turning on Yusuf the way he did," Asma says.

"That's probably why he messaged me," I say, recalling Liam's text. He hadn't apologized for being so hard on Yusuf, but at least he had the decency to reach out.

It helps a lot to have people even send a message. I quietly wish I would hear from Keith again but Christmas commands everyone's attention and is supposed to be spent with your own family, so I probably won't hear from him for a while. I flash again to the WhereHouse parking lot, seeing Keith and Danny talking to Larson. I feel a fresh wave of rage toward Larson.

I need to get some sleep. I'm seeing things inside out and upside down and need to be thinking straight now more than ever.

"Oh," Mona says, staring at her phone. She blinks slowly and turns it off, then shoves it into her pocket.

"What is it?" I ask.

Mona shakes her head and shrugs. She's trying to look unfazed but she's too transparent for that.

"Let me see it," I say. Asma looks from me to Mona, nervous for both of us. Nervous in general.

"Nothing important. Just junk."

"Mona," I say in a tone that persuades her it's better to share what she's seen with me now.

"It's just . . . I mean, the masjid posted about the vigil online and of course someone's going to have something stupid to say."

Asma looks at me, then shakes her head.

"Mona, just show it to us. This is making it worse."

Mona lets out a regretful groan but extracts her phone from her back pocket and pulls up the post for us.

Underneath the masjid's flyer about the vigil for Yusuf, a guy who goes by Paul B. Onion has added a paragraph that has attracted twelve reactions, a combination of stars and surprised looks.

Before everyone goes weepy for this man, don't forget that he tried to trick people into converting. That's immoral and criminal. This is America. We've all seen people hanging out at the mosque all days of the week and at odd hours too. Open your eyes, people.

"Oh my God," Asma says. "Does this guy even have a soul?"

"It's probably a bot. But plenty of people don't like what he said. This is classic attention-seeking behavior. We should do the opposite of paying attention to it," Mona advises, confident in her plan.

"And just let that exist out there . . . unchallenged?" Asma asks, waving her hand in the direction of Mona's phone. She's clearly uncomfortable with the plan.

In a reality where Yusuf never fell, I would show this to him so we could be angry together. He would type out some sarcastic, smart-ass reply and I would simmer, tongue-tied. Yusuf was the one with words and wit.

I am exhausted and only have the energy to close my eyes and wish, like a paintbrush heavy with ink, I could make everything and everyone disappear.

# 21

"Are you going to the restaurant?" I ask my dad, mostly to fill the silence. I have a strange new need to hear my parents speaking. I almost don't care what they're saying. What I really want to hear is a steady tone in their voices, confirmation that they're not on the verge of falling apart.

"No," Dad replies without looking my way. "It's closed."

He's assumed his regular driving posture. His left hand is at the six o'clock position of the steering wheel. His right hand rests on his thigh and he's leaning back into the seat. To the untrained eye, he probably looks relaxed, but I can see the tightness around his mouth. I know he never drives without his music on, mostly Afghan pop but also a bit of George Michael and Michael Jackson.

My parents close the restaurant only three days out of the whole year. The restaurant was last open on the night we found Yusuf. It's now two days after Christmas and it's still closed, a sure sign that our world has been turned upside down.

"Did the doctors say anything else about Yusuf after I left? Did they do any more tests?" I ask, wondering if I missed an update about my brother's status.

Dad shakes his head.

"No," he replies. "We just have to wait."

I exhale slowly, controlling the air so it doesn't come out as a shout.

"Dad?" I ask.

"Yes?"

Dad eyes me with curiosity.

"Do you think he . . . he just fell?"

My dad doesn't say anything. He slows the car to a stop at the intersection, then seems to be staring at the dry cleaner's across the street.

A loud blaring sound jolts me. My dad straightens up.

The light is green and the car behind us has grown impatient. The driver leans on the horn again. Dad lifts a hand in apology and moves through the intersection. I think of how resigned my father has been and wonder if he's still beating himself up for not finding Yusuf sooner. My dad shouldn't be the one feeling guilty. I don't want to believe someone could be so evil toward my brother, but I can't ignore the facts either. And I'm not the only one. Two people who commented on the masjid's post suggested there was real evil behind what happened to Yusuf.

"Some people are saying this was a hate crime," I say, and it feels like I've plunged into ice water.

My dad flinches.

"I'm just saying—"

"Yalda," he says, flipping into Dari as he does when he's frustrated or extra happy. His English only flows when he's at emotional room temperature. "I don't want to talk about this now."

I drop the conversation because my dad looks like the time he threw out his back and could barely go from sitting to standing.

I can see Keith's house ahead. I slip my phone out of my bag and scroll down until I find his name. I want to know what he knows and what he's been hearing through the grapevine.

Hey, you around? I text him, my screen angled out of Dad's view. By then, we've passed Keith's house and are close enough to ours that I can see the garage door is open.

"Dad, did you leave the garage door open?" I ask.

Dad shakes his head. "Your aunt is here. She took a flight this morning."

As if summoned, a woman emerges from our garage lugging a white trash bag. She tosses it into the garbage can and pauses when she sees our car approaching.

I don't need to ask which aunt. We're close enough that I can see for myself that it's Ama Leeda, Rahim's mom.

"She took a very early flight. I'm sure she hasn't eaten. Let's make some food and get her comfortable," my dad suggests, laying out the plan.

I haven't seen Ama Leeda since the funeral. I've overheard my mom talking to her on the phone plenty of times but the conversations are usually brief and Mom is always tearful afterward, repeating her prayers for God to keep all children safe and spare mothers such pain.

Ama Leeda looks different. She's gained some weight and a stripe of graying roots runs down her part. I step out of the car and walk over to her. She hugs me tightly while I mumble a greeting, blinking back tears that are awfully ready to spill these days.

"Come, sweetheart. Don't waste your time crying. Better to pray for your brother. And you should eat something. Your parents are worried enough."

Once inside, I can see Ama Leeda has gotten straight to work. The kitchen sink is empty and the counters are spotless. The rotating dish from the microwave is sitting in the drying rack, which means she's already made her way through the appliances. I hear the whir of the laundry machine coming from the hallway. We don't need to help her get comfortable. Ama Leeda is clearly here to fix us. For a split second, I feel hopeful. Like maybe with just the right amount of household cleaner and elbow grease, all our problems will vanish.

"Thanks, Ama jan. Maybe in a little bit. I've got some

homework I need to do," I say, and leave my dad and Ama Leeda to talk. I feel bad thinking it, but to be around her is to be too close to grief.

"Such a good girl," she says approvingly. "You've always been a good girl."

Ama Leeda turns her back to me. This is what she's said about me since I was a little girl and it became how the extended family thought of me as well. It's not that my cousins are derelicts. Most are just more comfortable than me sharing opinions or shouting at sports games or dancing when the music comes on. I run risk calculations and overthink and get lost in my own thoughts. It's not really that I'm a perfect girl. If I were, I probably wouldn't be retreating into my room to see if Keith has texted me back.

And he has.

> Been meaning to talk to you. I'm about to
> walk Fisher. Can you come out?

I give him a thumbs-up. I'm short on patience and words these days.

Ama Leeda is in the kitchen, her head in a cabinet.

"I'm going for a walk. I need some fresh air," I call out, then go down the stairs to the closet by the front door. I jam my feet back into my sneakers.

"You didn't eat anything yet. Where are you going?" Ama Leeda moves fast. She's at the top of the stairs looking down at me.

"Where? Just . . . out," I stammer, because I wasn't expecting to have to explain myself. I keep my hand on the doorknob but don't open the door just yet.

"Did you ask your father?"

"If I can walk outside?" I ask in a tone that surely conveys I think her question is insane.

"You should ask him. It's cold outside. Don't want you to catch pneumonia."

Will asking my dad for permission prevent pneumonia? I'm not a doctor but I don't think that's how pneumonia works.

"I'll be fine. I have a coat," I say, trying to sound polite.

Ama Leeda sighs heavily. "Okay, I just don't want you to get sick."

I don't want to come off as disrespectful to Ama Leeda within minutes of seeing her, especially when she's here out of kindness. But all of a sudden the house feels a bit less like home, and I wonder how long I'll have to sidestep her.

"I'll be back soon," I say.

I speed walk down the street, looking over my shoulder to make sure Ama Leeda or my dad haven't come out after me. Keith is crouched at the end of the block, adjusting the collar on Fisher's neck. When Fisher spies me headed toward them, he barks twice. Keith rubs his head.

"It's okay, buddy. That's Yalda. I think she likes you," I hear him saying.

Fisher seems to understand because his tail starts to wag.

"Hey," Keith says. "How's Yusuf?"

"Better," I say. "They might be able to take the breathing tube out soon."

"That's good," Keith says, his voice lifting. "So he's going to be okay?"

"I hope so. They still say it's too early to tell," I repeat my new auto-reply. "So, can we walk?"

"Yeah," Keith says, nodding. "That'd be nice."

We've gone half a block before he speaks.

"Look, I'm really sorry I didn't call you. We were away for a couple days. Spent Christmas with my grandparents."

"It's fine," I say.

"And I thought maybe you needed some privacy and some space."

A second reason. The plural of reason may not be reasons. It might be excuses.

But I am not in the mood to judge Keith. I remember closing my eyes and wishing for everyone to go away, even while I prayed my phone would light up with texts from friends. Maybe he was right to lie low for a while. Or maybe I didn't want to be as alone as I thought.

"Yeah, I guess it's hard to know what the right amount of space is." I am quickly learning that there's a fine line between space and distance. Keith nods. "And my aunt just flew in this morning to stay with us for a bit. It doesn't really feel like we have much privacy now."

"Yeah, I mean, I think almost everyone's talking about what

happened," he says. "How could they not?"

I'm not surprised. School may be closed for winter break, but that wouldn't slow down the spread of big news.

"What are they saying?"

"That it's awful," Keith says, looking at Fisher. "That the building was in shitty shape and someone should sue."

"So people think it was just the railing?"

"I don't know. People want to know what happened. And they want him to be okay."

So do I.

"I think somebody pushed him," I say. "I don't think that railing just popped out of the wall. And I'm trying to figure things out because . . . well, because what if the police don't?"

"I get it," Keith says. "If I can help, let me know."

"It would help to know who was really angry about Where-House. Someone wrote that stuff on his locker. It can't be a complete secret."

"I haven't heard anything, honestly. I would tell you," he says.

I want to believe him.

"Thanks. That would help. It just feels like . . . like everybody's holding back a little."

We take a few quiet steps together before Keith speaks again.

"I'm really sorry this happened to Yusuf," Keith says, his words more hurried than usual. "And I know I said that thing the other day about you guys being regular and not scary. That came out wrong. I'm sorry. I've been meaning to call you, but honestly I thought you might be mad and didn't think you needed to deal with me on top of everything going on with Yusuf."

And this is why I like Keith. Not enough people think *before* they speak. But even fewer people think *after* they speak. Keith didn't need me to point out to him that comparing us to extremists was offensive. He spent time thinking about what he had said.

This also means he spent time thinking about me and how I felt.

"I'm not mad," I say, looking over at him. "But it also seemed weird that you weren't saying anything at all."

"Yeah," Keith admits. "I didn't know what I was supposed to do. For some stuff, you know what to say. There are prepackaged words. But not for this."

I think about what Keith has said. Are we ever given a script for horrific injury or violence? Not really. What had Asma or Mona said? I can't remember their words. I only know it felt like they cared. And I know that Keith's silence felt like the opposite.

I don't want to make Keith feel bad right now, but I want him to know how I felt.

"I think it would have felt better to hear something— anything—from you."

Keith and I both have our eyes on Fisher, the safest place for our eyes to be right now.

Fisher has found a stick on the sidewalk, a tiny branch that

212

must have come from one of the oak trees on the street. He paws at it before picking it up with his teeth. Keith takes the stick out of his mouth and gives the leash a soft tug to get him walking again.

"And you should have heard from me sooner," he says. "I mean, I should have called you sooner."

We walk the second half of the block a little faster, like we've shed some weight.

"So, if you could just ask around. Somebody's gotta know something."

"Yeah, no problem. I'm on it," Keith says.

Fisher stops to sniff at the edge of a neighbor's lawn. Somewhere inside the house, a dog is barking up a storm. He lifts a leg and relieves himself on the already yellowed grass. We walk a few more steps and Fisher still has his nose to the ground. Before we get very far, he's relieved himself again and the barking intensifies.

Keith sighs.

"Try all you want, boy. Someone's already claimed this territory."

I turn every time I hear a car coming up the street. I look back, nervous that my dad will spot me with Keith. But first there's a red hatchback, then a green SUV, then a white sedan with music on blast.

I relax when we reach the neighborhood playground. A man is recording with his phone two kids ducking and weaving through the jungle gym. He waits for them at the bottom of the tube slide and pokes his head in when they take too long to pop out and has to jump back so they land on the rubber mulch instead of his head.

Keith and I wander over to a bench. We stand near it for a second before I sit down. The cold cuts through my jeans and shocks my legs. Keith sits next to me, close enough that he feels me shiver. He moves an inch closer. I have a quick panic attack, wondering if he's going to put his arm around me, but he doesn't.

"So, how are you doing?" he asks. "I can't even imagine."

I feel that lump in my throat again. I don't want to cry in front of him so I take a long, slow gulp of air and hope it ices that hot lump away.

"I'm fine," I say, because what else could I possibly say? I'm not the one in a hospital.

"You're allowed to be *not* fine," Keith says, as if he heard my thought, and it helps to hear him say that.

"I'll be fine when Yusuf is fine," I say. "And when I figure out who did this to him. That's all I need right now."

Keith kicks at the mulch for a beat, then speaks, his eyes on the leash in his hands.

"When Danny was deployed, we knew there was a chance we'd get a phone call with bad news. I was on edge the first couple weeks he was gone, but we didn't get a call. Things were okay. And some more time went by and at some point I forgot about being afraid of getting that bad call. I went back to thinking that my big brother was unstoppable. Our own hero

214

for serving. Then I came home from playing basketball with friends one day and found my mom crying in the kitchen."

It's my turn to feel like I could have done better. I've never asked Keith if seeing his brother come home bandaged up and limping was hard on him.

"That must have been scary," I say.

"It was. And at the time, my mom kept saying we were lucky the injury wasn't worse than it was," Keith says. "But we also didn't really know how bad it was. He still thinks a lot about what he saw over there. He doesn't talk about it much, but it's in his head. Makes him sad sometimes. Or angry or tired. And I feel bad because for a long time, I didn't really get why he couldn't just chill out sometimes."

"That's got to be rough on everyone," I say, and Keith agrees.

The kids have moved on to a suspension bridge. Their dad is sitting on a bench opposite us, looking at his phone. Before the little girl crosses to the other platform, she figures out that by jumping, she can make all the planks rattle and rock. Two feet behind her, her brother grips the railing and starts to cry. The little girl stops jumping and extends a mittened hand toward her brother.

"When Yusuf didn't come home that night, I called him a few times. Then it got late and he still hadn't come home. And do you know what I did?" My neck burns with shame, but I keep talking because I am not about to let myself off the hook. I let the splotchy heat creep up my face. "I fell asleep. Like it was no big deal that my brother was missing. I fell asleep."

"That's not your fault, Yalda," Keith says.

"I should have gone there earlier. If I could have gotten him to the hospital sooner or maybe even . . . maybe—"

"You didn't know."

"But I should have known," I fire back, because I haven't been in a very forgiving mood since that night, and no one's being held accountable.

I am rigid with anger, so tense that when Keith puts his arm around me and pulls me toward him, I am surprised I don't snap like a stick of dry spaghetti. His head touches mine and through my jacket I can feel his fingers on my arm, holding me together.

In truth, there have been times when I have gone full romantic in my head and imagined what it might feel like to be alone with Keith, to be so close to him that I could feel his chest rise and fall with each breath.

I just didn't think I'd be crying when it happened.

# 22

"I'll introduce you to Imam Jameel," Asma says, guiding my parents and me toward the masjid's entrance. "He thought it would be good for someone to say a few words tonight. Someone from the family, of course. Anyway, he'll talk to you about that once we get inside."

Dad stops to shake hands with two men he's recognized, guys who stop by our restaurant often for take-out orders. I wonder if he'll want to speak on our behalf. Mom's wearing her black puffer coat over a sweater and jeans. Her hair is tied back in a ponytail. She squeezes my hand, maybe unintentionally. On the drive over here, she gripped the steering wheel so hard her knuckles went white, and two days ago I saw her dozing with her phone clasped in her left hand. She's holding

217

on to everything a little tighter lately.

There are a few people following behind us, their eyes lighting on us briefly before looking away. As we approach the masjid's side entrance, I look back and recognize a couple of Yusuf's friends from school walking over from the parking lot. Mom and I have headscarves hanging loosely around our necks. She pulls hers over her head and I follow her lead, but once we're through the door, I remember it's not necessary. We're in the community center of the masjid, not the prayer area. I've been in this room only once before, when I volunteered with Asma to pack bags of groceries for the community food pantry.

The room looks very different today. First of all, no one's speaking above a whisper. And instead of stacks of pasta boxes, bags of rice, and jars of tomato sauce, the room is set up with rows of folding chairs facing a small podium. There's room for about a hundred people in here, and half the seats are already occupied by some adults, but mostly kids from school. The leader of the youth group, a woman Asma pointed out to me, is sitting on the end of a middle row, strategically positioned to spot anyone needing support. The coats are coming off and a woman wearing a headscarf is passing out small paper cups of water to people already seated.

Asma points to three empty chairs in the front row and then excuses herself so she can find Imam Jameel. Mom glances at her phone as we take our designated seats. She was reluctant to leave Yusuf but wanted to be here tonight.

I turn around to scan the crowd. The seats behind us are

partially filled. There are several people I don't recognize, men and women, mostly in hijabs or headscarves. Lots of people have gathered in the back of the room, as if they're afraid the imam might call on them to answer a question. Three rows behind us, I spot Nahal sitting with a woman and two other children. I think of the rooms we set up in the apartment, the clothing we gathered. Our eyes meet but, unlike other people, she doesn't look away.

"Why didn't Ama Leeda come?" I ask my mother. Ama Leeda backed out at the last minute. We were in the car waiting for her. Dad hates to keep an engine running so he went back in to gently hurry her along but came out of the house alone.

"She said she had a headache," Mom whispers. Someone at the side of the room catches her eye. I follow her gaze to Imam Jameel. "I don't know what to say to all these people here, Yalda. And your father . . . between us, I think he's afraid to say something."

"Why would Daddy be afraid?" I ask, as if I'm five years old and naive about the fact that parents are utterly human.

"He's so angry and upset. We all are. But he's afraid that if he says something in public, people will twist his words." She sighs. "Look at what they did to Yusuf."

Once she says it, I feel this might be what I'm afraid of too. People took my brother's comments out of context and now we're at a vigil. This is a friendly crowd, of course, but surely it will end up on social media, where every single post is a dinner bell for trolls.

The other issue is that when I think of speaking to this crowd, my mind turns into an empty canvas. This room feels way too funereal. Yusuf came so close to dying that night, and looking at these somber faces, a thousand frantic fists pound inside my chest and I have to remind myself that my brother is alive.

Yusuf. He's the one person from our family who could stand up in front of a crowd without fumbling, sweating, blanking. If he were here, he would smile and beckon folks in the back of the room to move toward the front. And for Yusuf, they would have, because everyone wants to be one row closer to him even if they don't know why.

In middle school, the art teacher convinced me to join the theater club so I could help with set design. That was all I was supposed to do, help create the backdrops for a play about pirates taking over a school. I was not supposed to be any-where near the stage during the performance, especially after the fourth-grade spider costume incident.

It's not that I have trouble saying no. I just have trouble saying no *out loud*, and that's how I ended up onstage, turning red and fumbling for the eight words that I was supposed to say. It's even worse if I'm supposed to come up with the lines. English becomes my second language and I'm searching for words the way I used to search for the right LEGO bricks in a bucket full of plastic pieces. I need time and quiet and privacy to turn my feelings into recognizable forms.

I inhale through my nose and out through pursed lips as

discreetly as I can because Imam Jameel is walking toward us.

I first met Imam Jameel at last year's Eid prayers and he caught me by surprise because he didn't fit the image I had in my head of an imam. He's an adult but looks young enough that he still might enjoy playing video games with friends. Today, he's wearing a quilted charcoal vest over a black sweater, and trendy, bold-framed glasses. A maroon checkered scarf is wrapped around his neck. On him, his beard looks more hipster than holy. In fact, if it weren't for the embroidered cap on his head, I'd guess he was here to help get a virus off a computer.

And even though the masjid board chose Imam Jameel, some people were reluctant to see him as a leader. As an American-born son of Somali immigrants, he doesn't look like most of the worshippers. People of color are experts at seeing and ranking every shade of skin. My dad's aunt would match a girl's skin tone to a food on some regressive color wheel she had devised to predict their futures. Milky skin meant a girl would have her choice of men. A girl with wheat-hued skin should stay realistic about her options and not pass up on a solid offer, and anyone unlucky enough to have skin the color of pine nut peels could plan to live at home and take care of her parents in their old age.

My aunts would laugh off her comments.

*Some people are too old to change. It's not polite to argue with an elder. She's had a hard life. It's just talk.*

The same excuses were made for the previous imam, a man

with a wispy white beard and a raspy but imposing voice. He would speak with his eyes mostly closed. After Mom heard him preach that women should spend less energy gossiping, she decided his was another voice we could ignore.

I'm not sure everyone wants to ignore the same stuff. I think back to Larson standing onstage at WhereHouse, some people getting swept up in his energy without realizing what he was saying. The police gave him a warning when they interviewed him. He was at a movie with friends the night Yusuf was hurt. He may not be guilty, but he surely isn't innocent.

Imam Jameel greets us with a gentle voice and asks my parents how Yusuf is doing. They give him a brief update, which seems to remind them both that they're not with Yusuf now. Dad clears his throat and excuses himself, saying he wants to give the hospital a call to check in.

"And you, sister. How are you holding up?" he asks me.

"I'm managing, I guess," I say, then remembering who I'm talking to, I blurt my gratitude to God. "I mean, Alhamdulillah."

A faint smile passes over Imam Jameel's face.

"If there's anything we can do, please let me know. Tonight is only one night. I'll be asking the community to keep your brother and your family in our prayers at every khutbah."

"Thank you," I say.

"Of course. I'm going to say a few words and when I'm done, I'm going to look your way. If you feel up to speaking, just give me a sign or come on up to the microphone. I know it's not easy but sometimes it helps to speak what's in your heart and know that people are listening."

I nod to be polite, but I have no intention of standing in front of this room, especially as it has continued to fill. I have so much to say that I don't think I can say anything. I am angry and I want justice and I want Yusuf to breathe and talk. Mostly, I want to rewind and go back to before WhereHouse. Imam Jameel turns and walks back to the center of the room.

Mona appears, hugs my mom, and then takes a seat next to me.

"Hey," she says, leaning into me. "This is an amazing turnout. So many people from school are here."

"Have you seen Chris or Liam?"

Mona cranes her neck. "That might be Liam . . . No, that's actually Garrett. Or someone else. I think I need new contacts. Oh, but that's Keith for sure."

Keith?

I turn around and spot Keith standing at the far end of the room. He's with a couple of other guys from school. I'm glad he's here.

Dad returns to his seat with a signal that nothing has changed with Yusuf. My mother has her head on my dad's shoulder. He's whispering something to her.

"I don't want to be here," I quietly confess to Mona, and immediately hear how ungrateful I must sound to everyone who has shown up on this cold night to pray for my brother.

She looks straight into my eyes.

"I don't want to be here either," she says. "I absolutely hate that we're here."

I want to hug Mona for getting me.

"Asma said you might thank people for coming," Mona says. "After Imam Jameel speaks."

"There's no way. I'm going to mess it up and I'll look so stupid. I can't."

"Don't worry about it," Mona says. "Imam Jameel will say everything that needs to be said."

Someone dims the lights just enough to appreciate the glow of the battery-operated tea lights that have been handed out. Imam Jameel steps behind the podium, leans into the microphone, and welcomes everyone. The room returns the greeting, a murmuration of peace.

"Tonight, we make certain that young Yusuf's family, the Jamali family, knows that they are not alone. Their heartbreak is our heartbreak and we have been and will continue to pray for brother Yusuf's recovery," he says, looking directly at my parents. My mom reaches out to both me and my father. Her left hand squeezes his and her right, mine.

"I would guess many of you did not know Yusuf but were summoned here by the compassion in your hearts. It is times like these that I am most proud of this community . . ." Imam Jameel's voice is soothing, so much so that I lose track of what he's saying and feel lulled by the rhythm and tone of his voice. He leads the room in prayer and I cup my hands and lower my head as well.

*Ameen.* The word covers the room like a warm blanket.

"We are also joined by a member of our county council. Councilmember Peters, thank you for being here," Imam Jameel says, raising an arm in the direction of the wings. There's a man with salt-and-pepper hair. He's wearing dark pants and a brown wool coat. A woman stands beside him in a belted black coat and a work bag slung over her shoulder. The councilmember raises a hand in acknowledgment. Imam Jameel motions for the man to join him at the front of the room and the councilmember obliges, sliding behind the podium with a faint air of reluctance.

"Why is he here?" I ask Mona.

"Thank you, Imam," the councilmember says, his head slightly bowed. The woman on the sidelines has her phone in front of her. She taps the screen. Did she take a picture? "My heart goes out to the Jamali family. As a father, as a member of this community, as a councilmember, I can only imagine how painful this must be. We will continue to keep . . . uh, Yusuf in our prayers."

He takes a step back and yields the podium to Imam Jameel again. He's hardly taken one step away when a voice breaks through the thick quiet of the room and halts the councilmember's departure.

"I'm sorry." He smiles and shoots Imam Jameel a quick glance before looking back into the crowd for the source of the voice. "I did not catch that."

"What can you tell us about the investigation?"

I turn around to see who's asking this question. The tea lights have made all the faces look eerie, exaggerating the hollows and the wet eyes. I can't tell, and from the way the councilmember scans the room, he can't identify the person either.

"Investigation? Well, I am fully confident that our police department is looking into all possibilities. Public safety is a priority. Now, whether that means building structures need to be kept up to code or . . . or whether we're dealing with a situation of malicious intent, that remains to be seen. Let us focus now on this young man's recovery, his healing."

Instead of sitting in this room, praying, I should be putting a third blanket over Yusuf because hospitals are surprisingly cold places. They should be warm with the smell of home-cooked food wafting through the vents and people's favorite songs playing in their rooms, just loud enough to drown out the beeping of the machines. The sheets should be made of flannel and they should ask that families bring in their blankets from home if they want people to get better. I want justice for my brother and I want to know how many candles we need to shine a light on what happened to Yusuf that night.

My throat tightens again. I take my scarf off because it feels a bit like being strangled, and I must have done it less than gracefully because Mona looks concerned about me.

I sink my gaze to the cold floor, to the scuffed toes of my boots, embarrassed that I can't even keep myself composed during a candlelight vigil with a room full of people gathered to pray for Yusuf. Why are these people asking the council-member about an investigation? Shouldn't I be the one pressing for answers?

"Do you really think this was just a building issue?"

*Breathe*, I command myself.

"As I said, I am fully confident that our law enforcement . . ." The councilmember repeats his canned deflection.

My eyes brim with tears. I am suddenly overcome with exhaustion. My sleep has been tortured for the past week and I might not be able to sit still much longer.

"We are concerned for our public safety, too," a woman declares. She's standing, so there's no issue identifying her. "Hate crimes are on the rise across America. What are you doing about that?"

Mom dabs her tears with a tissue. Dad's face is so tense, I can see his jaw muscles quiver. That's exactly how I'm feeling.

"I appreciate your concern . . . ," the councilmember starts.

I don't hear the rest of his response over the noise in my head. It's mercifully over soon after that. Imam Jameel con-cludes with a prayer and people stand up. People, including Asma's and Mona's parents, approach my parents to offer hugs, handshakes. Even some of our classmates stand a few feet away, timidly waiting a turn to say something. Keith is not one of them, so he probably slipped out with Garrett and the others. Asma and Mona are at my side, but when I see them get pulled into conversations, I use the moment to slip away.

I didn't make a conscious decision to leave, but in a flash

I'm in the bathroom standing over a sink, my eyes blurred with tears, when I feel a hand on my shoulder.

"Yalda, you have to breathe," Nahal says. I cover my eyes with my hand, fingers tented and trembling. Nahal waits. It feels strange to hear her say my name but shouldn't. We walk through the same doors. We know the same words. We eat the same foods. I've avoided her because I was uncomfortable with myself, not with her.

I am a mess, but a little less of a mess because Nahal's hand is still on my shoulder. Like the thin string of a windblown kite, it's enough to keep me from being lost to the winds. My breathing slows. I just need one more moment to face Nahal, to thank her for being here.

"There you are!" Mona says as the bathroom door swings open. "Oh, hi, Nahal! Yalda, are you okay? Oh my God, that was so intense."

Mona wraps her arms around me and squeezes tight. In the second it takes for me to blot the tears from my eyes and look up, Nahal vanishes.

# 23

"On the count of three. One, two . . ."

The doctor pulls the tube from Yusuf's mouth in one smooth swoop, and all of us in the room hold our collective breath as we wait to see if after more than a week of having a machine inhale and exhale on his behalf, Yusuf will take a breath on his own.

According to the nurse who took care of him last night, there were times the machine wasn't breathing for him. And she saw his eyelids flutter. And just an hour ago, this doctor showed us the scan of Yusuf's head that was done before the sun came up. Compared to the scans from the past few days, there hasn't been any new bleeding and the swelling has gone down a lot.

*This is actually a very strong recovery given his injury. His condition is more stable now*, the doctor had said in a flat voice.

Stable is not how I would describe anyone or anything right now. It feels like every time someone looks at a phone or I leave the hospital, there's a situation to deal with.

I think I see Yusuf's chest move. I look at the doctor's face while a nurse steps in and slides a long plastic catheter into Yusuf's mouth to suction out saliva. The skin around his mouth is raw from where the tape had held the breathing tube in place. His lips are chapped, nearly fissured. His eyes are roaming behind his lids, in search of something.

The doctor has already warned us that if he doesn't breathe on his own, they'll have to replace the breathing tube and hook him back up to the machine. The room is quiet now without the *whir-click-blow* of the ventilator.

"Yusuf," my mother calls. "You can do it. Breathe, janem."

She slips into Dari, sounding like she's trying to encourage a much younger Yusuf to ride down the sidewalk without training wheels for the first time. My father and I are silent. It should be Mom's voice he hears—if he's able to hear any voice at all.

"He's doing well," the doctor says approvingly. The nurse adjusts a coil of plastic tubing, placing prongs into Yusuf's nostrils to feed him oxygen. "This is a big step, but he's not out of the woods just yet."

We spend the next hour watching Yusuf breathe. My chest

goes up and down with his, as if my breathing is now dependent on his. Am I stealing his air? It's an irrational thought but I can't help feeling like there's just not enough in this room to go around.

"I'm going to take a walk," I say to my parents as I stand. My dad gives my arm a squeeze. Mom smiles weakly and resumes her vigil over Yusuf's chest, his hand clasped tightly between hers and pressed against her cheek.

I'm almost tempted to find an empty room, crank up the dial on the wall, and suck the oxygen into my own lungs. I skip the elevator and take the stairs, my sneakers squeaking on the linoleum tiles and announcing my escape to all the floors above and below me in the stairwell.

I slip into the lobby and don't notice that someone's come up behind me.

"You all right?" a voice asks. I spin around, caught off guard, and the woman behind me takes a half step back when she realizes how startled I am. I recognize her as the woman from the information desk. Her tight curls bloom from a high ponytail. She's wearing a blazer with dark jeans and weathered ballet flats that made it possible for her to get so close to me without making a sound.

"I'm so very sorry. I didn't mean to scare you," she says. "My name's Olivia."

"No, it's fine. I was just—"

"Who do you have here, baby girl?"

"What do you mean?" I ask, confused.

"Who have you been visiting?" she adds. Her voice is so soothing that I forget she's a stranger.

"Oh, my . . . my brother," I say. "He's in the ICU. He was hurt in a bad fall."

"I thought you might be related to him. I heard about that," Olivia says. "I've got your family in my prayers. I want you to know that."

I lift my head to thank her but can't do more than nod.

"And I can tell your brother's got a lot of people sending him light right now. I turned a few people away myself yesterday. Had some kids come in here hoping to get upstairs and see him. One kid came in with sunglasses on, trying to hide his tears behind a pair of aviators."

"People have always come around for Yusuf," I say, and smile despite myself, thinking of the way Yusuf's eyebrows lift, the way his face lights up when he sees someone.

But that's what's made all this smoke about WhereHouse even more unexpected. On top of that, something about the masjid's vigil makes me want to throw up, and it doesn't take a psychotherapist to figure out why. The last time I saw a whole masjid of people praying for one person was at my cousin Rahim's funeral.

"But then . . . then there are people who are saying awful things about him. Straight-up lies," I tell her.

Olivia shakes her head.

"Rumors. Prettiest kind of poison. People love to talk, especially when they have nothing worthwhile to say."

I laugh despite the lump in my throat. I can't let one person's rant get me down. And now that Yusuf is breathing on his own, it's easier to hope for a recovery. I keep telling myself that Yusuf will soon be awake and full of questions. I want him to know that I did more than pray for him.

While the masjid organized a prayer for Yusuf, some people were calling for the police to investigate this as a hate crime. I've heard about people being attacked for being Muslim after 9/11. And as proof hatred is truly ignorant, there are the Sikh people who suffered bigoted attacks by racists who took their turbans as a sign they were Muslim. Then there are the people who died because of someone's rage. It's not always easy to prove that rage was hate. I think of the young man in a gray suit and a soft pink tie, a smile that tells you he was the life of the party. The mom of six shot on the sidewalk of her quiet neighborhood. The three young adults who had been playing a board game, were summoned outside and shot by an irate neighbor. Though I've heard about hateful attacks, I still never imagined my family could be the victim of a hate crime and don't know how I feel about that possibility.

"You're right. It was one stupid post. I think I'm going to call the police and see if they've figured anything out."

"Good idea," Olivia agrees. "Don't let them forget about your brother, if you know what I mean."

Something in the periphery pulls Olivia's attention. Two women and a man are standing at the welcome desk. Three oversized helium balloons bounce between them—a pacifier twice the size of my head, a silver congrats, and a giant blue foot. She waves to them to signal she'll be right over.

"Just look at those balloons. Just how exactly are those poor parents supposed to cram those into the car with a new-born when they go home? Some people got money to burn. Let me get back to my desk, but feel free to stop by anytime. And I hope the new year is kind to your family."

The new year. It is so easy to lose track of hours and days in a hospital, but a new year begins tomorrow, changing nothing but the calendar. I watch Olivia as she returns to her desk to welcome the visitors with floating monstrosities, a tight smile on her face.

As I walk out the double doors, the chilly air sends a quick shiver through me. I sense a woman's eyes on me and want to be out of view, so I return to the serenity garden. In this weather, no one's interested in staring at a dry fountain.

I dig a pen and small notebook out of my bag and open to a fresh page. I write a single word at the top in block letters.
WHO?

I can't think of anyone who would want to hurt Yusuf. I know people wrote some nasty stuff on his locker, but I can't imagine any of them being so angry that they would try to kill him. Was it a random, deranged stranger? Possibly. Or maybe I just don't want to think anyone could have hurt my brother, but considering I'm sitting in a frigid serenity garden outside a hospital, that's some powerful denial. I bring the pen to the page.

### Larson

But the officer told my mom he was at a movie. Who else? There was, of course, the graffiti.

### Wyatt

Wyatt was apparently away for the weekend and some other kid ended up leaving the principal a sobbing voice mail, owning up to the graffiti. I think of the way Chris and Liam walked out of the principal's office, the way they turned their back on Yusuf.

### Chris

### Liam

Writing their names feels like another betrayal. I want to erase what I've written, but I learned long ago that ink is a commitment. I draw slashes across their names that only partially conceal them, like faces behind a fence.

My eyes fall on Larson's name again. Keith said Danny was trying to talk sense into him, but what if he wasn't? Keith has shared a lot with me about Danny, but I still don't know what he's thinking when he sees me. That goes double for Keith's mom. In fact, she may be even more uncomfortable around me.

### Danny

I look up, my breath a tuft of confusion.

Below the names, I write another word.

### WHY?

I take out my phone and see that Mona and Asma have both texted me to ask how things are going. Keith has sent a message too.

I'm glad Keith can't see my notebook.

I tell the girls Yusuf's off the breathing machine and Asma replies with a smiling emoji and hands in prayer. I give the same update to Keith and he responds with a string of thumbs up.

Yusuf's friends must be wondering how he's doing too. I've had a couple of people message me through Pic-Up but not anyone he hung out with regularly—like Liam or Chris.

I run my finger across the spiral of my notebook and sit back to think about this. When we were in fifth grade, Liam got called to the principal's office for etching half his name into a cafeteria table. The lunch monitor made a big deal out of it and I remember Liam's face flushing with embarrassment when he saw all the sandwiches hovering in midair, mouths gaping at the sight of him being led by the elbow out of the room. He must have wanted to get caught, though. Why else would he have been marking the table with his name?

But Liam's a good guy. And so is Chris. They're my brother's closest friends and I must have lost my mind to even consider they would hurt him. I open the notebook again and scribble over both their names, violently enough that the tip of my pen tears the page.

My fingers are feeling the cold. I call Chris and stuff my left hand into my pocket to warm up. I bet he's the one who showed up in the aviators.

Chris doesn't answer. The phone goes to voice mail before I can hang up. I debate leaving him a message but decide to try Liam instead. I'm hoping hearing his voice will help me forget the grim look on his face after WhereHouse or leaving the principal's office.

The phone rings four times. I'm about to hang up without leaving a message when Liam picks up.

"Hello?" he says.

"Hey, Liam. It's Yalda," I say.

"Oh, hey." He sounds surprised, or like he regrets picking up the phone. Maybe he hadn't saved my number after he texted me.

"I just wanted to say thanks for your message," I start. I listen closely, wishing I could see his face.

"Yeah, no. I mean, don't thank me," he says. "How's he doing?"

"A little better," I say. "He's off the ventilator."

"He is?" Liam asks. "So he's waking up? Did he say anything?"

I hesitate, wondering if I'm telling people too much. The hospital seems strict about keeping a tight lip when people ask about Yusuf. Maybe I should too.

"Yalda? You there?"

I feel a hand on my shoulder and my stomach jumps. My dad's face melts into an apology. He hadn't meant to scare me.

"It's too cold out here. Let me take you home," Dad says.

He looks at the phone in my hand, hears Liam repeating my name and asking if I'm there.

"Who are you talking to?" my dad asks.

"Liam," I reply. "He's asking about Yusuf."

Dad nods. Under normal circumstances, talking to a boy on the phone would get me a look. We're so far from normal that Dad just squeezes my shoulder. He hasn't shaved and the silver in his scruff catches the light and surprises me. I hadn't noticed it before.

"I'll meet you by the car," he says, and trudges toward the parking lot with shoulders hunched. He's wearing his leather jacket, the one he's had for so long that it's gone out of style and come back in.

I look back at my phone and realize Liam's hung up. There's a text message, though. I tap on it and see it's from him.

Is he out of the comma? Liam's written. It takes me a moment to realize he's misspelled coma. Such a small difference, such a thin line between a slumber so deep it could pass for the end and something as gentle as a pause, a chance for Yusuf to catch his breath and finish his sentence.

*Please let it be so*, I whisper to the cold garden.

# 24

Mona's sitting cross-legged on my bed. She called half an hour ago and told me she was coming over. She's not an overthinker like me and Asma. She won't worry that she might be intruding or wonder if she's disrupting plans. She just shows up. These days, I'm feeling a little more like Mona, like the distance between my thoughts and my actions is shrinking.

She takes my pillow and stuffs it between her back and the wall. I'm sitting on a beanbag chair I got at a garage sale last year when I was desperate to make a change in my bedroom.

"Girl, I'm so glad to hear it," she says after I share the news that Yusuf has been moving around more and even responding with some grunts and motions. "You gotta keep imagining him getting better and it will happen. This is a new year and you need to come into it with the best vibes."

"Oh, Mona," I groan. She's been following one of those influencers who deliver daily affirmations while she makes homemade granola and blends chickpeas into hummus. "This sounds like something that Food Queen would say."

"The Food Goddess," Mona corrects me.

"Goddess, my apologies. Yeah, I'll definitely take her advice. She sounds so down-to-earth."

"She also says judging others invites negative energy into your personal cosmos."

"Mona, there's only one person in my personal cosmos right now."

"And you love it!" Mona declares, flipping her hair back over her shoulder dramatically. "Who else is going to pry all your secrets out of you?"

It's obvious she's doing this to lift my spirits and distract me from the hurt, like *Finding Nemo* playing on repeat at the dentist's office. I do love her for it.

"Well, it's not a secret but I met up with Keith," I say casually. Or at least I thought I said it casually.

Mona's smile vanishes. She raises a serious brow.

"And you're just telling me now? Why was I not notified earlier?"

"Because it's not a big deal. We were walking his dog. We literally just went a few blocks to the park," I explain.

"Right, so you actually met up with Keith's dog and Keith

happened to tag along. Listen, Yalda, you don't need to rearrange details for me."

"Okay, but we were actually walking his dog," I insist, and feel my stomach tumble as I revisit the moment when I let myself lean into Keith, when he leaned into me. It felt like a lot more than walking a dog. "But actually I wanted to ask if he'd heard anything about that night."

"And?"

I shake my head. "Nothing, but he's going to ask around. And it was nice to be with him," I say. "I really didn't want to be home then."

"To be *with* him?" Mona asks, craning her neck and staring at me hard. "What does that mean?"

I hear the soft scraping of Ama Leeda's house slippers in the hallway, then the opening and closing of Yusuf's door. I must have rolled my eyes or somehow reacted because Mona slides to the edge of my bed and plants her feet on the floor.

"How long is she going to stay?" Mona asks in a stage whisper.

The walls are thin. I shrug and lift a finger to my lips so she'll keep her voice down. She salutes me, military style, to indicate she can follow orders. I don't know how long my aunt will stay. I came home to find my closet rod back in place and my clothes all neatly on hangers. She must be moving room to room conducting inspections. Maybe she'll leave when she runs out of things to fix or clean.

"Are you hungry?" she asks. "I've got an hour before I

have to take Sofia to tae kwon do. Want to grab something with me?"

I realize I am desperate yet again to get out of the house, to be somewhere other than inside this house or the hospital. I am on my feet and leading Mona into the hallway. We tiptoe so we won't alert Ama Leeda, who has been more of a sentry than a supporter. I keep telling myself she is still suffering the loss of Rahim, but I also know how hard she tried to change him, so I can't quite settle on feeling only sympathy for her.

We're out the door and in Mona's car. I text my mom to let her know we're going to grab a bite. Mom's been at the hospital since morning. Dad's planning on reopening the restaurant tomorrow. He's there now. Mom spent more than five minutes in the shower this morning and I saw her sit with her coffee. She didn't look anything close to relaxed, but we're also not the terrified statues we were the first couple of days.

Like Yusuf, we're showing small signs that we might just survive the fall.

Mona drives past Keith's house. I try not to make it obvious that I'm looking at his windows.

"You would make a horrible secret agent," Mona says.

"You know what? I miss Asma," I say.

Mona laughs.

"Me too. Text her. But tell her she has to come out. If we go in, her mom's going to feed us for sure."

I tap out a message. Asma must have been on her phone because she replies quickly.

"She'll be ready in two minutes," I report.

Mona pulls into Asma's driveway just as the front door opens. Asma comes down the front steps and opens the car's back door. I turn around to help her move the piled-up dry cleaning and reusable grocery bags. Mona convinced her parents to get her this car by promising to drive her little sister to all her activities, run all household errands, and apply only to schools with strong premed programs.

"Sorry about all the junk," Mona says, looking over the seat. "And if you stuff all those grocery bags together and hang the dry cleaning on the hook, I'll be your best friend."

"Not sure how I feel about that. I hear you make your best friends do a lot of things for you," Asma asks, hanging the dry cleaning as Mona backs out of the driveway and gets us on the road. She asks me about my brother and I update her. I hear her thanking God under her breath. In the first two days after Yusuf's fall, I prayed to God a lot, but not formally. I didn't roll out a prayer rug or even cup my hands together. My mom's been praying from the moment we found Yusuf. In the ICU room, I've spotted her holding my brother's hand with her eyes closed, her lips moving ever so slightly and her body rocking, as if she were trying to soothe a tiny, crying Yusuf in her arms. The first time I saw her do this, I had to look away. I ended up pulling out my sketchbook and drawing a baby sitting on top of a stone and staring into the murky heart of a forest. The baby's face is not visible, just his back and thin spirals of hair on his head. Something pulled my pen to a spot between trees and I added the almond eyes of a vigilant creature.

"So to celebrate this little bit of good news, what should we get? Sushi? Pizza? Burgers? You decide, Yalda," Mona says.

"I don't care. Asma, you pick," I say.

We're nearing the strip mall with the burger place. Mona slows down and looks in her rearview mirror.

"Well?" she asks, her eyes on Asma.

"Let's do pizza," Asma says. "Cheese is therapeutic."

"Pizza it is," Mona agrees. At the second light, she makes a left and pulls into the parking lot of the pizza shop. Red maple trees border the asphalt. Most of the leaves have fallen but some have hung on, desiccated and brittle. We walk in and head to the counter to place an order. The place probably hasn't had a single update in my lifetime, but people in town seem to prefer it that way. There are black-and-white photos on the wall of people sitting at the very same tables and one of a guy in a white apron with his hand on the door of the pizza oven.

Would this town ever turn on him? How long do you have to be here to earn that status?

My parents go over our restaurant's accounting at our dining table. Dad brings a big brown folder and Mom brings her laptop. She took an online class to learn an accounting program, so they sit together with a stack of invoices and a checkbook, paying bills and pecking away at the computer to record every transaction and calculate balances. We have expenses. We buy rice and oil and vegetables, all the ingredients for the items on the menu. We pay the staff's salaries and for electricity, repairs, insurance, tax, and rent. Customers pay for entrées and appetizers. Money comes in. Money goes out. In Mom's software, they're called credits and debits. If customers don't come in, there won't be credits to cover the debits. And if we can't cover our debits, we won't have a restaurant. And if we don't have a restaurant . . .

"Yalda! Hello? What toppings do you want?" Mona asks, pointing to the large menu sign above the cashier's head. "How about mushrooms, peppers, and olives?"

"No olives," warns Asma. "And sweet peppers, no jalapeños."

"Weakling," Mona mutters. "Yalda? You good with that?"

I nod. Honestly, the pizza could come out covered in acorns and postage stamps and I probably wouldn't notice.

We fill paper cups with peach iced tea and take a seat at a table by the windows with a view of the parking lot. Asma slides a straw out of its wrapper and drops it into her cup.

"Aren't those illegal now?" Mona asks.

"Are they?" Asma says, looking back at the straw dispenser. "I guess I grabbed it out of habit."

"They were. But then we got a new governor and plastic straws are back," I say, because restaurant-related trivia is my superpower.

The pizza store's door chimes. Two guys walk in and one of them glances at our table before saying something to his friend. I am extra suspicious of people looking in my direction now.

I worry about who they are and what they might be thinking or planning.

"Clearly not an eco-conscious establishment. Why would you bring back plastics? Did you see the video where they pulled one of those out of a sea turtle's nostril?" Mona asks. "He was bleeding for I don't know how long while they dug it out. I never knew turtles could cry until I saw that clip."

"I get it, Mona. I'm sorry, okay?" Asma says, her voice breaking a little. She takes her straw out and wraps it in a napkin. She stares at the napkin for a second, as if she's realizing she's responsible for another tree being chopped down.

"Can we not save the environment today? Or just for an hour," I plead. Mona's crusade to save the planet is a worthy one, but I don't want to think about crying turtles right now.

"Yeah, of course. Sorry, it just made me think of that—never mind," Mona says, flattened. She slides out of the bench. "I'll go check on the pizza and tone down my doomsday."

She returns a moment later with a large pie, the cheese hot and shiny. She sets the pizza on the table and breathes in the steam. A server follows her with a set of plates for us. There's a family sitting on the opposite side of the restaurant—a mom with two little children who are probably in elementary school. A little boy takes a bite of his slice and pulls the pizza away from his face. A thin bridge of cheese stretches, much to his sister's delight. Yusuf and I were once that little, learning about life cycles and stages of caterpillars and wishing we could sprout wings too.

"You know what's been bothering me?" I say. "Yusuf ended up hurt because he was standing up for other people. He was trying to make a point that the refugees aren't some evil alien invasion. But now the attention is on him. I wish there was a way to make people see what Yusuf was talking about."

"Well, Yusuf's sister, maybe you need to start that conversation," Mona suggests.

"I'm not an activist," I deflect. "It just bothers me that people are still posting signs and low-key refugee hating. This bothered Yusuf a lot, and I don't know why I'm just now understanding how bad it is."

"Yalda, you can pick up where he left off," Mona says. "But how would you do it? I mean, what type of campaign are you talking about here? A march? A protest? A boycott?"

"Who would I boycott? Maybe a protest or talk to a reporter? I'm not sure," I say, shaking my head. I don't see myself taping posters to street signs or tagging buildings with some message of peace and tolerance.

"You need to pick up a mic," Mona says.

"A literal mic or a metaphorical mic?" I ask.

What would I say? How do you get people to listen? I feel a little queasy and set my pizza back down on the plate.

"You need an influencer," Mona says before tapping and swiping her phone to life. "Asma, doesn't your cousin have, like, eight thousand followers on Pic-Up? Yes, here she is! Seven thousand nine hundred and eighty-five, to be exact."

"First of all, I'm pretty sure eighty percent of those are

bots," Asma says. "And second of all, she posts makeup videos. I don't think her contouring disciples are going to care much about immigrants in some random town."

"I tried her contouring tips one day. I was supposed to get a Disney nose, but I ended up with a Simba face. Blending is not that easy," Mona says, sucking her cheeks in.

"Maybe this is a bad idea," I say. "What if I open my mouth to speak and totally bomb—"

"Don't say bomb," chides Asma. "Literally any other word but that one."

"Ugh," Mona groans, darkening a napkin with her greasy fingers. "You know, in the celebrity world, there's no such thing as bad publicity. An actor can get arrested for drunk driving and guess what? Everyone's talking about him and his powerful apology and next thing you know he's starring in some rom-com. But Muslim bad publicity is real. One bad move and we're all on trial for it."

Had Yusuf put us all on trial? Will anyone be on trial for what has been done to him? Mona's face sobers.

"I'm sorry, Yal. I didn't mean to . . ."

"No, it's okay. I know what you mean," I say. I want to do the right thing, but it's not easy figuring out what I can do that won't make a bigger mess. "Sometimes I wish people would just stop talking about Yusuf so we could focus on him getting better and coming home. After the whole thing at WhereHouse, he actually wondered if opening his mouth was a mistake. Maybe he was right. Maybe him going off onstage was just him being impulsive. And maybe I should keep my mouth shut too."

"He wasn't just being impulsive. He was really upset about the hate in our town," Asma says.

"Yes, but he wasn't all that convinced he'd done the right thing," I reply.

"I don't think he regretted speaking up," she insists.

"No offense, but how would you know?" I say, suddenly prickled by Asma's assertion that she could know my brother better than me.

Asma purses her lips, as if she wants to hold back from saying anything else.

"What is it?" Mona asks, her head cocked to the side. "Something's up."

When Asma doesn't reply, I realize something actually is up with Asma. I go from prickled to confused. I've just been too wrapped up in what's happening with Yusuf to realize it.

"I didn't think it would be so hard," Asma says. Her face is aflame now, her cheeks wet. She covers her face with her hands. Asma is quivering, trying to hold her sobs in. I try to steady her with an arm around her shoulders.

"Girl, what's going on?" Mona asks, her voice gentle from across the table. "You have to talk to us."

"I'm sorry, Yalda," Asma groans, and my stomach drops. A gust of wind outside sets the brown, curled leaves on the trees dancing, hundreds of vacant cocoons. "I'm so, so sorry."

# 25

"I was studying at the coffee shop that night," Asma says. She swallows hard and breathes out slowly, steadying her breath. "I was headed back to my car and Yusuf was coming out of the studio. We talked for a while and then I left."

Mona looks baffled.

"I thought you were at the library that night. Since when do you study at Room without us?" she adds.

Asma presses her lips together. Her bottom lip is quivering.

"What time was it?" I ask. "Did you see anyone else there?"

"It was around seven. There was no one else around. No one I recognized, I mean. When I left he was going back up to the studio to get a new string for his guitar."

"But why . . . ?" I can't even put my thoughts into words.

Asma's eyes seem focused on some point beyond my head. Actually, her eyes seem anything but focused.

"I thought it would be too weird to tell you. And it wasn't . . . We just talk sometimes. I mean, we used to talk sometimes. By the music studio."

"Wait, you and Yusuf were . . . hanging out?" I am rewinding through every conversation to see if I missed something obvious. I remember Yusuf telling me he had run into Asma coming out of the studio a while back. He didn't mention anything after that, but come to think of it, he had been ultra-secretive about his phone lately. "And texting?"

Asma nods.

"I'm so sorry I didn't tell you, Yalda. But honestly, I didn't see anything that would have been helpful and I'd told my parents I was at the library that night," she says, her voice shaky. She's unraveling before me.

No wonder she's been acting so strange lately. Asma, who literally broke into hives when she forgot to turn in an essay in tenth-grade English, must be a hot mess to have kept their relationship, whatever that means, and her being with him that night to herself.

"Think back, Asma. Are you sure you didn't notice anything? Do you remember any of the cars in the parking lot? Anything?" There are strong undertones of desperation in my voice.

"Honest, Yalda, I've gone over it in my head a thousand times a day and if I could think of any little detail I would have

251

already said it. I'll meet with the police officer and tell them exactly what I told you, but that's everything. I hate that I left him there. If I would have just stuck around, maybe I could have seen something or stopped something or at least helped him. Or if I hadn't hung out with him, maybe he would have gone home before anyone could hurt him. I . . . I . . ."

I take Asma in my arms because I can see what's tearing her up is not a fear of what others will say she did wrong. She's had to live with the unforgiving voice in her head since she found out about Yusuf. My eyes well with tears that I wipe away with the back of my hand.

"What a goddamn mess," Mona assesses as she pushes away from the table. She goes over to the condiment table and comes back with a fistful of brown recycled napkins that are rough on our noses but better than nothing. Asma insists that I call the police officer who gave me his card, but that card is now in my desk drawer. I could call the police station and ask for him if I remembered his name, which is lost in the forest of all the names I've heard since we burst into the emergency room.

"Let's just go to the police station," Asma says. "I'll tell them right now."

"What about your parents, Asma?" It is one thing for parents to find out you've been talking to a guy and a whole other thing for them to find out you've been talking to a guy who caused controversy in town and ended up in a hospital.

Asma shakes her head. "Let me just figure out one conversation at a time."

I text my mom and dad that I'm still with the girls and I'll be home in about an hour. I don't need them worrying about me with Ama Leeda *tsk-tsk*ing in the corner.

"Where is the police station?" Mona asks, tapping the map icon on her phone. "Do you guys know?"

I don't know. I've seen police cars driving around but never needed to know where they came from or where they went back to. Though it turns out the station is only ten minutes away, the drive there feels like an eternity. Asma stares out the window. Her tears have dried and she looks oddly relieved, like she needed to get this off her chest.

I, on the other hand, feel like I'm turning my best friend in to the authorities. If Asma didn't see anything that night, there's not much she's going to be able to tell the police.

The GPS voice on Mona's phone cheerfully instructs her to make a left in twenty feet. Then she announces that we have arrived at our destination as if the police station is a five-star hotel. The first thing I notice are the seven police cars in the lot in front of the building. Along the side, there are even more black-and-white vehicles. There's a whole row of SUVs and something as big as an RV. I can almost picture a team of masked figures dressed head to toe in black jumping out the back doors with guns blazing. My phone rings just as I'm about to exit the car. It's my mom. I don't pick up but I text her even though I know it'll be read with a huff because it has already been established that texting is not a real form of communication.

We're dropping Asma off now. Be home
soon. Love you.

Asma's already out of the car. She looks so out of place here,
in front of a two-story brick building that is all corners and
metal trim. The glass double-door entrance is framed in blue
and the front is a perimeter of gravel, not a single plant.

"Asma, wait," I say, hopping out of the car. She turns and
looks at me, blinking rapidly, waiting for me to speak. What
will they get out of Asma's report that she was there that night?
What if they don't believe her?

The glass door swings open and an officer steps out, his
phone pressed to his ear. Asma looks startled, like he's come
out for her, but because we're mostly hidden by the car, he
doesn't seem to notice us. I recognize him, though. He's the
officer who came to the hospital that night. He walks to a car
in the parking lot, opens the trunk, and retrieves a bag. When
he slams the trunk closed, he spots me and Asma standing by
Mona's car, our breath forming small clouds in the cool air.

He says something to the person on the phone and then
slides the phone into the pocket of his shirt. He scans the parking lot and then starts walking toward us.

"Why is he . . . ," Asma asks.

"Hey. You're . . . you're the sister," he says. He's clearly forgotten my name. That's all right. I've forgotten his name, too.

"Yeah," I confirm, nodding.

"And you two. Cousins or something?"

"They're my friends," I reply.

He nods and introduces himself as Officer Song to Asma and Mona, who is still sitting in the driver's seat with her hands primly on the steering wheel. She smiles broadly, like she's been pulled over and is trying to convince Officer Song that she should be let off with a warning. He peers into the car.

"Right. What brings you all to the station?" he asks. "Did someone call you?"

I'm about to say no when I wonder why he's asking. Was someone supposed to call me?

"I thought if there were updates, we would hear directly from you," I say.

"I'm sorry, I should have made the call myself. I'm not the only one involved, though, and there's a process," he says, but I can hardly hear over my heart pounding. Something has happened.

Asma swallows hard. Mona opens the car door and stands with us, watchful.

"What's the process?" I ask.

"It's best if I go over this with your parents as well. Where are they now?"

"They're on their way over," I say with surprising ease given that they are most certainly not on their way over.

Officer Song puts his hands on his hips and exhales.

"All right, let's go inside and wait on them," he says, and turns toward the station entrance.

Mona has been doing a remarkable job of controlling her facial expressions, but as soon as Officer Song turns his back, she looks right at me with bewilderment. Asma looks frozen. I shrug and nod toward the station, a signal they should follow me. We've hardly taken two steps before he whirls around and realizes my friends are practically connected to me.

"Ladies, I appreciate you want to be with your friend, but I think it's best if you two went home," he says.

"Well, the thing is, I was going to—" Asma protests, but stops when I give her wrist a squeeze.

"We can talk more later, Asma. I need to do this now," I say. Asma chews her lip, obviously conflicted. I know she's steeled herself to do the right thing but is also relieved not to be entering the police station.

"Yalda." Asma says my name softly.

Mona looks from her to me through her kohl-lined eyes.

"Please," I tell her, so that she doesn't have to wonder if she's reading me right. I don't want her distracting the officer right now when he's on the verge of sharing information important enough that he wants my parents here before he opens up. "It's fine. You guys can go home."

My friends stay where they are, with Mona's arm around Asma's shoulders, until Officer Song and I have entered the station. A woman with her hair pulled back in a severe bun looks us over curiously when we enter. She raises an eyebrow at the officer.

"She's the sister," he replies. "Parents are on their way over—the Jamalis. I need to get them into a room. Call me when they get here and I'll walk them up."

She nods.

"Sure thing," she says. "You're going to take her up that way?"

"Yup," he says. "We'll be down the hall."

He leads me up a flight of stairs and down a corridor with doors on either side. Some are offices with glass windows; one has blinds drawn so I can't see inside. My mind is racing. Maybe when we get to wherever we're going, I can call my parents and tell them to come down here, but I also wish I could prepare them. I'm hoping with all my heart that this officer is about to tell us they've arrested the person who did this. But I'm also nervous that he's about to unload some news that will only break us more.

We make a left and the officer leads me into a small room with a gray metal table in the center and two chairs on either side. The blinds are drawn so there's no natural light coming into the room. The walls are a stark white and the flooring is light brown, mottled with scuff marks. It feels a solid five degrees colder in here than the hallway.

"Have a seat," the officer says. "How long do you think it'll be before your parents get here?"

"I'm not sure," I reply honestly.

"Okay," he replies. He clears his throat and checks his watch. "Are you . . . Do you want some water or something?"

"I'm fine," I say, and he nods.

"I hear your brother's feeling a little better."

Better?

"He still can't speak so I don't know if he's feeling better."

He nods, looking chastened, but being smart with him is misplaced spite and won't get me anywhere, so I forgive his poor word choice and recalibrate.

"It's going to be a very long recovery. That's what they tell us. It's still hard to believe this happened, so any information you have about that night or who did this to him would really help. Did anyone come forward with information? Or did you find a suspect?"

I scan his face for any reaction, a tell that will give away what they want to reveal to us.

"It's best we wait for your parents," he replies. "You said they'd be here soon, right?"

"I should check on them," I say, taking my phone out.

"Sure. I'll be back in a few," he says as he steps back into the hallway, leaving the door open. Do I call my mom or my dad? What do I tell them? I stand up, suddenly feeling the room shrinking in on me. I walk to the windows and find the metal wand to open the blinds. I peek through to see if Mona and Asma are still in the parking lot, but the edge of the blinds poke into my face. I pull the cord and raise the blinds altogether.

Mona's car is gone. I tap my phone again and decide I'll call my dad first. The phone rings once, twice, and then a third time.

"Hello?" he says.

But I don't answer.

"Yalda? Yalda, can you hear me?"

My eyes are transfixed on the parking lot—on the sight of two police officers standing on either side of a figure. I recognize the coat—a gray puffer with a red-lined hood. It's Chris.

"Yalda, are you okay?"

Chris is standing between two police officers, his head hanging low. Even from this distance I can see the tension in him, his shoulders pulled up close to his ears. My stomach knots. Chris? I think back to the conversation I had with Chris on the phone when Yusuf was still in the ICU. What had he said?

*I'm sorry. I'm really sorry.*

Sorry that Yusuf was hurt? Sorry he hadn't helped Yusuf? Or was he sorry for something worse?

"Yalda, where are you? What's happening?" my father demands. The controlled panic in his voice shakes me back to here and now.

"Dad? I'm here. Dad, you and Mom need to come to the police station now," I say, then repeat myself because he's not sure he heard me right. I press my face to the cool glass. Maybe the movement catches Christopher's attention because his eyes climb the side of the building and find me in the window above. When he sees me, his jaw goes slack. I look from him to the pavement, all the while imagining what it would be like to be pushed from this height to the cold ground below.

# 26

I am in the hall, then bounding down the stairs. I hold on to the handrail because I don't trust my legs right now. I collide with Officer Song as I round the corner.

"Whoa, whoa!" he shouts. "What's happening?"

"Chris is here. I saw him. I want to talk to him!" I reply, looking past Officer Song. I'm two doors away from the parking lot. Why is Chris here? Why does he look so devastated, so . . . guilty?

The officer from the front desk joins Officer Song. They each take me by an elbow and ask me to go back upstairs to the conference room. They tell me I can't talk to Chris right now. When I demand a reason, I'm ushered to a metal chair and asked to take some deep breaths and relax. This feels more like punishment than comfort.

"Can you cover this for a minute?" Officer Song asks.

"You go ahead and I'll sit with this young lady here," the woman says, and closes the door behind Officer Song.

"I'm Officer Janae," she says. "Emotions run really high anytime there's an arrest."

"So Chris is under arrest?" I ask.

She looks surprised.

"Chris? No. Did Officer Song not explain already? He's not . . ." Her words trail off as she shakes her head. She draws in a deep breath as if she's going to need extra air for the plunge she's about to take.

"Chris," she begins, speaking slowly, which is frustrating because I want to know everything right now, but also helpful because it's harder to hear over the noise in my head. "Chris contacted us to share information. Now, I know you're eager to hear more, but let's wait for your parents to get here so we can talk about this with them. It's probably best we do this once and all together."

I let out a breath. Of course it wasn't Chris. The thought of Chris harming Yusuf had rocked me hard, and I need a moment to gather myself before I can even guess at what information Chris might have shared with the police and who might be under arrest.

My parents must have broken some speed limits because they are at the station thirteen minutes later. We are seated together, my dad's face tense and stony and my mother's arm holding me close to her, when Officer Song returns and finally starts telling us what they've learned from Chris.

"He called and let us know that we should look into his stepfather's whereabouts that evening. Seems when Chris was talking to the owner of Crescendo about the security cameras, his stepfather overheard the conversation. He started acting spooked, as Chris put it. He asked Chris a lot of questions about the camera setup at the studio."

"But they told us the cameras weren't on," my father says, his voice guarded.

"That's right. They weren't. We still don't have any footage from the music studio, but we checked the traffic cameras," Officer Song explains. "We followed Chris's tip and were able to confirm that his stepfather's vehicle was near the studio around the time Yusuf left."

"Oh my God," Mom says, her body angled forward to catch every word the officer speaks. She's sitting between me and my dad with her feet flat on the cold, tiled floor. She squeezes my hand and my father's knee. "Why would he do this to a boy? I don't understand."

My dad stands.

"I want to see him," he says, each word measured and deliberate.

Officer Song gets up slowly, after I spot he and Officer Janae exchange a look. My dad doesn't look tired or worn down right now. He looks like he could walk through a wall if it would put him face-to-face with Chris's stepfather.

"Sir, at this point, we're going to handle this matter according to our protocols. We don't want to have a situation here that we all regret."

"Regret?" my dad repeats, wanting to confirm what he heard. "Here we will have a situation we regret? I want to know if he regrets what he did to my son."

"I understand, but there is a process that we must follow. It's in everyone's best interests—"

"But I just want to talk to—"

"As difficult as it is," Officer Janae says, "we're going to have to ask you to be patient."

Sometimes it's hard to work up the courage to do something. Other times it takes superhuman strength to do nothing. On the drive home, the car is an ark carrying every feeling that ever existed. Outrage. Relief. Confusion. Frustration. Fresh sadness.

Ama Leeda is standing in the living room when we enter the house, her face a question mark.

"They arrested someone," my mother says. Ama Leeda throws her arm around my mother and softly praises God. I slip into my room and pull out my phone. Mona and Asma have both texted me but I want to talk to Chris first.

I call but the phone goes to his voice mail. I call a second time. And a third.

On the third ring of the third try, Chris picks up.

Neither of us says a word. I can hear him breathing.

"I'm so sorry, Yalda," he says quietly. His voice is raspy, scared. "I'm . . . I'm not supposed to talk to anyone about this. They said I . . . I . . ."

"Please, Chris," I plead. "I need to know."

Chris starts to protest but falters. Then he starts talking.

Chris tells me his stepfather was supposed to pick him up that night. He had closed Crescendo and walked down the stairs to wait for his stepfather in the parking lot. He called a couple times but his calls went unanswered. He wasn't surprised. His stepfather had a habit of stopping by a bar for a drink or two after work and losing track of time. He thought about calling his mom but figured that would just start another fight between his mom and stepfather at home.

"And when they fight, it gets pretty bad," Chris says. "Like real bad. So I started walking. I caught a bus, then walked some more. Went to sleep when I got home."

Chris said he woke in the morning to messages about Yusuf being missing. On his way out of the house, he found his stepfather asleep on the couch, the smell of beer on his clothes.

"I don't know why I didn't put it all together. Part of me also thought I would get to school and see Yusuf was there. I was on my phone that morning, texting Yusuf. Calling him. My stepdad woke up and started in on me about being late for school. I told him he was the last person who should be talking about being late, seeing as how he totally forgot to pick me up the night before. And he sat up and told me I had it all wrong.

264

He wasn't ever supposed to pick me up because he had planned a night out with the guys."

Chris walked out then and didn't think much of it. His stepfather was a lousy person sober, and a wretched person drunk. And it wasn't like he had been looking forward to getting picked up by his stepfather. His mom wanted her husband to be more of a dad to Chris, but it wasn't working.

Chris didn't have reason to think his stepfather could have been the one to push Yusuf over the railing. Sure, after he'd heard about what happened at WhereHouse, he'd gone off on Chris's mom for letting her son hang out with a "future suicide bomber." He'd shoved her into the wall when she tried to argue.

"He gets that way sometimes with her," Chris says.

It doesn't take much imagination to figure Chris isn't telling me just how bad things are at home. He probably becomes violent with Chris, too, and has said a lot worse about Yusuf, but I get the gist. Chris didn't tell his mother about taking the bus home either.

"I knew he was bad, but I thought . . . I thought it stayed in our house. It didn't click until he asked me about the cameras. I'm so sorry I didn't figure it out sooner. And I'm sorry . . . I'm . . ."

"*I'm* so sorry," I tell Chris. "I know this wasn't easy for you. Thank you for . . ."

I can't put it into words for Chris. The silence is uncomfortable for both of us. He says that he better get off the phone, so I say goodbye.

What do I even call what Chris has done? It's like lighting a candle in a dark room. It's saying something true but also terrifying and painful. Yusuf won't heal any faster. I don't feel happy. I only feel like something is a little less wrong with this world.

# 27

My eyes open and I fumble for my phone, finding it on my nightstand. A quick glance and I realize it's four o'clock. My power nap somehow turned into a two-hour slumber.

"Are you hungry? There's warm aush on the stove. I made the noodles yesterday. It's so much better than the soup from the can."

How long has Ama Leeda been standing in my doorway and why does she hate on everything that can be purchased in a grocery store? Also, sometimes I think she forgets that I have access to a full menu of Afghan food while I'm working at our restaurant.

"Thanks, maybe later. I'm not hungry right now," I say, sitting up. My comforter slides off my bed and I am glad for the excuse to turn away from Ama Leeda. I pull it back up over my pillow and tug the corner to straighten it out. The heater kicks in and a gust of air blows through a ceiling vent. Did I not close my door before I slipped into bed? I should have, given that my aunt seems not to understand boundaries.

"You should put a sweater on. This cold is not good for your bones. You'll get arthritis like me," she says. "I can't sleep on my left shoulder at all."

"I'm not cold," I mumble.

"When you're young, you don't know how cold your feet are," she replies.

I consider my options. If I were to get up and put socks and a sweater on, would Ama Leeda walk away? Or would she see that as an invitation to offer me more advice? It feels important to choose carefully.

I do not reach for any warm clothing. Instead, I turn so that I'm facing her.

"If my feet were cold, I would know and I would put on socks," I say, trying to sound firm, but by the look on Ama Leeda's face, I think I skipped right over firm and landed on rude.

She blinks slowly, then leaves. I hear the padding of her steps down the hallway and groan because the conversation did not go the way I wanted it to.

I change into a black button-down and jeans. Dad hasn't asked me to come back to the restaurant yet, but I know he could use my help. I'm betting he wouldn't mind some company either. On my way to grab my bag and phone, I stop and peek into Yusuf's room. I can see the evidence of Ama Leeda's presence there. The bed has been made with the pillow on top of the comforter. The pillow looks perfectly smooth, like a website picture of a hotel room except for the handful of Star Wars decor pieces.

She's messed with his shelves, too. The books are lying on their sides and his LeBron James bobblehead figure has been moved down to the corner of the second shelf. On the nightstand is an unzipped, quilted makeup bag. Beside it, lined up like orange soldiers with white caps, are three prescription bottles, a bottle of pastel antacids, and a blue tin of Nivea hand cream. Her rolling suitcase sits inside Yusuf's closet, his belongings pushed aside to make room for hers.

I remind myself that there isn't another guest room in this house. Ama Leeda either sleeps here or moves into my room and rearranges my belongings. Neither are good options.

And I know I'm really on edge because I visited Yusuf. We've been praying over his bed with the foolish idea that Yusuf would wake up and be just as he was before the fall.

It's been a few days since they took him off the breathing machines. He's been more awake and aware but he's not able to respond yet. When our family spent four days in a hotel at the beach this past summer, I woke up every morning briefly confused by the lumpy mattress and the cheerful red crab on the wall.

Yusuf's slumber has been so much deeper and longer. He's

gone so much farther from home than the beach. In the past two weeks he's slept the number of hours a person sleeps in nearly two months. It's a time warp, like in movies about space travel.

Yusuf's awakening has been rough. The doctors and nurses check for signs of progress every day. When William, who quickly became our favorite nurse, tried to get Yusuf to squeeze his fingers, Yusuf pushed him away and growled. Mom was on him immediately, trying to steady him as he thrashed and apologizing to William.

*Agitation is normal*, William tells us. *We're all going to be patient with him.*

I had a new fear to keep me up at night.

What if this is the Yusuf who's returning to us?

I hear kitchen cabinets open and close, the clink of a spoon against a teacup.

I walk into the living room, my head sparking with frustrated energy. Ama Leeda has taken a seat on the sofa, facing the television. She's watching a Turkish soap opera with the volume so low she would have to read lips. Steam rises from a teacup on the side table. On her knee are two pairs of my underwear. In her hands is a third pair with a cute rainbow pattern, something I bought for myself when I was feeling a little silly. I feel like she's judging the underwear even as she folds it.

"You don't have to do that," I tell her. "I fold my own clothes."

"You do?"

I *can* fold my own clothes, rather. Whether or not I do is entirely irrelevant.

"Yalda jan, are you upset because I said something about socks? I was only telling you for your own good."

"Yes, but I'm not a child. I can look after myself. If *your* feet are cold, I'll gladly go get some socks for you."

"No, I do not need socks," Ama Leeda says slowly, glancing down at her fuzzy house slippers. "Yalda jan, I can see you are not happy that I'm here, but I am here to help. This is not a time for your parents to be alone. Especially your mother."

"My mom isn't alone," I reply, my tone softening. "I'm here."

"You're still young," she replies, and I want to throw something at the television because I'm not sure how old I have to be for my presence to count in Ama Leeda's world. "You have your own life, too. School and your friends. This is what you should worry about. Your family and your health are important. Thank God for these things and don't worry about other distractions. I worry about you when you're out at night in the streets."

"In the streets? What does that mean? Ama Leeda, I don't go out at night. And it gets dark by five o'clock, which is not really night," I say. She must have seen me walking in the neighborhood with Keith and Fisher, and yet she makes it sound like I've been lurking in sketchy alleys with Satanists.

If she considers my going for a walk or being barefoot in the house misdemeanors, I can only imagine how harshly she judged Rahim for the truth of who he was. It hurts to think about how stifled he must have felt. My heart squeezes at the thought of him and I want desperately to extract myself from this conversation before things get uglier, but Ama Leeda has more to say.

"Your father is quiet but I know him. He is under a lot of stress. As your aunt, I care for you. That's why I said something to you directly, because at this age, I'm sure you understand—"

Is she hinting at telling my dad that I've been hanging out with Keith? This feels less like her being a confidante and more like blackmail.

"Ama Leeda, I know my dad is stressed out, but that doesn't mean you can spy on me or judge me."

She seems taken aback. The living room feels like it's shrinking by the minute, as if the walls are closing in to get a better listen.

"I am not judging—"

"But you are. That's what you've been doing since you came here. Nothing is good enough, not the way we put our dishes in the cabinet or the way we do laundry or anything that I do. You want to fix everything, but not everything can be fixed. And maybe not everything needs to be fixed."

Dear God. If my mother were here, she would slap some duct tape across my mouth. Ama Leeda emits a strange sound, a note of bewilderment. She has every right to be bewildered. I've never had a sharp tongue and generally require a twenty-four-hour turnaround to think of a witty reply. Is this Ama Leeda's doing?

"Have mercy on me, God," she says softly. She's slipped back into Dari. "I don't want to fix anything. I know I can't fix. I know. I'm only trying to . . ."

She blinks a few times to hold back tears.

There's something different in her voice, something almost tender. Almost broken. It pokes holes in my puffed chest and makes me want to take back my harsh words.

"I shouldn't have said . . . I'm sorry," I say, my voice softened to match hers.

I want to touch her arm, to connect and steady her in some way. I wanted to get through to her, but I've clearly struck a nerve. I want to ask her about Rahim. I can see Rahim, Yusuf, and me sprawled on the living room couches late at night, laughing at the shadow puppets Rahim would make by lamplight. I remember the way he would sit with his arm around his mother's neck and Ama Leeda squeezing his cheeks together affectionately. Where did this memory come from? Why have I not thought of how much she must miss him?

I pull my sleeves over my hands and summon the courage to say my cousin's name.

"Yusuf and I, we think about Rahim a lot," I tell her.

She stares out the window, at the rustling leaves. It occurs to me now, seeing her sit impossibly still, that she has been in constant motion the entire time she's been at our house—reaching, rinsing, rearranging. A drifting cloud covers the sun and the room darkens by degrees.

"How the day passes," she remarks. "Let me soak some rice before . . ."

She sets a pile of my dad's folded undershirts back into the white laundry basket, then slips into the kitchen.

I want to run after her and undo what I've just done, but I don't think I have the right words. I hold still in her wake, replaying our hopscotch conversation that was all about me and my mother and Yusuf and my aunt, but I know in my heart we were both hopping around with one foot up, knowing any mention of Rahim would have sent us flailing and falling like clumsy children.

# 28

The bell rings and I slide out of my chair and head toward my locker. I can feel my teacher's eyes on me, but by now I've gotten used to it. People go out of their way to either talk to me or to avoid me. I don't blame them.

It feels strange to be back at school, a full week after winter break ended. Everyone else went back a week ago, but my parents didn't push. Maybe they need me around more because even though Yusuf's out of the hospital, he's still not at home.

Once Yusuf was able to respond to simple questions and get into a wheelchair with some assistance, the doctors decided he no longer needed the same level of medical care. His broken bones will continue to heal in the casts. He's been able to eat more, though he needs help with that too.

The rehab facility he's in feels like a hospital in some ways. There are nurses and therapists in monochromatic uniforms, like they were dipped in burgundy or blue on their way to work. But it's also clearly not a hospital. People aren't checking on Yusuf nearly as often and he's not hooked up to monitors. This makes Mom feel better, but it also makes her nervous. She's afraid something will go wrong, and no one will know. Yesterday, she took a thermometer from home so she could check his temperature herself.

"Hey," Keith says. He's already wearing his coat. His backpack hangs on one shoulder. I close my locker and give the lock a spin out of habit.

"Hi," I say. We usually meet outside and end up walking home as two people who happen to live a couple houses away from each other. But he's here now, standing at my locker, so we can walk out of school and into the cold together—like real friends.

Our conversation is slow on the way home, quiet. I'm not feeling very sarcastic or witty, but he doesn't look bored. We walk at a new, unhurried pace. He asks me about Yusuf and I tell him he's doing a little better. I decide he doesn't need to know what "better" looks like. Keith doesn't need to know that Yusuf walked to the bathroom with Mom holding his arm or that he's a little calmer. He's been complaining about his ribs hurting and really hates his cast, but before he couldn't complain at all, so even those are signs of progress. When he's ready, Yusuf can tell people whatever he wants.

We're being patient, just like William told us to, and it's just about the hardest thing I've ever had to do.

When we get to Keith's house, I wonder if his mother is watching again, and I'm tired of feeling uncomfortable around her. He starts to say goodbye but I cut him off.

"Can I ask you a question?" I blurt.

"Of course," he says, looking a little alarmed. Only complicated questions get announced. Simple questions are just conversation. "What about?"

"Does your mom not like me?" I ask to my own surprise.

"No, wait, what?" Keith scoffs. "Why would you even think that?"

If I had been a little unsure, I would have apologized for asking and told Keith to forget I ever brought it up, but I know what I've felt. I am sure his mom watches me, and not with a big, cheesy smile on her face.

"Don't do that," I say softly. "Don't try to convince me it's nothing."

Keith flushes. I can see it even as he looks toward the ground.

"I'm sorry. I didn't mean to—" he falters, but the truth is coming. I just need to be a little patient with Keith, too. "I should have explained. Here's the thing."

Keith tells me about Danny's friend, a marine who also served in Afghanistan. He was so close to coming home. All he had to do was help out at the airport while they got the last people out—American citizens and some Afghans who fought against the Taliban with the Americans. It was supposed to be

277

a few days and it was just an airport, not a combat zone.

"But then there was a bombing," I say, remembering the pictures, the video clips, the online commentary that had made my parents go quiet.

"Yeah. Danny's friend was one of the Americans killed that day. There were twelve others, mostly marines."

And almost two hundred Afghans died too. Besides the dead, there were also a lot of people who were wounded, Afghans and Americans. It was a horrible attack on desperate people.

"But what does this have to do with me?" I ask.

Keith nods. "Danny had been doing better and then this came out of nowhere. He was really broken up about his friend. It hit him hard. He was talking to other vets and it was hitting a lot of them hard, too. They were so mad about the way everything went down. Danny said they felt like everything they'd done, tours over there away from their families and getting shot—all of it was for nothing if we were just letting the enemy take over," Keith explains. "Anyway, it's taken Danny a while to get better. He wouldn't talk to us about it for a few months. He was just on his phone getting updates and reading and getting angrier. Mom had to call some crisis line and get him help. So, she's been worried about anything tripping him up again. Reminding him, you know."

"So she's worried I'll remind him of his friend dying in Afghanistan," I summarize.

Keith nods reluctantly.

And Yusuf too. Maybe that's true, but I only saw her reactions to my presence.

"But I have nothing to do with any of that," I protest. How is her reaction fair? How is any of this fair?

*Life is a most splendid biological miracle. Life is diverse and constantly evolving and adapting, but it is unlikely to ever become fair*, our biology teacher used to say.

"So the night we went to WhereHouse," I say, walking back through the times I've been around Danny. I remember him starting to ask me questions, but then we nearly got hit by that other car. "What was he really saying to Larson in the parking lot?"

"I told you the truth. Danny's really defensive about the people who got evacuated. He said there are people in there who fought shoulder to shoulder with Americans and he told Larson he was being a real shit about it." Keith looks adamant. He needs me to believe him and I do. This *feels* like the truth, and I'm learning that I can trust my feelings. "I'm really sorry. It wasn't anything you said or did, it was just my mom trying to keep Danny from getting his head into that place again."

Danny wasn't at the airport in Kabul during the bombing. He wasn't shot at or killed or trampled, but he was . . . wounded in another way. He lost a friend. Does any of this figure into the body count for that bombing? Will anyone ever be held accountable?

"I get it," I say, and it occurs to me that as much as I like Keith, I don't want to have to move along or feel bad when his mother sees me. I don't want to worry if I'm going to trigger something in Danny. Maybe I can't fix those problems. And maybe they're not mine to fix, anyway. "What does Danny think?"

"I don't know," Keith admits.

I look past Keith at the soft clouds dragged across a denim sky. The moon is a translucent dome, so easy to miss in the daylight.

"I think if she talked to you, you know. Like if she could just get to know you a little bit, that would help her see," Keith offers, and at first it sounds like a good idea. If I met her, I would be my most polite self, the one my parents taught me to be so that I could make a good impression. I think of my parents in the restaurant, wanting everything to be perfect because the customer is always right.

But I'm not serving customers here. I'm not waiting on Keith's mom and hoping for tips.

"Maybe it's time for her to ask Danny how he feels," I suggest, and Keith flinches slightly at the edge in my voice. I can't help it. "I want Danny to be okay. I really do. And I'm so sorry for everything he's gone through and that he lost his friend. But me disappearing isn't going to make Danny better."

Keith glances at his house and puts a hand to his forehead, like he's getting a headache trying to find the right words, trying to figure out how to make this right. But maybe it can't be right, at least not yet. I touch the sleeve of his jacket.

"It's okay," I whisper.

"But it's not," Keith replies quickly.

"No, it's not. But it's also not on me to make it okay," I say, and I feel like I've slipped out of a lead jacket. "Please tell Danny I'm sorry for everything he's been through. See you tomorrow, Keith."

I don't turn around to see if Keith is watching me.

When I enter my house, I can smell the rosewater and cardamom. I know Ama Leeda has made roat, the heavy cake Mom doesn't bake because it's all carbs. I love it, though. As a kid, I loved watching Ama Leeda press patterns into the dough with the tines of a fork, a thimble, a bottle cap.

I have been thinking a lot about Ama Leeda after our last conversation. I need to cut her a break too. She and my parents were raised in a different time and a different place. I know they grew up with rules and traditions and that they've spent their lives trying to figure out which ones to save and which ones to surrender. I know they all lived through some awful things in Afghanistan. I've heard stories about rockets flying into their neighborhoods, and trying to decide what they were more likely to survive—staying or leaving. And ultimately, she's the one who lost a son. I know she loved a version of Rahim, even if it wasn't exactly who Rahim was.

As I start to climb the stairs, a ring breaks the silence and nearly makes me jump. Ama Leeda, unaware I've returned, sniffles and clears her throat as she plucks her phone from the coffee table. She lowers the volume on the television.

"Are you home?" she asks in Dari.

Her tone surprises me. I've heard her take plenty of calls since she's been here and she answers the phone like my mom does—with a greeting and asking about the caller's mother, father, daughter, son, aunt, uncle, fifth-grade teacher, mail carrier, and anyone else she can think of. Then she goes into their health. The older the person on the line, the longer I hear Mom cluck her tongue and ask what the doctor had to say about it.

Ama Leeda doesn't do any of that.

"Did you take the meatballs out of the freezer?" she asks. She must be talking to Uncle Zahir. It occurs to me that he's been home alone the whole time she's been here. Does she really have to tell him what to eat?

"Well, it's on the third shelf of the freezer. Maybe the second. One of those two. Don't forget. And the rice cooker takes only fifteen minutes. Don't be lazy."

I slip into my room but linger in the doorway. I'm not sure what I was planning on saying to her and at this point, I'm really just eavesdropping.

"I don't know," she sighs. "Maybe tomorrow. Do you think you can find a flight? Even if it's in the morning, I can find a way to get to the airport."

I feel a knot forming in my stomach. Why am I not relieved?

"No, everything's fine. Yusuf's improving every day. They're lucky."

I wince at that comment.

"I know, I know. I just wish we could have been lucky too.

Call me back and let me know what you find. I want to come home."

She sets her phone on the table and runs her hands over her hair, patting it down. She picks up the remote and turns off the television, then tosses the remote onto the sofa cushion. She is still for a moment before I see her back straighten.

In another winter's Yalda celebration, my mother had read a line from Hafiz that made Yusuf sit up straight and nod: *The words you speak become the house you live in.* I step back into the hallway and move toward the living room, pulled by some new feeling in me that nothing important should go unsaid.

We see each other, our reflections appearing on the darkened screen. I break the silence.

"I'm sorry, Ama Leeda."

Ama Leeda swivels her head and nods in acknowledgment.

"Forget about it," she says in Dari, but I don't want to dismiss this like it never happened.

"No," I insist, coming into the living room and taking a seat next to her on the sofa. "I don't want to forget about it. I was . . . I was frustrated and I didn't mean to be so harsh. I know you're trying to help. But I'm also used to doing things my own way. Or the way our family does things. When you tell me to be good, it sounds like you think I'm being bad."

Ama Leeda shakes her head at this.

"No, no, no. You're not bad. You're a very good girl, Yalda jan. Oh, what can I say? You're a good girl and Yusuf jan is a very good boy."

"Like Rahim," I say softly.

Her eyes are shining with unwept tears. She nods.

"He was a good boy," she says. "God forgive him."

It's a saying in Dari, rolling off our tongues every time we mention someone who has passed, something close to "rest in peace." But to hear her pray for Rahim's forgiveness makes me hurt for him.

"Do you think he needed to be forgiven?" I ask.

Ama Leeda examines the palms of her hands before curling her fingers closed.

"We all need to be forgiven," she replies.

I don't know what to make of that response.

"Rahim liked to dream," she says wistfully. "From the time he was a little boy, he would talk about buying a house big enough that he could have one room for me. He told me he would make sure it had very big windows because I love sunlight."

Maybe she used to love sunlight. The only light I've seen Ama Leeda getting in the time she's been with us is the synthetic glow off the television screen. I cannot imagine how hard it is for her to face each day without Rahim. She is an open wound, and I'm not sure there are any right words to say to her.

"I'm sorry he was in so much pain. I miss him a lot," I say. I put my hand over hers and squeeze, which seems to release something in her. Tears stream down her cheeks and her chest shakes with sobs.

"There was no one like him," she says. "He always knew

284

how I was feeling. 'Don't be sad, Madar jan. Go for a walk.' That's what he would tell me. And he wanted to teach me how to breathe. I told him I've been breathing my whole life. 'You are holding negative feelings in your chest.' So much he talked about breathing. Breathe in and count—I can't remember how many seconds—then breathe out. He would ask me if I did it and I would tell him yes, of course, because I didn't want him to feel bad."

Through her tears, Ama Leeda lets out the tiniest laugh, and I realize I'm smiling at this memory she has of Rahim; him guiding her through conscious breathing.

"He would have been a great therapist. He had a peaceful soul," I say, thinking of the times I realized after a couple of hours of cousin conversations that Rahim had been the one asking questions and listening, keeping a circle of chatter alive without saying very much.

"One day before, he called me," she says.

She doesn't have to name it. I know the day she's referring to.

"I didn't want to talk about anything else with him. I just wanted everything to be simple. I wanted him to talk about the dreams he had when he was little, a house with big windows. A room for me. We were both tired of talking about anything else, I think, so I talked about the weather. 'I went for a hike today, Madar jan. Halfway down the mountain, the sun was setting and there were no other sounds, just birds and a little wind. Go for a walk today, Madar jan. Let the birds sing for you.'"

Picturing Rahim halfway up a mountain trail pausing to listen to birdsong gives me a sense of peace.

*Let the birds sing for you.*

My heart knots to think of this parting instruction. But it's more than an instruction. There's a touch of forgiveness in there too. And not just on that day, I realize. Rahim must have forgiven his mother every day that he picked up the phone and called her, every time he went home for dinner, every time he thought about her. And if Rahim forgave his mother, isn't it wrong for me to resent her?

"He was different. Not like other guys," I say.

"Yes," Ama Leeda readily agrees even as she wipes away a stray tear. "Very much. No one had a heart like him. People always told me I was lucky to have a son like him."

"Ama Leeda, why . . ." I pause, giving myself a chance to reconsider asking this question, but I need to know. "Did you try to make him marry some girl?"

My aunt lets out a sad laugh.

"I could not change my boy," she says. "He told me one day that I should tell people I am finding a girl for him. We had too many people asking questions about him. Nosy people. And I didn't want people to hurt him or talk about him. So I told one or two people what he said, then I stopped. I don't need to explain anything to people. It's his life."

I am stunned. I assumed she had been trying to "fix" Rahim, when that rumor had been Rahim's idea. And as his mom, in her own broken way, she was trying to buy him some privacy.

I'd never even considered that there was more going on than what I heard through my mom.

"I didn't know that," I say.

"No one knows that. Just me and his father." She sniffles. "The doctor tells me he died from a disease, just like some people die from cancer. But what can I think when I saw him young and healthy? How can I not feel that my son left me because I did not know how to take care of him?"

"Rahim loved you very much," I say, feeling at a total loss for words. The hurt I see on Ama Leeda's face is equal parts grief and remorse. She shakes her head and tries to compose herself again. "I'm so sorry for talking to you that way."

"I did what I thought I was supposed to do as his mother," she says. "Good or bad or right or wrong, I don't know. What good is it to know now? He's not here to forgive me."

Ama Leeda would do things differently if she had another shot. We probably all would. But this life isn't a video game and we don't get five tries to get it right. I've been feeling resentful of my aunt, but I'm also resentful of myself. I had not months but years to reach out to Rahim, to call and ask how he was doing. In the couple of years before he decided to leave this world, I probably sent a million text messages to my friends but not a single message to Rahim to wish him a happy birthday or happy Thanksgiving or to tell him I missed hanging out with him. Would knowing that have changed anything? Or is it arrogant to even think that I could have swayed him?

The possibilities are haunting.

I go back to the day Yusuf and I almost talked about Rahim—how I didn't want Yusuf to blame himself. I'm not willing to feel guilt-free just yet, but I can see that I shouldn't carry this either. "Maybe you should forgive yourself," I offer ever so meekly, because we only ever talk about being forgiven by God. But why not? It hurts to resent the face in the mirror.

Ama Leeda considers this a second, then puts an arm around me. I lean into her and feel a warmth I hadn't expected.

"Are you really going to leave?"

Ama Leeda nods. "I came only to take some pressure from your parents. And I want to see Yusuf jan get better. Thank God soon it is time for him to come home and your mother and father can have their son again. It is time for me to go home too."

"Will you come back?" I am almost surprised to hear myself ask this.

Ama Leeda looks at me and I see just how fragile she is.

"Oh, my sweet niece. How can I stay away?"

I hug Ama Leeda a little tighter and we breathe together, setting something free with every exhale and listening to birds sing songs of forgiveness just outside the window.

I peep through the window and see two people at the door; the taller figure has on a wool headscarf.

The door opens and I hear my mother greet someone in Dari. There's conversation I cannot make out, so I creep into the hallway to get a better listen. Are these relatives? If so, they're not ones whose voices I recognize.

"Nahal jan," I hear Mom say. I know what's coming next before my mother calls my name. "Yalda! Come and see who's here."

I walk down the hall to the top of the stairs and see Nahal and her mother being ushered into the foyer by Mom. Their noses are pink with cold. Nahal's mother has the same round eyes and dark hair as her daughter and is holding a foil-covered dish in her hands.

"Salaam," I say, and wave. Nahal smiles back. She looks much more at ease than she does at school.

"Salaam, sweet girl!" her mother says in Dari, then turns back to my mom. "Dear sister, we should have come much sooner, but I did not know how to find your home."

"I'm glad you're here," Mom says, closing the door behind them. "What a pleasant surprise! Let me take your coats."

"No, we didn't want to trouble you. We won't stay. I only wanted to bring a little something for you," she says.

"Stay just a few minutes, at least."

"Another time," she says. This is an Afghan dance of formalities, and I know it well, though I've always wished we could just skip the fancy footwork and get to the finale.

"You can't possibly come and not sit for a cup of tea," Mom insists. "Yalda jan, can you hang their coats?"

I take a couple more steps down to get to the landing, reminding myself to smile so my surprise is not misread as unwelcoming.

"Sure, let me take them," I offer, but Nahal's already taking her mom's coat. She plucks a hanger out of the open coat closet and hangs her mother's jacket first, then drapes hers over the same hanger.

"Oh, I would have done that for you," I say when I reach the landing. The mothers are up the stairs and chatting.

"It's okay," Nahal assures me, and closes the closet door.

Mom points Nahal's mother to the living room and takes a seat next to her on the sofa.

"Yalda jan, can you put on some tea?" my mother asks when Nahal and I come up the stairs. She locks her eyes on mine, a transmission of reminders to add the cardamom and bring the glass cups, not the red Christmas mugs with the white Santa mustache.

If Ama Leeda were here, the water would already be boiling. I went into Yusuf's room after she left and was surprised at what I found. The bobblehead was back in its place and Yusuf's closet had been restored to what it looked like the night he didn't come home, as if Ama Leeda had never been here. Still, something's shifted in our home after her stay with us. I realize we really didn't feel alone because she was with us. And that I didn't know everything about her and Rahim. I don't know why I thought I did.

"I can do it with her," Nahal offers, and follows me into the kitchen. She has the foil-covered tray in her hands and asks where she can set it down.

"You can set it on the counter," I say in Dari, which probably sounds terrible to her, though she doesn't react. She's looking at the pictures on the fridge, one of Yusuf with a reluctant arm around my shoulder at a wedding when we were thirteen years old. Mom realized I needed professional help with my hair but took me to the kind of hair salon that has loyalty punch cards, so instead of beachy waves, I ended up with hurricane hair.

I fill the electric kettle with water and turn it on. I hope

Nahal doesn't really think I need help to boil water.

"How is Yusuf jan doing?" she asks in English. I'm surprised at how good her English is and then kick myself a little for assuming it would be more stilted.

I lean against the counter and face her.

"He's getting stronger," I say, relieved to switch back to English. "He'll probably come home in a couple of weeks."

"Inshallah," she adds, just like my mother would, but it feels more like protection than correction and I feel myself start to relax.

"How are you doing?" I ask, wanting to change the subject. "How's your family?"

She smiles. "My mother got a new job. She's working in a grocery store," she says. "Back home, she was working with computers, but this is okay for now. She says she is learning a lot about America from this place. There are so many ways to get milk without a cow."

I laugh, thinking of the half gallons of oat milk and almond milk my mom has in the fridge.

"I imagine it was a hard year. There must have been so much to get used to," I say.

"Yes, a lot. But people helped," she says, looking through the window over the kitchen sink and into our backyard. "When we came to our apartment, there was nothing. Khala jan, your mom, she brought us chalow and kofta. When we were on the base and then in the hotel, I was missing our rice so much. Spinach is my favorite too, so the sabzee your mom brought made me feel better. And when she gave my mom the spices so she can cook too, my mom was crying."

I remember Mom packing the big containers of cumin, masala, and ground garlic into a cardboard box. I considered going with her, but the thought of making small talk with strangers overwhelmed me, so I had finished an essay that wasn't due for another three days.

The kettle whistles. I spoon green tea leaves into the thermos, add a pinch of ground cardamom, and then the boiling water. I let the fragrant steam warm my face before twisting on the cap.

"She loves food and she loves to help," I say. I peel the aluminum foil back from the white ceramic plate. There's an artful halo of green raisins, walnuts, and sprigs of fresh mint leaves around a center pile of cubed, fresh cheese. It's beautiful, vision-board worthy. Because I'm a restaurant kid, I almost want to take a picture and add it to our menu as an Afghan cheese board.

"Can I take these out?" Nahal asks, pointing at the teacups in the glass door cabinet. I can hear our mothers talking in the living room but can't make out what they're saying. A month ago, I would have been sweating at the thought of sitting with people I hardly know, but I was a different person a month ago. It's like some Afghan genes have just been activated.

"Sure, those are good," I say. My phone buzzes on the counter, just below the cabinet where the cups are. From here, I can see the screen light up and Keith's name appears. He's in my contacts now—a list that has grown so much since Yusuf's fall. Nahal glances down and then moves the phone toward me.

I feel the same heat on my neck that I felt the day she passed us in the hallway. I think of all the restrictions they have in Afghanistan now, all the ways Nahal's life would be different if she were still there. She wouldn't be allowed to go to school or walk through a park or go to a gym. With all the beauty salons forced to close, she couldn't even go for a haircut. And if Nahal and her family dared to express their outrage out loud, they might disappear as other protestors have. Last week, I saw my cousin post that a young woman and man were publicly flogged for texting each other.

Life is terrifying when the people in charge of your life are terrorists.

Nahal's mother got her family out so they wouldn't have to suffocate under those rules. But even here, our culture still blushes at dating.

"He's not my boyfriend," I blurt, slipping my phone into my back pocket. "He lives down the street. He texts to ask about Yusuf."

Nahal looks confused.

"Yalda jan, I did not say anything. I did not ask," she says.

"But I didn't want you to think—" I start, then cut myself off because it occurs to me I might need to talk less right now.

My mother walks into the kitchen then, her eyes floating from the thermos to the tray.

"Yalda, did you remember to add the— Oh, wow, look at this kishmish paneer!"

She pauses, taking it in. I'm sure she's thinking of my grandmother because that's who came to mind when I saw this tray.

"Bring the tea, girls," Mom says when she's recovered from the tidal wave of nostalgia. "And, Yalda, grab some plates. Let's enjoy this together."

Nahal and I follow her out and take seats in the living room. Mom shoots me another telepathic look that gets me back out of my seat to pour and serve the tea. I never drink tea, but here I am nursing a cup because I will otherwise be forced to sit on my hands.

Mom takes a bite of the cheese and shakes her head. It's as if my grandmother has just planted a kiss on Mom's cheek. Not even the most expensive, most organic store-bought cheese could have this effect on her. If Ama Leeda were here, she'd have something to say about my sudden realization.

"I watched my mother make this when I was young, but in all these years, I have never been able to make it taste like hers. May your hands not ache," Mom says, expressing her thanks.

Nahal's mom shakes her head and insists my grandmother's must have been far better. She does the usual self-deprecating thing and claims she wanted it to come out much better but hopes we enjoy. She takes only the smallest piece of cheese for herself and touches Mom's wrist when she tries to serve her more. Our mothers are at ease with each other, speaking a common language of words and gestures.

"I'm so glad that there's another Afghan family in the school with Nahal," she says. "People have been very nice but even then, it's different to know there's one of your own people nearby. Nahal was not always this shy. In Afghanistan, the principal of her school told me Nahal had more control over the classroom than her teacher."

Mom shoots Nahal a mischievous smile. My phone buzzes again. When I take it out to silence it, I see it's another text from Keith. I shouldn't but I have to peek.

Going to walk Fisher. Busy?

"Yalda, did you know that Nahal jan is also a musician?" Mom asks.

"Violin," Nahal's mother says proudly. "She is very good. Maybe not like Yusuf jan, but she started only two years ago. We bought a violin for her only one month before we left."

"It was a surprise. I never expected anything but clothes for my birthday." Nahal laughs.

"And what happened to it?" Mom asks gently, because it's safe to assume the violin did not survive the urgent evacuation at the Kabul airport; the crush of people trying to flee.

"It was left behind," Nahal says, and pats down the hem of her shirt.

"But we are here," her mother insists, waving away the loss. "And we came to tell you if you need anything, please let us know. We have prayed for your precious son since Nahal jan told us about what happened."

Mom thanks her again and gives her a rundown of the

improvement Yusuf has shown, the signs that he will recover more. It is unlikely he will be the same person he was. The fall he survived has changed his speech, his movements, his balance. He is quickly frustrated and slow to smile. He struggles to find words. He's often asleep during the day and awake at night, like a jet-lagged traveler.

Yusuf's fall has changed me too, but in ways that others cannot see and I cannot name.

We walk Nahal and her mother to the door. They have taken a bus to get here and will not entertain my mother's insistence on driving them back. Nahal's mother says doing so would mean they would never feel comfortable visiting again, and she is very proud that Nahal has practically memorized the town's bus routes.

If I were thrown from my home into a new country, how long would it take me to navigate the local transportation system? How would I feel needing so much help? How long would it take me to feel like I could help others?

I think of how I've avoided going with my mom to drop off coats or food, how much I wanted to help only from out of view. How uneasy I was at the thought of being around people like Nahal and her mother.

When they leave, I return to the living room to gather the dishes. Instead, I find myself at the window, watching Nahal and her mother walk down the street, passing Keith walking Fisher, and making a left to meet the bus at the end of the block. Keith pulls Fisher onto the grass and yields the sidewalk to them, raising his hand in a half wave. Nahal does the same and her mother nods.

*I did not say anything. I did not ask.*

No, Nahal hasn't said anything or questioned me. But somewhere along the line, I started to hear judgments in my head and was sure it was her voice I was hearing.

Maybe it was my own.

# 30

Watching Yusuf recover is like watching trees change through the seasons. On a daily basis I don't see a difference, and yet here I am in the rehab hospital on a Thursday afternoon at the end of January thinking how much better he is today than the night we found him. He has gone from breathing on his own and squeezing Mom's hand back to getting out of bed and telling the staff that the green beans taste like shoelaces. Here, he's allowed more than two visitors at a time so our friends can finally come see Yusuf instead of texting me to ask about him.

My mom's influence on me is clear because I've been cleaning up his room, a space that's meant to look a little cozier than a hospital room. It has generic artwork on the walls—children riding bikes past a field of flowers and other similarly sappy scenes. The room is large enough for an armoire, a small sofa, and the hospital bed. It is a far cry from home, but we won't be here forever.

I put a tube of ointment, a pink water pitcher, and a pair of sweatpants in the armoire to clear the area. I set the tray from Yusuf's half-eaten lunch in the hallway. I ask Yusuf to get up so I can make the bed, folding back the top edge of the blanket before I let him sit on it.

"Too bad Mom isn't here to see this," Yusuf says, his voice a little rough. He clears his throat, sits up a little higher, and starts to zip up the sweatshirt I brought in for him. I was so tired of seeing him in a hospital gown. "You might have a chance at being her favorite."

*I am grateful for your sarcasm.*

"Yeah, unlikely, but do me a favor and tell her all about it. I think I have a shot at being her second favorite," I reply. I open the door to make the room a bit more inviting for our friends.

Mona appears in the doorway first.

"Found them!" she calls out to whomever may be listening in the hallway.

Asma is right behind her, followed by Liam and Keith. As they file into the room, I keep looking back at the door to see if Chris has decided to come with everyone else. I don't know what it would feel like for Yusuf to see him now and can't imagine what Chris is going through at home. He's been quieter at school, plodding through the days without saying much. Mona told me he meets with the school counselor every other

300

day. He sent a single message to Yusuf, one line to say he hoped Yusuf was doing better. Since then, he sometimes replies to Yusuf's texts, but it takes him a while and he doesn't say much.

Mom and Dad told Yusuf not to bother talking to him right now.

*You need to get better first. Remember what the doctor told you. You don't need more stress*, Mom said.

"Hey," Liam says, his fist raised for Yusuf to bump. "How are you doing, bro? Glad we made it past security."

"Yusuf! My goodness, look at you with your own private room and staff. Royalty, huh?" Mona says.

Asma walks around to the other side of Yusuf's bed. She looks unsure how to greet him. Yusuf offers her a hand and she squeezes it.

"It's good to see you," she says.

"Yeah, you too," he replies. He looks down and groans. "I'm . . . uh . . . also really glad to see the rest of you, but I'm not going to hold your hands."

Asma laughs then, her head tilted back and her eyes full of feelings.

Keith, Mona, and I sit on the vinyl-covered sofa. Liam and Asma take the chairs.

I look at Keith and smile. We still walk to and from school together, but we're pretty clear now that we're just friends. Maybe "just" is the wrong word. Friends are a big deal, and the kind who want to hang out even in a rehab hospital are precious.

Before long, we are talking about school and our teachers and which one of us is least likely to become a nurse and why.

"I don't think I want to be that far up in people's business," Liam says. "But I think I've got the bedside manner."

"Bro," Yusuf says, shaking his head.

"Okay, maybe not." He shrugs.

"How's the food?" Asma asks. "Any better than cafeteria food?"

"Bro," Yusuf says again, and shakes his head. Laughter brightens the room. A nurse peeks in and smiles at this small band of friends, another vital sign.

"Yusuf, I don't know if you've heard, but Mr. Dempsey is not doing well without you," Liam says. "Tried talking music in class and pretty much cried when Clint asked if Aerosmith was a department at NASA."

"Oh my God," Yusuf groans.

"What does Aerosmith mean?" Mona asks. "Actually, what does The Hipper Campus mean?"

Yusuf and Liam shoot each other looks.

"It's your call." Liam shrugs. "But I think if the people want to know, give it to them."

Yusuf smiles.

"Have you heard of the hippocampus?" he asks.

"The half-horse, half-fish mythological sea monster," I say with authority. "But why a sea monster?"

"No, not that hippocampus," Yusuf replies. "It's a part of the brain. This little area shaped like a sea horse; a little curled thing that's pretty deep in there. It's where memories are stored; new ones and old ones, and it helps with navigation. Like understanding dimensions, I think. And somehow all of that is tied to feelings. I wanted us to make the kind of music that could take people to a place where they feel good or better. Or at least feel something worth remembering. And so, a Hipper Campus."

I look down because there are tears in my eyes. I wish I had known what the band's name meant. But maybe it resonates differently with me now, after what we've lived through.

Yusuf's eyes float to the binder by the window. I brought it in a week ago. One of the counselors at school collected notes from teachers and classmates to let Yusuf know everyone's looking forward to seeing him back in school soon. I don't know how soon that will be. It's already been a month since the night of Yalda, and Yusuf's still got a lot of recovery ahead.

Fifteen minutes go by. We do not talk about the longest night of the year. We do not talk about whether we should measure the time it will take for Yusuf to recover in days, months, or years. We do not wonder aloud what changes might now be woven into Yusuf's identity and what parts of Yusuf we've lost. No one wants to make Yusuf self-conscious about his injuries or take him back to the moment his head hit the ground, pushed by someone filled with contempt for him. Or maybe just filled with contempt. No one talks about what people in town have been saying about Yusuf or what people in school are now saying about Chris. We keep the conversation gentle, avoiding all the sharp edges. It reminds me of the game Operation. We are reaching carefully into dark holes for little plastic targets with trembling hands, hoping not to light up the splayed patient with red, buzzing pain.

Avoid. That's exactly what we're doing.

A void. That's exactly what we're tiptoeing around, trying not to slip in.

We almost succeed.

"Have you talked to Chris lately?" Yusuf asks Liam. The room goes still as we look straight into the dark. There's not an ounce of surprise in the air, though. Yusuf is here, casted and sutured together, because he chooses to face problems head-on instead of dodging them.

We have a lot to deal with—in our own families, in our neighborhoods and schools, in our towns, and in our world. Maybe the best way to start is small, a conversation with an aunt or a friend. But I know in my bones now that it can't end there. One of these days, I'm going to find a way to bring more people into the room.

Liam shakes his head, flashes his phone on and then off, like he's checking to see if Chris has messaged him in the last few minutes.

"He's been real quiet. And actually he's been absent a lot since his stepdad got taken in."

Yusuf looks at me, then Asma. We've kept Yusuf up to date on the proceedings, as much as we know. Chris's stepfather was charged with assault. A prosecutor called Dad and told him that he would do everything he could to get justice for Yusuf.

"Chris shouldn't feel bad. This isn't his fault," Yusuf says.

"He's barely talking to me either," Liam adds.

"I would not want to be him," Mona says. "Hey, what did the judge set for bail? I hope you get a judge that's hard on violent offenders. Some of them have applied the whole criminal justice reform movement a little too widely, if you know what I mean. Is there going to be a jury trial? You know, your family should consider pressing civil charges too."

"Looks like listening to all those podcasts is finally paying off," Asma says.

"If you don't know how the system works, the system won't work for you," Mona replies.

"Oh my God, Mona," I say, but I do envy her activist energy.

"Who listens to podcasts, anyway? What are you, like, forty?" Liam asks.

"Did you really just say that to her?" Keith groans.

Mona raises an eyebrow.

"Okay, in my defense," she begins. "Podcasts can be incredibly informative. I listen to one about business backstories. Did you know that Adidas and Puma were started by two brothers who couldn't stand each other? They had factories in one town and people were either Team Adidas or Team Puma. You could tell by looking at their feet."

"Are you making that up?" Keith asks. "That sounds made-up."

"Don't question her," Asma warns.

"Why would I make up . . ."

I look at Yusuf. He's listening to the back-and-forth and smiling. Today's visit will leave him exhausted, but it's still the best day he's had in a long time.

# 31

Two weeks of T-shirt weather have tricked the cherry blossom trees into an early bloom. On our drive to the restaurant, we watched delicate white petals flutter to the ground, mimicking snow. Spring is right around the corner.

"What if I cannot do it?" Nahal asks after she's set her backpack on an empty chair. "I am nervous."

"Nervous is okay. Nervous is normal," I reassure her. "You'll be great. And honestly, Yusuf used to be nervous before playing in front of people, but after a couple of times, having people watch him became normal. He even pretended to have a broken leg to get out of his first performance. Right, Yusuf?"

"Yalda, that was the third-grade talent show and I had

sprained my ankle that morning so it really did hurt," Yusuf groans.

I am more grateful than I can say to have my brother here, remembering a sprained ankle as a distant memory. Every day, he moves further away from his recent injuries. His arm was just freed from the cast and his bruises have faded. His leg will need more time, but he's gotten pretty good at moving around with a pair of crutches. His scars are there but healing. He is a slower, stiffer version of himself, but he is here.

Nahal smiles.

"Okay, I will not say my arm is broken," she jokes. "But I am still a little nervous." I don't tell her that I'm nervous too. Having her play at the restaurant was my idea, but I wonder if maybe it won't go the way I've imagined it in my head. Why did I insist we do this on a Saturday night instead of a Tuesday? Business has been picking up again, but we're still not back to where we were a year ago. Whenever Mom says it's because of crazy inflation and gas prices, Dad agrees. Maybe they're right. Maybe the few tables that sit empty on weekday nights have nothing to do with Yusuf or the storm of comments about us in town and on social media.

"I'm nervous, too," I admit. My sketchbook is no longer hiding in my nightstand. When I gave the hippocampus drawing to Yusuf, he asked to see more.

*People should see what you've created, Yal. You're an artist. Every one of these is a story.*

*Artist.* That was the word that got me because he's right. I haven't just been doodling. I've been creating art—because that's what artists do.

I used a blade to cut pages of drawings out of my sketchbook and slid them into black frames. When Mom came into my room, she was stunned. She spent an hour on my bedroom floor, looking at each piece.

*Yalda, these are amazing. How did you come up with these? What do they mean?* she had asked. I must have squirmed because she closed her eyes and shifted her tone ever so slightly. *Maybe later you could tell me more about them.*

We've used removable hooks to make a gallery wall. Against the brick-red walls of the restaurant, the ink drawings stand out. I am nervous for people to see them and am not sure what kind of conversations they might spark, but that's okay, too. I've gotten more comfortable with being uncomfortable.

"You've done things that are much harder than this. There will be a lot of people here tonight who already know you. And everyone who's coming here is very excited to hear you play," I tell Nahal. "By the end of the night, we won't be nervous anymore."

Nahal takes in the space, the array of tables and the makeshift stage my dad and I built out of a couple of pallets, plywood, and an Afghan carpet we brought from home. There are two chairs on the stage, two microphones, and a portable speaker. I added a few candles at her feet, tall and tapered with fake flickering flames. It's not the most sophisticated setup, but from a distance, it is just the right mood.

"Okay," she says, looking down at the violin case in her hands. She smiles then, the kind that floats up and seeps from her eyes as well. "Yes, it will be okay."

"And you won't be alone up there," I remind her. "If you want, you can warm up or just relax for a while. We still have some time."

I would love to stay and hype up Nahal some more, but I need to run through my checklist too. No one, not even my parents, knows that the mayor and a few of the teachers will be coming tonight. There will also be at least a dozen people from the interfaith group that worked with families like Nahal's in the last year. These people have donated cars, assembled furniture, and taught people how to speak a language that is full of silent letters, homonym traps, and exceptions to grammatical rules.

"Yalda." Mom stops me mid-step with a hand on my elbow. "You think Nahal's okay to do this?"

I look back at Nahal, who has taken a seat next to Yusuf. She is showing Yusuf her violin, the one that was gifted to her by the owner of Crescendo after he learned of her aspirations. Yusuf takes the violin from Nahal's hands and holds it like a guitar, even strums a couple of notes. She laughs and brings her hands together for applause. She offers to teach him how to play, but he shakes his head and returns the violin to her. She adjusts the strings with a tenderness that also tells a whole story.

"Yes," I say, and give my mom's hand a confident squeeze. "She'll be fine."

Mona and Asma enter together. Asma's eyes connect with Yusuf immediately, and they both break into grins that would make me gag under normal circumstances. There's definitely a spark between them, and I'm kicking myself again for not seeing my twin's romantic interest sooner. Maybe I was too wrapped up in my own awkward situation to notice.

"This is going to be so great! My parents are going to come too, and a few other people they told. Hope there's enough room," Mona says.

Enough room? I was scared we'd have an empty restaurant. I give Asma a quick hug.

"Oh, I'm so glad you're both here," I say. "Those are your seats, right by Yusuf. He's been waiting for you."

"But, Yalda, hold up! Are those your drawings?" Mona gasps, pointing at the wall. "Finally, she reveals her secret talents!"

Asma beams. "I'm so proud of you!" she calls out as Mona yanks her by the hand to get a closer look at the artwork.

I run back to the kitchen, where Dad is pulling salad dressing out of the fridge. Our cook lifts the lid on a pot and gives something a stir with a wooden spoon. She inhales and her eyes flutter closed in appreciation. The kitchen feels alive again after a few wilted weeks.

I am back in the dining room, which is filling up by the minute. Keith and Liam are with Yusuf as well, Keith in a chair and Liam standing in front of him.

"Hey, guys!" I call.

"I'm here for the bread," Keith announces. "I hear it's pretty good."

I shake my head and laugh at a conversation that happened a hundred years ago, when we were just getting to know each other. We're not done getting to know each other, but I also want to get to know myself better. I'm not the same person I was when winter started—none of us are.

"And we've got two more people coming," Keith says, glancing at the door just as Keith's mom and Danny enter. I walk over to greet them. Keith's mother gives me a hug. She got my number from Keith a couple of weeks ago and texted me to ask if we could meet up. Keith and Danny weren't home when I stopped by, so it was just us, Fisher, and two mugs of hot cocoa. She told me she realized that what Danny really needed was to be closer to people who understood what made him sad. She didn't mean to make me feel like I was the problem. We talked for over an hour, a conversation I could not have predicted back when she used to stand at her front door clearly wishing Keith would just walk to school on his own.

*You don't get to choose who you share a street with, but you do decide what kind of neighbor you want to be*, she had said. The PROTECT OUR NEIGHBORHOOD yard signs are still around. I take them as a reminder to do just that, in my own way.

Four more people enter and I check the time on my phone

312

once more. When I look up, my breath catches at the sight of a face I was not expecting in the window. I walk across the restaurant and out the door. It is dusk but a few moments before the parking lot lights turn on. By the time I reach the pavement, Chris has turned his back and is walking toward his car.

"Chris!" I call out, aware that I have no plan. What will I say to him? What will he say to me?

Chris turns and looks at me, then runs his hand through his hair. He looks torn.

I walk toward him and he squints and looks away, as if it physically hurts him to see me.

"Chris," I say.

"I just . . . I can't . . . ," he stammers, then stops. I cannot imagine what he's been through, living with someone capable of such violence and anger. I am glad that he and his mother have been freed. I've written to Chris that we're grateful he chose to come forward with what he'd seen. Some people at school have been judging Chris for not speaking up sooner, but he must have been terrified, too. I don't know what I would have done in his place.

"Please come in," I say.

Chris looks past me to the restaurant, which twinkles with the string lights and candles I've set up inside. As I stand with Chris by his car, another couple walks in and the door chimes. Chris shakes his head.

"Not tonight," he says, then wills himself to meet my eyes. "But some other time. I promise."

I nod, accepting his promise and vowing to hold him to it. I'm worried about Chris. He's been injured too, though not the kind of injury that leaves visible scars or needs bandaging. He lumbers back into his car and raises a hand to say goodbye before pulling away.

I walk back into the restaurant and exhale, but I don't want to tell anyone about the conversation with Chris just yet because Nahal is looking at me and the clock on the wall. She has apparently gone from nervous to eager to get this started. I walk over to the corner setup and turn the microphone on.

"Hi, everyone. Looks like it's time to begin," I say, and the chatter in the room dies down. Liam slips behind me and adjusts the volume on the speaker. "My name is Yalda, and on behalf of my family, we're really glad to see you all here tonight."

My parents are standing behind Yusuf. Mom gives his shoulder a squeeze as Dad presses his lips together and nods for me to go on.

My heart is pounding so hard I think it might fly out of my chest, but the faces I am seeing give me courage. I look down at the note card in my hand, but it's flapping like a flag in a storm, so I tuck it into my back pocket and decide I'll just have to wing it.

"We've been through a lot since December and it's been

really tough. The one thing I can say is that we didn't feel like we were alone during any of it. Our town isn't perfect, but we've got a lot of great neighbors and friends who have been there with us when it really counted—the vigil, the hospital, our school, our restaurant, our home, and even some online as well. I'm really glad my brother, Yusuf, is sitting here tonight." I glance over at Yusuf. Before I can speak again, the room has erupted into applause, giving me time to muster up the courage for the rest of what I want to say. Yusuf shakes his head and laughs. My mom hugs him from behind and kisses the top of his head. "I am not going to be cheesy up here, but I will say that I love you, Yusuf. And I am looking forward to annoying you for the rest of our lives."

Light laughter ripples through the room.

"And now, I'd like to introduce our guest musician for tonight. Nahal and her family moved here from Afghanistan a year ago, and she is a junior in high school. She started to learn violin in Afghanistan because a year ago, girls could do that. Now that music is forbidden and girls aren't allowed to go to school, I'm really glad Nahal is here. She and Yusuf are going to perform together. Yusuf wrote the lyrics and Nahal did her own take on the melody. I hope you enjoy it. I mean, I know you will."

There are soft cheers this time. Yusuf grins. My dad offers his arm and Yusuf grips it to help him stand and, with one crutch, joins me at the microphone.

"Yeah, bro!" calls Liam, and there's another round of snaps and clapping.

"Thanks, everyone. I just want to say thanks to all of you for being there for me and my family," he says, and then puts a hand over his heart and nods before taking his seat.

"Nahal?"

Nahal steps up to the microphone, tucking a strand of hair behind her ear. She looks out at the faces before her and settles on the older couple, the Petersons, who helped her and her mother learn to drive.

"Thank you, everyone," Nahal says. She shifts on her feet and clears her throat. "It has been a very difficult time and we are every day still worried about our family back home. But here, we have a chance for music and life. I wish all of us could be here, but . . ."

Nahal's voice trails off. I worry that this is all too much for her.

"But I will keep studying, and I hope that one day I will go home and play music and help my country to be peaceful, for girls and boys. For men and women."

The applause is not gentle this time. There are whistles and whoops and even some sniffles. There is so much good energy in the air that I can almost see it. I hang on to this feeling fiercely because I already know there will be days ahead when I will need to remember a night like tonight is possible.

Nahal and Yusuf only rehearsed together a couple times. It isn't easy to coordinate schedules and we've been worried about Yusuf tiring himself out. He fatigues pretty easily and needs frequent breaks, all of which frustrates him. We're trying to celebrate his recovery but it's such a slow, thorny process that most of the time it doesn't feel like anything worth celebrating.

Nahal steps up to the second microphone and gives Yusuf a nod. He taps his foot and lowers his gaze to the floor as Nahal starts the mournful melody. It's a heartbreaking sloweddown variation of the one the band played at WhereHouse. Yusuf comes in with the lyrics, singing at half his usual volume but with twice the heart. The lyrics make my eyes well up. Mona must have noticed because she wraps her arm around my shoulders.

*If we stay or not, all the battles we fought*
*They cannot steal this*
*They take us apart, but we're a work of art.*
*And they'll never unsee this.*
*I come in peace,*
*Breathe with me or*
*I'll leave in pieces.*

Yusuf's eyes close. He doesn't look at the people before him, this crowd of old and new friends. It's him and the song, the truth of the lyrics resonating in a way that is personal and powerful. The night of the fall, the longest night, changed us all. We will never be the people we were before, but maybe we were never meant to be those people—unaware and unconnected. I am certain there will be more long nights, but I'm also certain,

317

looking at the faces of people who have chosen to gather with us, that we won't be alone for them. The music weaves through the room, binding us, echoing in our heads and hearts long after Yusuf sings the final word, long after Nahal strums her final fragile note.

We are works of art and they can't unsee this.

# A NOTE FROM THE AUTHOR

Yalda and Yusuf are imagined characters who inhabit a fictional world. But buried in their story are the hard truths that inspired *Spilled Ink*—the reality that hate and fear cause immense harm to people, property, and communities. This story is also about the truth that while Afghan refugees received during Operation Allies Welcome were not always met with open arms in every American community, there was a remarkable outpouring of hands-on support to soften their landing.

*Spilled Ink* is the story of Muslim, Afghan American siblings who come face-to-face with Islamophobia and xenophobia. I wanted Yalda and Yusuf to help me think through the impact of a bias-motivated assault by following the journey of one family. On a side note, I feel the word *Islamophobia* is incomplete. *Phobia* implies a passivity or an avoidance, but what we witness is active and consequential.

The FBI's Uniform Crime Reporting (UCR) Program registered over 7,000 hate crime incidents in 2021. Because of a shift in reporting mechanisms, this is most likely an undercount. These crimes occurred in places where we should feel safe—homes, roads, schools, restaurants, and playgrounds. In my own community, we've seen a rise of ugly antisemitic graffiti and markings in schools and playgrounds, as well as hate speech directed at Muslims or those perceived to be Muslim. Asian and Black communities have experienced the same physical and emotional violence. The UCR website tracks the motivations for bias incidents—race/ethnicity, religion, sexual orientation, gender identity, disability, and gender. What is more difficult to record are the incidents motivated by a combination of these identities. ProPublica has curated a comprehensive list of resources for victims of hate or bias crimes, including organizations that offer guidance on immediate steps for victims to take, options for legal recourse, and emotional/mental health support. There are, thankfully, local resources in many cities and counties—too many to list here.

Hate crimes are notoriously difficult to confirm because unless a perpetrator explicitly declares their motivations, the motivations of a crime remain unknown. As I write this, all but three states have laws criminalizing bias-motivated assaults or intimidations. Not all those forty-seven states and the District of Columbia have laws that cover biases based on gender identity, sexual orientation, gender, or disability. A few federal laws exist as well, named after the victims of egregious crimes: Emmett Till, Matthew Shepard, and James Byrd Jr. But while laws can provide avenues for punishment and move us toward justice, they are unlikely to be preventative. The real work happens outside the courtrooms and in our sacred spaces—our homes, schools, houses of worship, and sports leagues.

In this story, I also wanted to acknowledge that even communities and individuals who have been on the receiving end of bias can carry their own intolerant beliefs. Prejudice is an equal-opportunity affliction. We are also, thankfully, learning how to prioritize mental health individually and as a society. I hope that our dollars follow our intentions. For anyone struggling, please know resources are available. The Suicide & Crisis Lifeline (dial 988) provides free and confidential support for people in crisis or for those supporting an individual in crisis.

Here's the happy truth at the heart of this story. Very often, people are building bridges and helping strangers with total disregard for what makes us different. During Operation Allies Welcome, when tens of thousands of Afghan evacuees were being received and resettled across the United States, I had a chance to see just how welcoming we can be. Both working on a mental health program for evacuees and in my interactions with community groups, I was astounded by the generosity of spirit. Volunteers gathered to set up new homes, assemble furniture, and stock refrigerators. Case managers took on the very daunting task of guiding fresh starts in a new country. Attorneys provided pro bono legal services. Afghan Americans offered to translate for strangers, and doctors organized vaccine clinics to get newly arrived children ready for school. Mental health providers eased distressed minds, and veterans advocated on behalf of the Afghans who fought shoulder to shoulder with them against a common enemy. Teachers have signed up for trainings that would help them to connect with their new Afghan students. People have shown up in creative and vital ways to ease a difficult transition.

I'm proud to have served on the board of the Afghan-American Foundation and the leadership council of Welcome. US, two organizations that have been at the heart of advocacy and welcoming efforts. Little would have been accomplished without the many allies, organizations, and individuals who have banded together to help newly arrived families. Resettlement is a long game with evolving needs.

Just as spilled ink cannot be recovered, some harm cannot be undone. We are imperfect creatures and too often approach others with assumptions and stereotypes, stigmas and hesitation. But we are also all artists in a way, creating our stories and drawing connections. We are continually evolving beings at every stage of our lives and judgment can give way to grace.

There's plenty of ink left in the bottle.

# ACKNOWLEDGMENTS

No one gets this far without many to thank. I will surely fail to name everyone because so many hands, seen and unseen, help usher a story into the world. I'm deeply grateful to Rosemary Brosnan, a gracious and keen-eyed editor. Reading over your comments with a cup of coffee is a dreamy way to spend any day. To my agent, Sarah Heller, and the team at the Helen Heller Agency, thank you for the brainstorming and the encouragement every step of the way. To Marsh Agency, thank you for helping share these stories with readers around the world. And to the incredible team at Quill Tree Books and Harper-Collins Children's Books, this story would be quite naked and raw without your expertise and creative energies. Thank you to Courtney Stevenson, Alexandra Rakaczki, Joel Tippie, Meghan Pettit, Allison Brown, Patty Rosati and her team, and

Audrey Diestelkamp. Thank you to Muhammad Mustafa for the compelling cover illustration.

I can't possibly name all the book clubs I've connected with over the years, but please know you have a special place in my heart and my calendar. These conversations, in which someone inevitably asks me what I'm working on, keep me writing. Thank you for your patience and your impatience. Shout-out to the Physician Mom Book Club, a Facebook community like no other. I'm ever grateful to the people, especially the newly arrived, who shared their personal experiences with me. No specific individual is depicted in this book, but the challenges they described are part of Nahal's story.

To my children, who interrupt sentences mid-construction and can't find their jersey and need to report what a sibling has done, thank you. Thank you for asking me when you'll be able to read this book and for sharing these stories with your friends and teachers. Thank you for wanting to know what the story is about, for joining me in celebrating our culture and other cultures, for growing and learning with me, and for inspiring parts of stories. Zoran, your line made it into this one and I hope you'll keep spinning words into verse. We can talk about your compensation now. Zayla, my thoughtful reader, this one's ready for you now. Thank you for giving me permission to share the story of the substitute teacher "welcoming" you into class as if you had just trekked here from a foreign country. So proud of how you handle this messy world. Kyrus and Cyra, my exploring duo. Thank you for the tight hugs and for making me laugh each and every day.

A heart full of gratitude to my parents, for saving the day. Every day. To the Amini clan, my chosen family, you brighten my days with your love, and I'm lucky to have you.

And to Amin, for insisting on these stories, for the thoughtful journey, for the curbside neurosurgical guidance on this story, and for (literally) building with me a home that reflects and celebrates us, all my love.